YOU CAN'T ALWAYS GET WHAT YOU HAUNT

ELLEN RIGGS

Free Prequel

Rescuing this sassy dachshund would be a lot easier if he were actually alive.

Novice psychic Janelle Brighton has been framed for murder and a cocky canine ghost holds the key to the mystery. Can they rescue each other before a killer prevails?

Join Ellen Riggs' author newsletter at **ellenriggs.com/mystic-mutts-opt-in** to get this FREE prequel to the Mystic Mutts Mysteries series

You Can't Always Get What You Haunt

Copyright © 2021 Ellen Riggs

ISBN 978-1-989303-91-7 eBook
ISBN 978-1-989303-90-0 Book
ASIN B09752RB3N Kindle
ASIN 1989303900 Paperback
Publisher: Ellen Riggs

www.ellenriggs.com
Cover designer: Lou Harper
Editor: Serena Clarke
2301140512

CHAPTER ONE

Home.

It was a small word—only four letters—but it packed a big wallop of emotion. Whenever I thought about our old family manor in Wyldwood Springs, sweet nostalgia flowed through me like water from the cool streams that defined our town. After the nostalgia passed, anger followed, then sadness, guilt, and finally fear. I'd left that town in a hurry, once upon a time. Still, I was relieved to be heading home now and grateful for the adrenaline that had kept me awake at the wheel all night.

Pushing my sunglasses onto the top of my head, I rubbed my eyes. We'd been on the road nearly 12 hours and still had quite a few to go. I was used to long road trips, having worked at resorts all over the country. I was even used to taking the back roads to avoid being tailed.

Beyond that, nothing about this trip was normal.

For starters, I hadn't visited Wyldwood Springs in 15 years, give or take. An epic blow-out with my mom over a teenaged prank sent me out into the world early, and I'd been running from memories ever since. But enemies of our family had recently come out of the woodwork to make me face my past.

A showdown had begun last night at the Briar Estates, my grandmother's gated retirement community in the sunny south, and ended in a nearby jewelry store. I won the round by a narrow margin and the next would take place on home turf if I had anything to say about it. It had been clear I'd need backup from Mom and her most trusted advisor, aggravating as they both were. I figured they owed that to Gran, my cousin Jilly Blackwood and her best friend Ivy Galloway. Until we got Wyldwood politics settled, no one would be entirely safe.

My first priority was making it home alive. One of Gran's neighbors had tried to kill me to prevent that from happening and I'd put the woman out of commission long enough to climb into my beat-up bronze sedan and hit the road.

"I should have left sooner," I said, flipping my shades back down.

"But then you wouldn't have met me." The voice startled me. My traveling companion had been quiet for a couple of hours. "No time for regrets."

My fingers tightened on the steering wheel. His voice was lovely and deep but his tone rather patronizing. "It's a long drive," I said. "There's plenty of time for regrets."

I regretted not leaving the Briars on a high note, for example. There should have been cocktails and kudos for my success in getting the place stabilized after two murders shook the community and exposed corruption on the condo board. There should have been hugs and tears with my beloved Gran, and a bittersweet parting from the best man I'd met in... well, forever. And there should have been a brief pause to strategize before I set off for Wyldwood Springs to take out another load of trash.

Nothing about my departure had gone as planned after a murder in that jewelry store revealed a plot against my life.

"All credit to me for exposing the nefarious scheme," my passenger said, "when you were just flailing."

"It's normal to flail over a murder victim," I said. "And you did give me a bit of a shock, just appearing like that."

My fingers reached for the pendant that had taken me into the jewelry store in the first place. The little gold dachshund charm had practically burned my palm when I first touched it. Today it gave off a warm glow that was actually quite comforting.

"I've always had impeccable timing," he said. "Except for one moment long ago I'd rather not dwell on. Yesterday, things worked out beautifully."

"I was savagely attacked, Mr. Bixby," I said. "I don't see the beauty in that."

"Then see the beauty in the scenery, Miss Brighton," he said. "Look at those trees."

Checking all the mirrors, I sighed. "That's all there is to see. Miles and miles of trees."

Initially, I'd mapped a scenic route through quaint towns to inspire the new business I wanted to start in Wyldwood. I'd also planned to visit pet rescues to see if my dream dog—a Belgian shepherd I'd already named Lilith—was waiting for me.

There was no time for any of that now. Knowing that people were either in pursuit or waiting at the other end for me took all the fun out of the journey. I had to push Elsa, my trusty sedan, much harder than the old girl liked and I hoped she wouldn't throw one of her hissy fits. We couldn't afford unnecessary stops. I wouldn't be safe till I reached the old manor, where the main risk would be Mom and I duking it out.

"Would you lighten up, please?" Mr. Bixby said. "I'm having a blast."

I let my shades slide down my nose and glanced at him. He was savoring the breeze from the open window, as he had been for most of the ride. All the fascinating sights, sounds and smells had mostly kept him quiet. Even so, sharing space was a major adjustment—not because Mr. Bixby took up room in the car, but because he took up room in my head. My talent for mind-reading was unreliable and what I picked up from others was often involuntary and usually unpleasant. I hadn't yet mastered the art of keeping intruders out. Hopefully, Mom could show me the ropes. Her abilities were far stronger than mine.

In the meantime, Mr. Bixby mostly had a free pass into my private mental landscape, and he had no compunction about commenting on what he saw there.

"Wouldn't *you* have plenty to say after being silenced for so many years?"

He spoke out loud, although he didn't need to. He probably just liked the sound of his own voice.

"I suppose," I said. "I just wish you'd knock before entering. My brain is my private domain."

"Why so secretive?" He gave a sly chuckle that might become charming when he became less irritating. "Mostly what I hear is complaints about your hair. Who cares about your hair with all you've got going on?"

I ran my fingers through long, tangled curls. His insistence on having the window open had turned my dark mane into a chaos of frizz.

"I care about presentation, Mr. Bixby. Looking good is half the battle in this world."

"In the world you left behind." He turned from the window and stared at me with big brown eyes. "Normal people care about lustrous curls. You're not normal anymore."

I wanted to protest but couldn't. "Never was, I suppose. I faked it pretty well for a long time."

I'd been the life of the party at every resort. On the strength of my social skills and a good work ethic, I'd climbed the ranks from housekeeping, through bartending to public relations and then management. No boss was happy to see me go. I'd made sure to leave before trouble found me.

"Sounds like a lonely life," Mr. Bixby said. "I was trapped in that jewelry store for years, yet I had more friends than you. Maybe you should have worried less about your curls and more about honing your special abilities."

There wasn't much to hone. On top of dubious mind-reading skills, I could deliver a zap of energy through my hands. Not always on command, unfortunately, although things had improved lately in the human taser department.

I could also see ghosts. Two, specifically. One was waiting for me at the old manor. The other was sitting beside me now.

At least, Mr. Bixby *had* been a ghost until yesterday. Our savage encounter with a murderer had seemingly corporealized him. He had come back from the other side with plenty of energy and some unexpected talents.

At least, unexpected for a dog.

A pedigreed tan-and-black dachshund, to be precise.

Obviously, Mr. Bixby was far more than your average doxy, but as he stuck his long nose out the window and sucked in a gusty snort of fresh air, he was most certainly still a dog.

"The answer to your question," I said, "is that my mom cares about my hair. She'll take one look at me and rip me to shreds in three seconds."

There was plenty to criticize. The altercation had done a number on my favorite little black dress and pumps. I didn't have time either to pack or to shop.

"Why do you care so much about her opinion?" Mr. Bixby's voice swept into the car on the wind. "You haven't seen her for years."

Easing the seat back and then forward, I tried to find a comfortable position. "Spoken like someone who can't remember his mother."

"On the contrary," he said. "Mine was mostly sweet with a nasty nip when you crossed the line."

"Well, my mom has a nasty nip twenty-four seven."

He fell silent again, probably sifting through my memories to verify my statement. "Sounds like she was scared for you. Knowing you'd be heading out into the big bad world without a strong armor."

"I had to leave home before I developed that armor."

Turning, he gave me an appraising look. "Or you just resisted her at every turn."

"I was a teenager. That's what teens do. Establish their independence."

"Look where that got you." He succumbed to the call of the window again. "A head of frizz and nowhere safe to go."

I glared at his shiny black ears as they lifted like the wings on my pendant. "How about you keep your opinions to yourself for a while? I've been driving nonstop for ages."

"On that note, I could use a potty break," he said.

"Another one? Did you have to eat and drink so much on our first break?"

"If nothing had passed your lips in decades, you'd relish it, too," he said. "Dog food has gone upscale since my first life. I want to sample every brand."

A trickle of drool flew out of his mouth and hit me in the cheek. "Ew, gross."

"Then don't talk about food," he said. "Talk about potty."

"You're going to have to hold on a little longer."

"Your decision, but I fear for your upholstery if you continue." He shifted to inspect the seat. "This cracked leather could use a refresh anyway. The whole car could use a refresh."

"I like this car," I said. "Elsa's seen me through some tough times."

"You nearly wept over the state of your dress. Haven't you noticed the car clashes with your image?"

I noticed, but Elsa was more than a car to me. She was a

companion, and for a brief, sad time, my home. Even if I could afford a sharp car, I wouldn't give her up.

"This was my favorite dress," I said. "I wore it on some amazing dates."

"Such a shame that handsome police chief will never get to see it. How many times has he texted now?"

"Too many," I said. "I have to ignore them for his own good."

"I liked him well enough," Bixby said. "Somehow he managed to walk around me and not through me. As a dachshund, you worry about being punted like a football."

"I liked Drew, too. But romance is a no-fly zone for me now."

"There's such a fine line between hero and martyr," he said. "I'd stay on the side with the hot cop. But that's just me."

"We were talking about my dress. I wouldn't have worn it if I'd known it would get—"

"Staked?" he said. "How does one ever predict that? Oh right, you're a psychic."

"Not a good one. Clearly."

That didn't used to bother me. I didn't want the gift or the title. Now I had second thoughts about second sight. I would need all the help I could get to protect myself and Mr. Bixby in Wyldwood Springs. He was my responsibility now. I owed him. Not to mention Gran, who wasn't as safe in her gated community as I'd thought.

My fingers left the wheel to explore the puncture in my dress. The makeshift wooden spear could have done far more damage. I had literally been sparring for my life when—

"I saved you." Mr. Bixby jumped in to complete my thought. "Surprising even myself."

"You didn't know you could do that?" I asked.

"No idea. I would have attacked someone long ago if I thought it would help me escape." He cocked his head and his ears flopped fetchingly. "Guess I was never motivated enough. Last night, I was dying to give that lady a bite to remember, and ended up living."

"It was very brave," I said. "And thank you again."

"I appreciate the appreciation." He cleared his throat, which still gave him a little trouble after years of disuse. "But I was already dead, remember? There wasn't much to lose."

"We don't know what someone like that is capable of doing. I imagine there are worse fates for a ghost dog than kicking around a jewelry store with a friend like Sinda Joffrey."

"I'll miss Sinda, but fate had bigger plans for me," he said. "I gave up a cushy eternity to ride along on this misadventure with you." Now he sighed. "I'll probably get killed all over again. I hope it's a little less dramatic than the first time."

"What happened the first time? If you don't mind my asking."

"It's not a tale I can tell on a full bladder. How about you pull over?"

I checked the mirrors again. The slower, safer route wasn't entirely risk free. "It's not a great place to stop, Mr. Bixby."

"When you gotta go, you gotta go."

I was going to ignore him but a routine scan of the dash showed the needle on the temperature gauge had crept into the red zone. Elsa's radiator was about to boil over.

"The car's overheating." I turned quickly to the dog. "Did you do that?"

"Me! I don't have that kind of power—if I have any at all. I'm just a regular dog." He poked his nose out the window. "Luckily, there's a picnic area ahead. I can smell campfires and old wieners." A disgusted snort followed. "I hate that word."

"I'll erase wiener from my lexicon, and no great loss," I said, turning onto a dirt road. "But you're no regular dog, Mr. Bixby. In fact, you could give Ivy Galloway's brilliant crime-solving sheepdog a run for his money."

I pulled into a gravel parking lot. There were half a dozen picnic tables and barbeques in the clearing ahead of us.

His beefy paws pounded the seats eagerly. "I met Keats, you

know. He came into the store once with Ivy and I'm quite sure he saw me."

"I think Ivy saw you, too. When I said I wanted a Belgian shepherd she told me to 'think longer and lower.' Must have had you in mind."

"I'll thank her for the vote of confidence," he said. "As for Keats, he didn't seem overly impressed." Mr. Bixby shook himself, as if he'd been doused in cold water. "Hopefully, his attitude will change when we meet again."

"Probably intimidated," I said, opening the car door. "You're both heroes, but remember you have a few assets he doesn't."

He walked over to stand at the edge of the driver's seat. "There is one thing I envy about Keats, though."

"Ivy's farm?" I asked. "It sounds like an idyllic life. Something I can't give you."

"What would a dachshund want with thundering hooves and manure?" He grunted as I scooped him up. "It's his legs I envy. Being hoisted like a sack of flour is uncomfortable as well as undignified. I'm capable of jumping down on my own, you know."

"I've read about dachshunds and back trouble. You won't end up with a wheelie cart on my watch. They make doggie staircases, though."

"Now you're talking," he said, when his paws were on the gravel. "You have coolant?"

I reached into the car to pop the hood. "Yeah, but we'll need to give Elsa a few minutes to breathe, first. Go stretch your legs."

There was a chilly silence and I looked down.

Way down.

"It's a figure of speech, Mr. Bixby. No offence intended."

"Well, if you don't mind, I'd like to appreciate nature without your incessant babble."

"Fine. How about you stay out of my brain, too? There's a door and you can knock first."

He trotted ahead of me. "More like a bead curtain. Anyone can stroll right in."

We spent the next 10 minutes exploring the vacant site. There was a lovely stream that might have soothed my frayed nerves if it hadn't reminded me of Wyldwood Springs. Besides, the burbling seemed like a distraction from something on the fringes of my awareness.

Something dangerous.

I turned suddenly and headed back to the parking lot.

"Excuse me," Mr. Bixby called after me. "Didn't you promise to stoop and scoop?"

"No time. We've gotta roll, and fast."

After collecting the jug of coolant from the trunk, I leaned under the hood, removed the radiator cap and poured in the fluid.

Mr. Bixby joined me, lifting his long nose. "Miss Brighton, the window for flight is closing." He cocked his head and turned. "There's a car in the lane."

"Picnickers?" I asked, hopefully.

"Only if they smell like very bad magic."

I slammed down the hood and ran around to do the same with the trunk. Then I hurried to the driver's door with the dog at my heels. "What does bad magic smell like?" I asked, practically tossing him into the passenger seat.

"Rotten eggs," he said. "And fermented yard waste. Plus a hint of old roadkill."

I turned the key in the ignition. "That's bad."

"It comes in deceptive little puffs, too." Mr. Bixby's voice was surprisingly mellow. "But don't worry. The two of us are more than a match for magical flatulence."

CHAPTER TWO

"Maybe we should try running," he said, as I bumped the car over the curb and onto the grass. "They must have better wheels than—"

"There's no better car than Elsa," I interrupted. "And she'll see us through this."

"You're afraid of ruining your heels," he said.

I steered around the picnic tables. "I'm worried about leaving Elsa. And what's in the trunk."

"Ah, yes," he said. "*Everyday Spells for Everyday Magic.* The book you liberated from a witch and wrapped in a slinky dress."

"I don't know about the witch label. I've been called that myself and I hate it. But I do know I can't run through heavy bush—"

"In heels—"

"With a heavy book *and* a dachshund in my arms," I said. "I'm not leaving the car, the book or you to our magical enemies. Anyway, I've got a plan."

"The ATV trail behind the playground equipment?"

"Exactly. So, hold on, Mr. Bixby. This ride's about to get bumpy."

"Like it wasn't already."

I let momentum carry us down the small incline toward the stream, willing myself not to look back. Elsa charged into the creek but her rear wheels got stuck in the mud and spun for a few moments.

"Easy now," Mr. Bixby said, as I pressed the pedal. "Your nerves are showing."

"Your nerves would show too, if you knew these people."

"I do know these people, or people like them. They're all the same under the surface." He turned and rose on his hind legs to peer out the rear window. "Black sedan. Looks almost like a limo. Ring a bell?"

"Unfortunately, yeah. The people of the roadkill cologne. The ones who likely hired or hexed someone to kill me."

"Ease up on the gas and let the car coast through the creek," he said.

"Like you've ever driven," I said, although I did as he said.

He gave another chuckle. "I've been on car chases worthy of action movies. Anyway, it's not like you to get so flustered."

It wasn't like the former me—the one Ivy Galloway called Janelle Bond. That Janelle was polished and poised, at least on the surface. Recent events had stolen my best traits.

Elsa finally rolled out of the creek and up the rocky ATV trail, bouncing us both around. She wasn't built for a smooth ride and this terrain brought out the worst in her.

"You don't know me yet," I said. "I get plenty flustered when the Wyldwood magical crime syndicate rears its ugly head. I've had a target on my back with them since I was a teen. Even if I get home, how can I manage to live there?" I wanted to look over at him but the path ahead took all my focus. "I'm sorry I got you into this, Mr. Bixby. Here you are ready to enjoy your second life and it's already in peril."

"Janelle." He used my given name for the first time. "I know you well enough. You've got an 'open' sign in your brain and I took a little tour before I committed to this gig. Your intentions are good." All four paws lifted off the seat with the next bump. "Your execution leaves something to be desired."

"Let's remove execution from our lexicon, too," I said.

"Onto the pile with witch and wiener," he said. "And sausage, for that matter."

A giddy giggle escaped me as I piloted Elsa around a torturous turn. This trail was likely too rocky for that sleek black sedan to negotiate. I knew my car's strengths and she could handle this. If they wanted me badly enough, they'd have to follow on foot. Or by other means if they had them. Broomsticks? Batwings? Teleportation? I had no idea of their abilities.

A chunky paw landed on my leg. "Take a deep breath. The Force is with us."

"The Force is...? Did you just make a Star Wars reference?"

"Focus," he said. "I've watched a lot of sci fi, thanks to Sinda's late husband. Sinda herself inspired my fondness for rom-coms, and the dearly departed Lexie gave me a penchant for reality TV."

"How interesting. I never expected that."

"Television addiction is probably common in ghosts, whether human or canine," he said. "What else do we have to do?" He stuck his nose out the window and inhaled deeply. "On the bright side, TV keeps you relatively current. Otherwise, the deplorable state of the world today would come as quite a shock."

"What do you smell?" I asked.

"The stench is fading. I'm cautiously optimistic that you've shaken them for now." He turned to look at me. "What do *your* senses tell you?"

"I'm not a human antenna, Mr. Bixby. Normally I need to touch something to get much of a reading. Stones and natural objects are the best."

"I say this with all due respect, but you'd better up your game if we're going to be dealing with magical crime lords."

"No argument there. Mom had better up her game, too. Fifteen years and she hasn't been able to make peace with these people?"

"I'm sure she'll be glad to have your expert social skills on her side," he said.

"Is that a joke?" I gripped the wheel even harder. "Because you're never that nice."

"You don't know me, either."

He was right about that. While the dog could seemingly rifle through my mental file cabinets at will, he was not an open book to me. If we were going to get into more situations like this, we'd have to learn the best way to work together. I'd been a stellar team player in all my jobs, but I trusted no one. That would be my biggest challenge now. Trusting Bixby. Trusting Mom. But it could be done. I had shown my potential in trusting Ivy, Jilly, Keats the sheepdog and Percy the cat.

Elsa's engine screamed as we crested a steep hill. At the top, I pressed the brakes, facing two forks in the ATV trail.

"Which one takes you home safely?" the dog asked, prodding my bare arm with a damp nose.

Staring down at the heavy foliage, I tried to discern any signals over the pounding of my heart. "I think—"

"Don't think. Use your other skills." I started to protest and all it got me was another jab with a wet nose. "Here's a hint," he added. "One smells like supernatural flatulence."

"Is this a test? I dropped out of college over my test phobia."

Actually, I'd been kicked out of freshman year because someone framed me for setting a dormitory fire. There was zero evidence pinning me to the crime, but with my police record in Wyldwood Springs, I was an easy target.

"Thinking," Mr. Bixby said. "Ruminating. Spinning mental wheels so hard there's more smoke coming out of you than Elsa. May I suggest you blurt out your first reaction about the right trail? There are only two choices, after all."

I'd waffled back and forth so many times I couldn't remember. The pressure of knowing the magical bad guys might still be on our tail had short-circuited my instincts.

"I've got an idea." Putting the car in park, I opened the door. "Hang tight, Bixby."

"We don't have time for—"

I was already out of the car, picking my way over uneven turf on the balls of my feet. At the head of one trail, I crouched and placed both hands on the soil and rocks.

"Ow!" I nearly fell over backward from the force of the negative energy. It felt like pythons had coiled into my body to squeeze my vital organs. Panting, I pushed myself up and staggered back to the car. Normally I moved with stealthy grace, but now I teetered like a drunk.

"Get out, get out," I said, reaching for the driver's door.

"I'm not going anywhere," Mr. Bixby said. "Not with you looking like that. You're as pale as a— Well, never mind."

"I meant the snakes." My voice sounded choked, as if reptiles were still blocking my windpipe. "Some kind of dark energy hit me like pythons. I used to go snake hunting and one time I saw this eighteen-foot pregnant Burmese python. She just woke up in my brain."

The dog shuddered. "I felt it. And I'd be nothing but a light canapé for a creature like that. But I trust you got the message."

"Loud and clear. We take the other trail."

"Couldn't be worse than pythons," he said.

It could, though. I only hoped we got home before we ran into any of them.

CHAPTER THREE

M r. Bixby didn't request another pit stop for the last few hours of our drive. Instead, we fell into what felt like a more companionable silence. Maybe conquering another challenge together had made us both less prickly. I tried harder to close the door on my thoughts, and he had the decency to stay silent about the worries tumbling around my mind like laundry in an industrial size washer.

In all my years of tuning into other people's thoughts, either accidentally or intentionally, I'd never felt anything like the negative energy emanating from the rocks on that trail.

If I'd realized the people I was heading home to face were *that* powerful, maybe I'd have kept running. Until recently, I was sure Mom could handle absolutely anything. Then I heard about the cars tailing Jilly and Ivy on their drive down to the Briar Estates. They'd seen a man in uniform like the one worn by the Wyldwood Springs underground magical police force. The fact that an officer was following my cousin and her friend told me snakes were loose in Wyldwood, and the magical good guys weren't winning.

"There's still time to run," I said. I'd meant to use my inside voice but it wouldn't have mattered, since Mr. Bixby could hear that, too.

"Patience you must have, my young Padawan," the dog said.

I rubbed my forehead to ease a pounding headache. "I'm driving to my doom with a dachshund who thinks he's Yoda. What an interesting day."

"The Force is strong within you, Janelle." Mr. Bixby laughed in delight. "More than you know. Otherwise, no one would give a hoot over your homecoming. People don't make this big a fuss over a harmless housefly."

"Housefly? You can't do better than that?"

"The glittery metallic one," he said. "A bluebottle."

"Not helping. How about a butterfly?"

"Still a caterpillar you are," he said. "Let's see what you meta-morphosize into here."

That made me brighten a little. "Wyldwood Springs is the perfect place for transformation."

I took the final turnoff onto a country back road. We weren't far from my hometown, and I didn't need road signs to prove it. The big ugly snakes coiling in my unconscious washed away with images of clear rushing water.

I hadn't been here in about 15 years, yet it still felt like home. Smelled like home, too, with the scent of pine needles and wild-flowers on the breeze. Rolling down my window, I heard the song-birds marking their territory. I could even taste home on my tongue —a bittersweet combination of the cinnamon buns Gran used to bake and the stalks of crisp rhubarb Jilly and I dared each other to eat every spring.

"No time for nostalgia," Mr. Bixby said. "There are threats on every corner."

I had no doubt about that, but I drove down Main Street anyway. First, I wasn't going to slither in by the back routes like a common criminal when I had every right to be here. And second, I was dying to see how the town I loved had changed. One thing I had going for me here was that the magical police were probably on high alert to quell skirmishes for the good of the community. I couldn't depend on them to keep me safe, but it was something.

"Maybe I should buy a gun," I said. "Mace probably won't do me much good."

"Just try to stay out of everyone's crosshairs long enough to turn into a butterfly," Mr. Bixby said, rising up on his haunches to peer around. "I can see it might be difficult in a dinky spot like this."

"Dinky! It's gorgeous."

"Spoken like a lovestruck teen," he said. "I see nothing remarkable about Wyldwood Springs."

"That's because you haven't seen the actual springs. Or the quaint bridges and little rainbows that seem close enough to touch." I reached out to stroke his back, surprised by how silky his coat felt under my fingertips. I hadn't dared to stroke him like a regular dog, before. Mr. Bixby wasn't the snuggle bunny pet I'd envisioned.

"Snuggle bunny, indeed," he said with a sniff. Nonetheless, he leaned into my hand, and when I rubbed his ears, let out a long groan. "That does feel nice, I must admit."

I put both hands on the wheel again to maneuver around the rubberneckers on Main Street. Wyldwood Springs was one of the oldest of the many towns in hill country, mainly because it sat at the base of the long craggy range that stretched past Ivy's hometown of Clover Grove. A couple of centuries ago, the founders had put careful thought into Wyldwood's design. I suppose they had to, with so many streams running through it. Quick getaways were challenging in a town with so many bridges, yet there was always a need for escape routes. Even in its earliest days, Wyldwood had been full of magical rabblerousers. Or so Gran had told me, and her gran had told her. Magic and crime were baked into the soil and constantly rinsed away by the creeks, only to renew again.

"It hasn't changed as much as I feared," I said, rubbernecking myself to check out all the stores on Main Street. "There are a few trendy new cafés and upscale boutiques, but the bakery, butcher and candy store are all still here."

I was glad the town leaders hadn't adopted hokey mystical naming conventions, despite the magic that abounded. The store-fronts were quaint and tasteful, with planters spilling over with flowers and trailing vines climbing the walls.

It looked as peaceful and picturesque as any other hill country town, and in many ways, it was. But there was a hum under the surface that confirmed looks could be deceiving.

"There's the Achilles Heel shoe repair," I said. "Maybe these stilettos can be salvaged."

"I wouldn't count on it," Mr. Bixby said. "And since I spend time milling around your ankles, remember those heels could kill with a single misstep. That's not how I'd choose to die the next time."

"Duly noted." I hit the brakes hard. "Whoa, look, Mr. Bixby!" I pulled into an illegal spot by a hydrant. "It's our store."

His head swiveled. "Our store?"

I pointed to the real estate sign in the window. "The old book-store is for lease."

"Mabel's Fables? It's a wreck."

"When I was a kid, it was a tearoom. Then it changed hands countless times. Every business failed, which was strange, because it's a prosperous town."

"Cursed?" he asked.

I shrugged. "People said it was haunted."

"Then forget about it," he said. "Another ghost we don't need."

I gave him a curious look. Though he'd spent plenty of time poking around my mental archives, he'd overlooked something significant. Perhaps now wasn't the time to break the news about the other ghost in my life. He'd find out soon enough. Meanwhile, I considered adding a third apparition by leasing this property to open a jewelry and gift store that showcased Sinda Joffrey's designs.

My fingers reached again for the dachshund pendant Sinda had created. The shiny little charm had led me to discover and rescue Mr. Bixby, and according to its designer, every piece in the collection represented a ghost dog stuck between life and the hereafter. She said they needed to be liberated to fulfill a new calling in the present. What's more, she believed I was their bridge to move from one plane to another. I had no idea how the process had worked with Mr. Bixby, but it was certainly a project I could put my heart into and a town full of bridges felt like the right place to do it.

"It's our store, I sense it," I said. "And if it's haunted, we could probably get it for a good price. My start-up fund is a little scanty."

"Maybe you should have thought of that before buying so many shoes," he grumbled.

"Right again, Mr. B," I said. "But they're pets. Like Elsa."

"I don't care for nicknames." His ears came forward as he propped himself up to watch the flow of pedestrians. "Shouldn't we deal with the evil snake people before setting up shop right here on Main Street? You'll be rubbing your existence right in their faces."

"Whimsy," I said.

He turned. "Pardon me?"

"It's the name of our store, as long as Sinda agrees." That's what she'd called her jewelry store before her niece renamed it Haute Baubles. "We'll sell her pieces, and I'll source other suppliers as well." Someone pounded on the horn behind me, so I snapped a quick photo of the store with my phone and signaled before pulling out. "The real estate agent is Laverne Billings, an old friend of Gran's. We'll set up a viewing as soon as she'll see us."

"A viewing? Of another spirit who can't rest?" His paws pumped impatiently on the seat.

"What have you got against ghosts? It seems hypocritical, Bixby."

"What's so hard about saying mister? Two easy syllables."

I moved slowly along Main Street till the first intersection. "We're a team now. Mister feels so formal."

Stopping at the red light, I grinned at his expression. Those big brown eyes sure could cast a chill.

"Where's the old manor?" he said, changing the subject. "Is it a dump or a diamond?"

"A little of both, probably. Gran kept it in good shape but Mom probably got slack."

"Lazy?" he asked.

"More like flighty. She can't focus on anything longer than... well, that bluebottle fly you mentioned."

"What else do I need to worry about with this lady?"

"Hair-trigger temper," I said. "Blurts out whatever crosses her mind and alienates people. Oh, and she hates dogs, too. Or at least, she'd never let me have one."

"Lovely," Mr. Bixby said. "Did you inherit anything nice from her?"

"Green eyes." I turned off Main Street and headed for the outskirts of town. "I can't think of anything else right now. Ask me again after our big reunion."

"She can't be *that* bad, because she loves you," he said. "And your gran."

"Maybe, but she doesn't accept either of us. My powers weren't what she hoped, and Gran has none at all. Then there was her sister, Jilly's mom, and Jilly herself, who both came up empty. Seems like Mom got most of the magic and all of the responsibility."

Mr. Bixby's skinny tail drooped. "I'm sure it's hard for everyone to think they don't measure up to her standards."

A lump formed in my throat and my chest seized up. This feeling used to derail me, but after what had happened at the picnic site earlier, the fear of disappointing my mother diminished a little. There were bigger problems ahead.

"Maybe she's changed," I said, easing my foot off the gas as Elsa chugged the last half mile to Brighton manor. Long before I could see it with my eyes, I felt it in my heart. Once again, the sensation of home surged through my veins. Even if Mom had let the place go to seed, it would be beautiful to me. I would restore it to its former glory and treat it like the most precious of jewels.

All I had to do was convince Mom to leave.

"You want to evict your own mother?" Mr. Bixby asked.

"Not evict, per se. I want to send her down to watch over Gran and manage the Briars. I'm confident I can smooth over the magical politics here better than she could."

He gave a snort of laughter. "Did you really just say that? After nearly getting stabbed? And pursued by criminal hometown neighbors?"

"It's a stretch, I know, but I figured Mom and I could work together for a bit. And then she can..."

"Shove off?" he said.

"Exactly. She deserves a nice tropical vacation. I'm sure it's been stressful here."

The manor was exactly as I remembered it. Large, but not massive. Red brick with white accents. There was a salute to Tudor design, and a bow to gothic with the understated turret. Overall, while the house was imposing, it was more welcoming than forbidding. It helped that the gardens surrounding it were lush and inviting. Plus, our weathervane with four roosters still spun merrily on the roof. That made me smile, despite a growing unease.

Mom wasn't on the porch to greet us, as I'd expected. As I'd *hoped* if I were being honest. Gran must have called her, and Mom's own psychic powers would have announced the return of her long-lost daughter.

"She must be out," I said, pulling into the driveway. "There's no sign of her car."

I opened Elsa's door and sat there so long that Mr. Bixby

crossed over my lap and jumped down on his own. He trotted toward the porch and I got out to follow. After turning back to get the spell book from the trunk, I caught up with the dog at the bottom of the stairs and stooped to lift him with my free arm. At the top, he struggled to be set on his own paws again, which only made me clutch him tighter.

"Something's wrong, Mr. Bixby. The door's unlocked."

Opening it slowly, I stepped into the spacious front hall and then gasped.

"What?" he said, wriggling so much I finally set him down.

It was early afternoon but the house was dim inside, as always. Flipping the switch on an ornate chandelier, I stared around.

"Mom's no neat freak but this place looks like a frat house after a keg party."

The hall table was on its side and the antique oval mirror that sat over it was cracked. Half a dozen coats and even more shoes were scattered over the parquet floor. The coat rack itself lay broken on the curved oak staircase.

"Not impressed so far," the dog said, strutting ahead of me. "It's a dive."

"It's been ransacked. What do you smell, Mr. Bixby?"

He stopped, lifted his long nose and sniffed. "Nothing. Absolutely nothing." There was a note of uncertainty in his voice now. "It's like everything's been neutralized."

"Mom? *Mom!*"

CHAPTER FOUR

"Stay calm," Mr. Bixby said, trotting ahead of me into the living room. "I hear something. If I'm not mistaken, it's *Survivor*."

"*Survivor?* The TV show?"

"One of my favorites," he called back. I couldn't see him now, but a sharp bark alerted me to danger. "Stay back, Janelle. There's an intruder."

"It's probably not an intruder," I said. "It's—"

Another harsh bark cut me off, followed by an assertive, "Who are you and why are you here?"

No one answered so I hurried after the dog, who turned in the doorway.

"There's a man in a tuxedo lounging on the couch like he owns the place," Mr. Bixby said. "Is he your mother's paramour? And why on earth is he wearing formal attire in the afternoon?"

I stepped inside the room just in time to see a tall, dark and slightly transparent man rise from the couch in one fluid motion. He looked like Mr. Darcy in my favorite *Pride and Prejudice* adaptation. His big hands fluttered and something like confusion filled his eyes. It was as if he were waking from a long sleep, or more likely, a *Survivor* bender.

"Miss Brighton," the man said, in his impeccable English accent. "You're home. Thank goodness."

"And you are...?" Mr. Bixby demanded. "You've scared the life out of us."

I couldn't help smiling, despite my unease. "Mr. Bixby, it's okay. I know him. Very well, in fact. There's nothing to fear."

"I'll believe that when he accounts for himself," Mr. Bixby said. "Something's greatly amiss here."

The tall man's eyes cleared somewhat and he stared down at the dog. "Miss Brighton, please tell him to stop that infernal yapping."

"What did he say?" Mr. Bixby asked, sniffing at the tall man's shoes. "All I heard was babble. All I smell is... nothing."

"All *he* heard was barking," I answered. "You two don't understand each other, which is going to be a little awkward."

"Are you speaking to that... that cur?" the man asked, surprise clearing his eyes even more. But now there was a different sort of confusion.

"Yes, I am. And I'd thank you to be more respectful of my dog, Sir Nigel," I said. "Allow me to introduce Mr. Bixby, my pedigreed dachshund. And while you may not be able to understand him, trust me when I say he's extremely articulate. What's more, I owe my life to him."

"Correct," the dog said. "Sir Windbag."

"Mr. Bixby," I continued, "Allow me to introduce Sir Nigel Boswell."

"Sir?" the dog said. "For real?"

"For real," I said. "He fell on hard times and became our family's butler."

"A butler?" Mr. Bixby stared around. "I don't get it. Why would you need a butler? It's a big house, but not that big."

He really didn't get it. Neither of them did and I could hardly blame them. This was a strange new world and I was only learning the rules myself—if there were any rules.

"It's a long story, Mr. Bixby," I said. "The important thing to know right now is that Sir Nigel is... what *you* were, until very recently."

The dog's eyes widened to show a crescent of white and his ears came forward. Then he did a full-on head tilt. "You mean, he's deceased?"

"Very much so and for more than a century. He came over from the old country with my ancestors. Sir Nigel and I haven't always seen eye to eye, but he's an important part of my family."

"It's wonderful to hear you say so, Miss Brighton," Sir Nigel said. "We didn't part on the best of terms and it's troubled me more than you can know."

The last time we saw each other, I was 17, and in a blind rage. I'd slammed doors and shouted words I'd never use today. Sir Nigel had intruded on my life to the point where I lashed out and got into trouble. Got my entire family into trouble. Mom made it worse by backing "Boz" over me, whereas Gran had played peacemaker. After a prom prank gone wrong, I left early for college. And when that didn't work out, I joined some carnies on the road, thus beginning life on the run.

It wasn't the time to air old grievances. Whatever Boswell's failings, he had our family's interests very much at heart. I could see that quite clearly in hindsight and was ready to bury the hatchet.

"Speaking of Mom, where is she, Sir Nigel? I expected a greeting." Maybe not a warm welcome, but something.

His hands flew to his mouth in a comical gesture that was entirely out of character. I'd been observing this ghost since before I could walk. He was my first babysitter.

"Gone," he mumbled.

"Gone? Gone where?"

"I have no idea, Miss Brighton. One day she sent me up to the attic to dust and reorganize the old journals. When I came down, the hallway was in complete disarray, and she had vanished. That was some time ago, I'm afraid. It seems she's ghosted me."

Panic started fluttering like dark moths in my belly and worked their way up to my chest. There was nothing like a brand new problem to shine a light on the past.

There was only one thing I knew for sure in this moment: my mom would *never* ghost our family ghost after well over a century in our care.

"How long has she been gone?" I asked.

"I'm not sure," he said. "It's all been a blur."

I suspected he hadn't moved from the TV since Mom left. It could have been weeks.

"Why didn't you let us know, sir? I've been staying with Gran for the past three months. Jilly's nearby and she would have come down. I'm sure you know that."

It was interesting to see a grown ghost squirm in his permanent double-breasted waistcoat. "I—I assumed you and your grandmother, and perhaps even the rest of the family, knew more than I did. You know I'm forbidden to leave the house or attract notice."

"A rule you conveniently ignored at my high school prom, as I recall. Among other occasions."

While Boswell was tied to the house and invisible to most people, there was a charmed talisman that liberated him on both fronts. The charm had been controlled by Mom, so I never knew whether he'd borrowed it, or she'd sent him after me.

"That was when you were just a girl. It was my duty to protect you from curs." He looked down at Mr. Bixby. "Of the human variety."

"Why is he looking at me?" Mr. Bixby said. "I don't like him. He smells like trouble."

"He doesn't smell at all," I said. "You've already said so. And there are more pressing matters at hand, Mr. Bixby. It sounds like my mother may have been kidnapped."

"Judging by the front hall she put up a good fight," the dog said.

I turned back to Boswell. "There is no way Mom ghosted you. We take our obligations seriously, sir."

He gave a little sigh and said, "I'm so glad you're home."

I looked down at Mr. Bixby, who was more likely to be of help than the overwhelmed butler. "We'd better figure out what happened to Mom, and fast. She could be... well, she could be..."

My voice quavered and faded. Only now did I realize how much I'd looked forward to seeing my mother on that front porch. I'd rather have her here, ripping my appearance and skills to shreds, than...

"She isn't dead," Mr. Bixby said. "No matter how deficient your psychic skills, you'd most certainly sense your mother throwing off this mortal coil."

"Do you think?" My voice was still all wobbles.

"When your gran was in trouble, you knew it, right? And when your cousin got in over her head, you knew that, too. Isn't that why you went to the Briars?"

"Yes, but Mom and I were estranged, and she was very proficient at shielding her thoughts. I never should have let our squabble go on so long. She was just so annoying."

"She still is," Mr. Bixby said. "For the moment, she's annoying someone else."

Sir Nigel cleared his throat conspicuously. "I believe she did mention a conflict, Miss Brighton. Before she left."

"Mom always had conflicts," I said. "A new feud bubbled up every week."

"This one seemed more significant than the others, I'm afraid. Normally your mother took everything in stride. This time she became weary." He wrung his hands, and I was struck by just how real he looked. He could fade out of view and yet be substantial enough to push the tea cart around and keep the house organized.

Or more like perpetually reorganized, as he enjoyed moving the furniture around almost daily.

"What's he saying?" Mr. Bixby asked. "I can't pick up as much from your thoughts when you're frazzled. Things are flying around and colliding in there."

"That's exactly what it feels like," I told the dog. "It seems like Mom got into something over her head. Someone probably got frustrated and forcibly removed her."

"They haven't killed her," Mr. Bixby said. "There must be a reason for that. What do you think that is?"

I pushed frizzy hair out of my eyes, looked down at my tattered clothes and then sighed. "Me, maybe? I could be the reason for that. We've already seen that someone was willing to kill me to keep me from coming home. Those two things probably aren't a coincidence."

"Someone tried to kill you?" Sir Boswell sounded horrified. "Why, Miss Brighton?"

"Who knows? Maybe they wanted to keep me from finding Mom."

"Or keep you from getting your hands on that," Mr. Bixby said, sweeping his long nose up to the spell book still locked under my arm.

"So many possible reasons," I said. "We can only tackle one at a time, and that starts with finding my mother."

"Then that's what we'll do," Mr. Bixby said. He glanced at Sir Nigel and sniffed imperiously. "You'll need to ditch the stiff."

I shook my head. "I'm afraid I can't do that. With Mom out of the picture, Sir Nigel is under my care."

The butler straightened, and the light came back on in his eyes. "And you under mine, Miss Brighton. We'll solve this mystery together. You'll need to find my talisman and then crate the cur. We can't move about freely with a yappy... What do they call them now? Oh yes, wiener dog."

"Mr. Bixby doesn't like that term and we've banished it from our lexicon," I said, as the dog put two and two together and growled. Using my index finger, I drew a circle between the three of us. "Welcome to the team, gentlemen."

CHAPTER FIVE

"Could I ask you a favor, Mr. Bixby?" I said, backing out of the driveway an hour later and directing Elsa toward town.

"You can ask," he said. "Keeping in mind I already know what it is."

"Well, then. Will you?"

"Shut up?" he said.

I gave him a glare. "I did not put it that way, even in my own private thoughts."

He stuck his nose out the window. "That's what I heard. Your intention more than the words themselves."

"I don't want you to shut up entirely. Not when you can help keep me alive." I took the longer route into the downtown core on purpose. "I just don't want to embarrass myself by answering you out loud when I'm trying to make a good first impression."

"Sounds like that ship sailed fifteen years ago." He poked his head right out as we crossed one of the many quaint, old wooden bridges that spanned the twisty network of streams. "Burned a few bridges from the sounds of it."

I wanted to give him another glare but the bridge was a single lane and it paid to be careful. Normally, only crazy teens drove around at breakneck speed but many cars had careened off these bridges and it hadn't ended well.

"Some of the old contingent has either moved on or passed on," I said. "There are no completely fresh starts in Wyldwood Springs, but it might not be as bad as I fear." I pulled out my phone. "Which reminds me to call Gran. This would be one of those moments you could practice being a normal dog who doesn't offer witty rejoinders she won't hear."

"I'm enjoying the breeze anyway," he said, sending another stream of drool wafting in my direction. A few droplets landed on the floral print dress I'd borrowed from Mom's closet. Normally I didn't do prints, let alone florals, but when you arrive without so much as a suitcase, you take what you can get. A quick shower and change had made me look and feel better, even without a wink of sleep.

"Do you mind controlling the drool as well as the chatter?" I asked.

"I smell cookies," he said. "A bakery. If you promise to stop and get me a treat, I'll simmer down."

"Deal," I said, pressing Gran's number. "This is a sensitive conversation. I need to tell Gran her daughter is MIA."

He turned a brown eye on me. "Then get it done and stop worrying about your hair."

"I am not worrying about my hair," I said, letting my hand drop from damp curls. "But like I said, first impressions count."

Gran answered on the first ring. "Janny! Oh, my darling, I've been so worried about you. Are you home?"

I put her on speaker and locked both hands on the wheel. "Home. Yes, if you can call it that. I've been to the manor and am driving into town now."

"I haven't slept since Sinda Joffrey's call. Your texts were rather cryptic."

"I know and I'm sorry. I just wanted to stay on the alert." I was relieved Sinda had shared at least part of the story. "Did she tell you about the attack, Gran? Someone tried to impale me."

"After trying to cast a deadly hex on you. Yes, Sinda told me. I was beside myself, but it sounds like you acquitted yourself brilliantly."

Mr. Bixby turned and stared at me, clearly waiting for his share of the credit.

"I had help, Gran. My new dog, Mr. Bixby, was the true hero of this story."

"I hear he's no longer a ghost." The tension in Gran's voice eased. "I'm so glad you have a partner in crime, as it were."

The dog's mouth opened in a happy pant but still he said nothing.

"I'm glad, too," I said. "Because we're in a bit of a situation here."

"Already?" Gran said. "You can't have been home long. How did things go with your mother?"

"Therein lies the problem, Gran. There's no easy way to say this: Mom is gone."

"Gone! What about Sir Nigel?"

"He's still at the house and very confused. It's like he has amnesia. I'd almost think someone cast a spell on him but that's impossible, right? He's a ghost."

There was a long sigh at the other end. "I wouldn't have thought so, but I don't actually know what's possible. Your mom would never willingly leave him, though. Sir Nigel is our responsibility."

"That's what I told him." I ran my fingers over Mr. Bixby's sleek coat absentmindedly. It was quickly becoming a soothing habit. "She must have been abducted but Boz only remembers there was tension in town. Gran... I would sense if Mom were dead, right?"

"Definitely. And so would I," she said. "I may not be wired for magic, but a mother knows these things."

I let out a sigh of relief. "Thank goodness. If she's alive, I can find her." The big eye turned again. "With Mr. Bixby's help and possibly Boswell's, if he recovers. I had to leave him at the house because his ticket to ride is gone, too."

"Do be careful, Janny. Wyldwood folks have long memories and they won't hesitate to punish you for whatever trouble your mom's gotten herself into."

"Understood. I may not have her command of magic, but I do have some genes she didn't inherit."

"Tell me more." Gran had a smile in her voice.

"The Brighton charm. Jilly and I both inherited that from you."

"You're sweet to say so. I used to think we could only have the charm *or* the magic, but you've proven me wrong."

"I don't have enough magic for what's going on around here, so I'll need to rely on other skills," I said. "I'm meeting Laverne Billings in half an hour to talk about renting a store. Mabel's Fables is still empty."

There was a pause, as Gran no doubt chose her words carefully. "Janny, do you think you should be opening a store? It's like putting a target on your back."

"Exactly what I said," Mr. Bixby muttered, unable to contain himself. "And that was before I knew about your mother. I was only worried about evading the regular magical miscreants who no doubt followed us here."

"Never mind that," I said. "Gran doesn't need to know."

"I do need to know," she said. "I hear grumbling sounds. Are you talking to your dog? And does he talk back? Sinda said he corporealized."

"Yes and yes," I said. "Mr. Bixby is a dog of strong opinions, Gran, and doesn't like to be left out of the conversation."

"Well, if he saved my granddaughter's life, I welcome him in any conversation."

His skinny tail whipped back and forth. "Your gran is grand indeed. I hope to meet her sometime."

I couldn't help laughing. "He said he'd like to meet you, Gran. And I wish you could be here, too, because I don't have many allies." I crossed another bridge, slowing to admire the view. "What can you tell me about Laverne Billings? You two were friends, right?"

"Not exactly," she said. "What's that term you and Jilly use? Frenemies. Laverne was very well connected, so I did my best to stay in her good graces."

"She's on the non-magical side, as I recall?"

"Yes, as much as she might try to suggest otherwise. As a real estate agent, she does business with everyone, and the magical clients get preference. So, tread carefully. Charm won't help you much with Laverne."

"I figured Laverne is well enough connected to have information about Mom. Leasing the store would be a bonus."

There was another long pause. "Honey, I really don't like this at all. Where is that spell book, by the way?"

I trusted my grandmother with my life, but I also knew her phone could be bugged. "It's safe, Gran."

"Ah. You're afraid someone is standing with a knife to my throat?"

"That hadn't occurred to me, so thanks for that image. But I do want you to be safe, and the less you know, the better."

"Unfortunately, I agree. There's no one powerful enough at the Briars to protect us now. Anyway, be careful with that book. Don't start using it casually."

"Gran, I'm not about to crack it open and hex people. I'm not a witch."

"Aren't you?" This question came from Mr. Bixby. "If not a witch, then what?"

"We don't use that word," Gran said, as if answering the dog she couldn't hear. "But many would say it applies to your mother."

"Do you think whoever came after me wanted to keep the book

from falling into her hands?" I asked. "Because Mom wouldn't hesitate to use it."

The sigh on the other end sounded like it came from the soles of Gran's daisy-studded hippie sandals. "Honey, I think someone wanted to keep it from falling into *your* hands. And they wanted to keep you and your magic book from coming back to Wyldwood Springs. Do you understand what that means?"

"Yeah," I said, turning onto Main Street. "It means you and Bixby are right. There's a target on my back and any hope of a peaceful life in this town just went down the drain."

"Long before now," Mr. Bixby said with his wry chuckle. "I heard the sucking sound the day we met. It's a matter of staying out of the cesspool."

"Dachshunds aren't built to keep their head above sewage," I said. "Are they?"

Gran laughed freely for the first time. "Our conversations are going to be so interesting from now on. This dog of yours is so much funnier than—"

"The butler stiff?" Mr. Bixby interrupted. "Bridie, you are so right about that."

"Boswell," Gran continued. "Though I feel disloyal even saying so. Sir Nigel defended your great-great-grandfather with his life. When he was still alive."

"That doesn't make him interesting," Mr. Bixby said. "It's a crime to be around that long and still be dull."

"What's he saying?" Gran asked. "I can tell I'm missing some fun."

"Bixby is working on his comedy schtick and I don't want to encourage him," I said. "I'll call you back later, Gran. Please play it extra safe and keep in touch with Drew Gillock, okay?"

"You've filled him in on what happened?" she asked.

"Not exactly. I couldn't tell him the real story, could I? And I haven't had the mental bandwidth to make up a good lie."

"Let me see if I can help with that," Gran said. "Coverups are a family speciality."

I told her I loved her as if it were the last time, because it might be. Then I pulled into a parking spot not far from Mabel's Fables. Elsa's engine sputtered out before I turned the key.

"I demand a better ride," Bixby said. "A broomstick would be an upgrade."

"Broomstick with a sidecar," I said. "Coming right up."

CHAPTER SIX

The Beanstalk Café was one of the early "cool" venues on the Main Street strip. As a kid, I'd loved perching on the tall stools at the old wooden counter and stealing sips of Gran's coffee. It made me feel like a grown-up. On special occasions, Gran would buy me a milkshake from the old-fashioned machine.

Everything about the store was intentionally old-fashioned, from the sign outside to the wood shelving that held bags of coffee beans and, strangely enough, books. It was a collection of classics that weren't for sale. The owner, Mitzy Lennox, liked encouraging the town to peek into *Huckleberry Finn* or *Oliver Twist*. It was a noble cause that didn't catch on, except with Gran and me. She'd choose a book and read the first chapter aloud. If we got hooked, we'd trade off reading it all the way through during our after-school visits. I loved running my index finger along the spines to see which of the books got the most wear and tear. Many had been pristine, and likely still were. It would be the first thing I checked after ordering a coffee and staring down the many prying eyes.

"Remind me why we're doing this?" Mr. Bixby said, grunting as I hoisted him under one arm. "And I'll remind you that I'm not a designer handbag to be dangled at your whim."

"It's not a whim," I said. "The sign says no pets allowed. We should get therapy certification, like Ivy has with Keats. They can go anywhere together."

"Newsflash," Mr. Bixby said. "I'm not Keats. Sheepdogs are bred to obey. To perform tedious drills."

"Whereas dachshunds are bred to...?" I prompted.

"Scent, chase and flush savage badgers out of tunnels."

I walked over to the window of the Beanstalk Café and peered inside. "That'll be handy if we develop a badger problem at the manor. My research tells me doxies are inclined to be stubborn. Belligerent. Hard to housetrain."

"I've heard the slander. Some say we're way down the intelligence scale, whereas border collies rock the charts. But I ask you... do I seem dumb?"

I laughed. "Nope. You could probably train the trainer in service class."

"If I deemed it worth my while, which I don't."

"Then you'll need to play handbag and cross our fingers no one tosses you out of stores. It's not a particularly dog-friendly town."

The sun disappeared behind a cloud, and I caught a look at my reflection in the glass. For a second, I thought it was my mother, because of the dress. We were the same size, but our taste couldn't be more different. I favored sleek and stylish, whereas she liked down-home country girl—girl being the operative word. I couldn't imagine why a woman in her late fifties would wear the wholesome frocks lined up in her closet. The row of shoes underneath were equally stodgy, with a focus on Mary-Janes with a modest heel.

"Oh, my goodness," I said. "I look like Anne of Green Gables."

The dog laughed in my arms. "On the bright side, the flared skirt and low heels are better suited to your new lifestyle."

"Which new lifestyle is that, specifically? The one where I'm a total nerd?"

"The one where you blend in until you need to run like heck. If pressed to turn and fight, you'll be able to kick hard and fast." He cocked his head as he stared into the glass. "But there is something terribly wrong with this picture if you take a close look."

I did as he suggested and noticed everyone at the round tables seemed to be staring. "It's the dress," I hissed.

He gave one of his more sarcastic chuckles. "It's not the dress. At least I doubt it."

"What, then?"

"Probably the fact you're having a prolonged conversation with your reflection. That's what they're seeing. You're staring inside and chitchatting away."

"Oh gosh, you're right, Bixby. I look crazy." I turned and walked to the door. "You're making me look crazy."

"You could use your inside voice, remember," he said. "I can hear you just fine without your lips moving, and it might save you some embarrassment. Pretty sure you said first impressions matter."

I walked into the café, keeping my eyes on the counter. "Well, I just blew that opportunity, didn't I?" This time I *did* use my "inside voice."

"Helpful tip from a friend? Using your inside voice is only half the battle. Your expression shows you're arguing with a silent adversary. Eyes narrowed. Mouth set in a grimace. Turn that frown upside down and flick the switch to ignite the Brighton charm you brag about."

"I don't brag," I muttered internally. "Or maybe I do. I can own that." I straightened my shoulders under the floral frock and plastered on my hospitality industry smile. "It's showtime."

"Less teeth," he said. "You look like a—"

I joined the coffee queue. "Never mind. You're baiting me."

I must have said something out loud because the man ahead of me turned, looking somewhat startled.

"See?" Mr. Bixby said. "You scared him with your teeth. No

one really likes a clown, no matter what they say. They were invented to terrify children into behaving."

I could feel irritation and amusement battling for supremacy on my face, which was probably scarier than the clown smile. "Stop it," I told the dog, mentally. "One more smart remark and you're going back to wait with Elsa. Are doxies bred to survive steamy cars or cool tunnels?"

The dog subsided into an audible grumble, and I turned down the wattage on my smile for the man ahead of me. He was middle-aged and well groomed—the type of man I could often charm without much effort. At least, in my own clothes and footwear. I'd always relied on my wardrobe as a buffer against the world.

"Hi there," I said. "Is the coffee here still amazing? I haven't been around for about fifteen years."

"Best in town," he said, and his eyebrows settled where they should be. "Maybe the best in all of hill country, although I still have a few towns to check off."

"Sounds like you're building a treasure map of all the best coffeehouses in hill country."

His alarm vanished completely. "Pretty much. With special mention of the baked goods on offer. You'll find they've improved since you left. The baker here is a whiz with scones."

"Thanks for the tip," I said. "I'll try one."

It was his turn at the cash register, and after placing his order, he turned to me. "What will you have? It's on me. To welcome you home."

"Oh, how sweet," I said. "I'll take a black coffee to go and... what type of scone do you recommend?"

Before he could answer, the silver-haired woman behind the counter pinned me with sharp blue eyes behind big rimless glasses. "Blueberry is the most popular, Janelle."

Hearing my name fall so easily from her lips made my eyes widen.

"Uh-oh," Mr. Bixby said. "Am I allowed to point out trouble before it happens? Or are your skills online?"

I didn't bother to answer. It was too risky. Instead, I looked at the nametag on the woman's mustard-colored uniform smock to confirm, and said, "Hello, Mitzy. Nice to see you again."

"Wish I could say the same." Mitzy's voice was crisp. "No one's forgotten the devastation you left in your wake when—"

Mr. Bixby let out a strangled sound, no doubt deliberately calibrated to derail Mitzy's diatribe.

"My poor dog has hairball problems," I said. "I'm quite sure it won't come up in here."

"I should hope not. There are no pets allowed," Mitzy said.

"He's not a pet," I said. "He's a service—"

"Don't bother," Mitzy interrupted. "You probably lie as much as your mother." Her eyes sharpened even more. "Where is Shelley, anyway? Haven't seen her in weeks and she does like my coffee."

I'd prepared for this by running a few scenarios while in the shower earlier. "Mom's headed down south to see my gran. I promised to keep an eye on the house while she's gone."

"Really?" She didn't buy a word of it. "After fifteen years you come home only when your mom is gone? What kind of daughter—?"

Mr. Bixby unleashed another retching hack.

"I will take the blueberry scone, since you recommend it," I said. "I hear you're a talented baker."

"Not me," she said. "Renata Scott is my baker. I believe you were friends once." She turned and bellowed, "Ren, there's an old familiar face here."

"Not that old," I joked, as my heartbeat quickened. Renata and I had been the very best of friends... until I blew it.

"True," Mitzy said. "Your mom's dress ages you, although it does fit like a glove. Shelley's kept her figure and you're the spitting image of her."

Mr. Bixby squirmed under my arm. "Stop squishing me. I'm enjoying being alive and have no desire to cross back over anytime soon."

Renata Scott came out of the back room, wiping her hands on her apron. Her jet-black hair was confined under a net but she was still stunning. Her dark eyes were heavily lined, and her lips ruby red with a shiny gloss. Not everyone could rock a hairnet, but Ren had classic features and white, even teeth, which she showed now in a hesitant smile.

"Hey, Ren." My voice sounded nearly as strangled as Mr. Bixby's just had, hopefully minus the fake hairball. "Good to see you. This gentleman was singing your praises as a baker." I turned to find the man in question had vanished. The exchange with Mitzy had obviously tarnished my charm. "Is the blueberry scone my best option?"

"You'd prefer the chocolate raspberry cupcake," she said. "Unless your tastes have changed."

"Dogs can't eat chocolate," Mr. Bixby said. "I'll take the scone."

"We'll take both, then," I said. "A lot has changed, but not my love of chocolate."

Ren's eyes—as intense and dark as bitter chocolate—scanned me. "You look great," she said at last. "*Are* you?"

A laugh escaped the dog first, but I echoed it. "Am I great? No. Merely average in some regards and below in others. But I'm doing okay." For the first time, my smile felt genuine. "Glad to be home."

Her eyes widened. "You're staying? After—"

The hairball hack started again as Mr. Bixby steered the conversation out of dangerous Wyldwood water.

When he stopped, I jumped in quickly. Ren deserved an honest answer, or at least as close to honest as I could offer at this point. "Home for now. Watching over the house while Mom is away. I hope we can—"

Another retching cough started, and the dachshund practically convulsed in my armpit. "Would you mind, Mr. Bixby?" I said it aloud. "Sorry, Ren. Sometimes this dog is too much."

She laughed. "Good thing he's cute, then. I've never seen a handsomer dachshund. His coat is so shiny and his eyes are like the richest fudge brownie. And those paws... I could eat them."

"I doubt they'd taste too great. You have no idea where they've been."

"Do they smell like corn chips?" she asked. "That's what I always loved about my old lab. She's gone now."

"I—I'm not sure," I said. "Never really thought about it." I grabbed one of Mr. Bixby's paws and bent over. He squirmed and uttered a few words no dog should say even in my head. "Not really. More like... You know, I'm not quite sure what they smell like."

Ren started walking around the counter. "Let me sniff."

"She will not," Mr. Bixby said. "Flattery will get her nowhere with me."

"Don't you want to know what your paws smell like?" I asked, as he writhed harder.

"Renata," Mitzy said. "Do I need to remind you this is a café? We serve food here, most of which you prepare. A discussion of dog feet is off-putting for some, including me." She turned her eyes to the door. The middle-aged man was just a speck in the distance. "Janelle's already lost me one customer."

"Not a chance, Mitzy," I said. "He said you serve the best coffee in all of hill country and there's no way he'll give that up."

Mitzy looked somewhat mollified as she pushed a paper cup and a paper bag across the counter to me. "Well, don't let us keep you, Janelle. That'll be ten dollars. Even."

It was pretty steep for coffee, a scone and a cupcake, but I fumbled to find my card while jockeying the dog.

Ren rolled her eyes behind her boss and then said, "I've got you covered, Janny. Welcome home."

CHAPTER SEVEN

"I've changed my mind," Mr. Bixby said, trotting ahead of me down the sidewalk. "I like her."

"Ren?" I asked. "She's awesome. We were very close until... the incident. Which you probably know all about."

"I don't, actually." He stopped in front of Mabel's Fables and looked up at me. "Your mind is mostly a wide open space, like a factory showroom, but there are a couple of trunks with padlocks. That incident must be inside one of them."

"When we have a little more time, I'll unlock it for you," I said. "It's important for context. Right now, I see Laverne Billings heading our way."

The real estate agent moving toward us was about Gran's age but looked older because of the mauve tint in her hair. She was fleet of foot, however, in black, rubber-soled lace-ups that seemed jet propelled.

Her arms came out to hug me and I automatically stepped back, stumbling over a planter and nearly falling. As a young teen, I learned that touching people—especially their jewelry—could raise a host of unwelcome images from their memories. So, I tried to keep my distance and normally I was more graceful about it. Mom's stodgy shoes were throwing me off my poise game.

"Laverne, it's so good to see you," I said, smoothing my hair with both hands. "Gran was just singing your praises and asked me to send her best."

She let her red-framed cat eyeglasses slide down the bridge of her nose to evaluate me. "I was always fond of Bridie," she said. "It was a shame what happened."

"Gran's very happy at the Briar Estates. It's like a luxury spa and I don't think we could drag her out of there now."

The glasses slipped a little more. "And your mother's joined her? That doesn't sound like Shelley's style."

There was a coffee cup in Laverne's hand. She'd visited the Beanstalk Café and filled up on gossip before meeting me.

"They'll enjoy some quality mother-daughter time," I said, turning my fake smile up a couple of notches. "And as for me, I'm looking to stay in Wyldwood Springs for a while." I gestured to the store. "Set up a little business."

"Do they think that's a good idea?" she asked, shoving her glasses back up her nose. There was a ring on her finger with a large green stone. If it was an emerald, it was worth a bomb. If it was a green diamond, even more.

"Gran sent me home," I said. "And Mom's been asking for years. So yes, I suppose so."

She set her coffee on the rim of a planter and sorted through dozens of keys on a ring. Then she said, "Others probably think your setting up shop on Main Street is a bad idea."

"That's a shame because I want to breathe new life into this place. It's been empty for years, right?"

Laverne sighed. "Couldn't get a tenant to stick, although it's full of character."

"Too full, from the sounds of it," Mr. Bixby said, pushing through the gap as she opened the door.

I followed, but Laverne stopped in the doorway. When I turned, I saw a tremor pass over her. Then her disapproving frown turned into a grimace and her feet didn't budge.

I saw the reason why immediately, even if Laverne couldn't. On the long seat in front of the wide window sat an adorable poodle cross. She was medium sized and fine-boned, with a mop of unruly apricot curls.

It hadn't taken long to find the resident ghost, or at least one of them. If that's all I had to contend with, I would consider myself lucky.

Mr. Bixby also saw the ghost dog and took issue immediately. His sharp, insistent yapping made Laverne step backward onto the sidewalk. "What's wrong with him?" she asked.

"Who knows? Dogs pick up on the strangest things."

He charged across the hardwood floor and stood under the window seat, yelling canine accusations at what would have appeared to Laverne to be thin air.

"How very odd," she said. "Janelle, I'm sorry, but this place really isn't right for anyone."

I glanced around and smiled. This place was everything right... for me. It had soft lighting, high ceilings and plenty of old oak accents to add to the charm. It wouldn't take much effort to clean up the garbage strewn around. Someone had probably left in a hurry.

"I love it and I'll take it," I said.

"You haven't even asked the rent," Laverne called through what was now just a crack in the door.

"I'm sure you'll give me a fair price," I said. "Since you haven't been able to keep it leased."

"I can't in good conscience let you open a—what kind of business did you say?"

"I didn't, because I don't want to spoil the surprise." I spun around with my arms flung wide as Mr. Bixby continued to scold the poodle. The ghost dog had shifted into a play pose. Then she pranced along the edge of the seat, baiting him. He followed, his voice getting shrill to the point of hysteria. "Laverne, I'm sure you can see there's something strange here. My dog is very unnerved."

"That's why renting it is a bad idea," Laverne said. "You'll find it hard to bring customers through the door. The stories date back long before Mabel's Fables. Strange footsteps. Heavy breathing. Growling. Eerie wailing. The list goes on. Some insisted on giving it a try but either got too spooked to stay, or their businesses..."

"Tanked," I said. "I get it. I've heard the stories about the place being haunted. It'll be different for me, Laverne."

She rolled her eyes behind the cat eyeglasses. "Everyone else said the same thing. What makes you think your chances are any better?"

I gestured to Mr. Bixby, now pacing back and forth under the windowsill, growling. He sounded like a regular dog. In fact, he hadn't said a word to me since we stepped inside.

"My dog's a ghost hunter, Laverne. I wouldn't be at all surprised if the resident spirit—or spirits—decided to leave." I grinned at her. "Maybe they'll move down the street to one of the other stores and give this place a break."

"Don't even say that," Laverne said. "All my tenants are good people and they don't deserve trouble like that."

"Your tenants? Do you own this strip, Laverne?"

Her face flushed. "Not me, of course. I'm just the property manager."

"Well, won't the owner be thrilled to hear a ghost hunting dachshund wants to take over this long-empty store? I'm your best hope of leasing the place anytime soon."

"The owner is fine with letting it sit empty," she said. "I only agreed to show it to you because of your grandmother. She'll need help to sell the Brighton manor when the time comes. Its reputation is even worse than this store's."

Ah. So this was about earning a commission on the house. Well, the time for that wasn't coming anytime soon, but I'd use whatever leverage I had.

"That's a good point, Laverne. It'll be tough to keep up the manor and the store on my own." I shrugged and directed my words through the crack in the door. "I'd want to confirm my mom is on board before making any big decisions, of course."

"Of course." She shoved her glasses back in place. "If she comes back, I'll be pleased to help."

"That's so good to know," I said. "I don't have many friends in town and I assume my mom has detractors, although she's never said so to me."

Laverne's glasses slid down again. "I learned long ago not to speak ill of someone's parents, Janelle. It's one thing for you to criticize and quite another for me."

"Well, Mom could be a thorn in my side and I'm sure others agreed. Part of my reason for coming back was to work through these things. I hope she doesn't stay away long."

My last words sounded plaintive, and it seemed to soften Laverne a little. A gust of minty breath came through the crack in the door as she sighed. "No one's seen Shelley in weeks, and I'm not sure I buy your story that she's with Bridie."

"Where else would she be?"

Laverne shrugged. "No idea. People leave Wyldwood without a forwarding address all the time. Especially when they've crossed the wrong people."

"Did Mom cross the wrong people?"

Another minty sigh. "Shelley crossed nearly everyone at one point or another. In my view, she had too much time on her hands. Those of us holding down a job don't have the luxury of having big opinions on how the town should operate."

"Sounds like Mom," I said. "Lots of opinions."

"Take it from me, Janelle—someone who's moved among all ranks in town—sticking your neck out in Wyldwood Springs is never a good idea. Shelley seemed oblivious to the repercussions, and I worry that caught up with her."

The minty smell started to make me feel lightheaded as Laverne confirmed my fears for Mom were warranted. If I wanted to keep the information flowing, however, I'd need to sound nonchalant. Luckily, I had plenty of experience with that.

"Laverne, the Briar Estates is exactly the right place for my mom to lie low until tensions die down. Is there someone I could speak to on her behalf? To smooth the waters?"

She shook her head hard enough to dislodge her glasses. They dangled from a red, beaded string that matched her frames. I remembered her pretty eyeglass strings from childhood. She had a color for every season and special holiday editions. It was her signature touch.

After a pause, she leaned heavily on the doorframe. "Janny, I don't mean to upset you, but you probably know that the waters only got rough for your family after your high school prank."

"That was fifteen years ago. Surely I can get a second chance now?"

She toyed with the beaded string and pursed her lips. "Folks here have long memories."

"Well, I intend to run a respectable business and contribute to the community. Gradually I'll redeem the Brighton name."

"That's the wrong way to go about it," she said, putting the glasses back on. "The right way is to head back to the Briars."

"I can't do that." I looked around the store and shook my head. "This is the right place for me, Laverne. I can feel it and I bet you can, too."

Her head did the hard shake again and dislodged the glasses once more. No wonder she needed those chains. "I feel nothing of the sort."

This wasn't going as I'd hoped. Laverne was determined to hold onto the keys, and my persuasive powers were failing.

Mr. Bixby finally stopped yapping at the ghost dog and threw me a quick glance. "If you actually want this place, I suggest you test out your other powers. Isn't that what you came home to do?"

"No," I said.

"No *what?*" Laverne asked.

I turned on my best hospitality smile again. "No, I just can't give up on my dream. I'm utterly convinced this is my store, Laverne."

"It's not in the cards," she said. "Come on out of there."

"Let me talk to the owner and make my case." I eyed her fingers on the door. "Please, Laverne?"

Reaching out, I touched her hand, targeting the big green stone. An image instantly appeared in my mind of a tall, silver-haired man. He was as handsome as an aging movie star, but his smile was feral. Laverne had a great deal of respect for him so I suspected he was the owner. I tried to pour reassurance into her that leasing to me was the right thing to do. I didn't have much experience influencing someone's thoughts, but I knew from Mom it was possible.

"Oh my," she said, moving her hand away. "I don't feel so great all of a sudden. Must be the heat."

"Are you okay?" Her eyes looked glazed and I reached through the crack in the door to give her arm a squeeze. "Thank you so much for agreeing to let me lease the place, Laverne."

"I didn't agree... did I?" Her voice was filled with doubt. "I had better check with the owner first."

"How could he possibly object when I'm transferring the full year's rent now?" My visit inside her mind had provided the lease amount and it was reasonable for a space on Main Street. Handily, it had also provided important personal information I'd need to make this official quickly. "That proves my commitment to treating this store like the gorgeous gem it is."

I pulled out my phone and transferred most of my savings to her and tapped out a quick email. "Now, if you could just reply to confirm, we're as good as done." I waited while she pecked out the words with her long red nails. "Thank you so much," I said when I heard the ping. "Come by for a signature when you can, Laverne, but consider it a deal." I held out my hand, palm up. "Keys, please."

"I—I don't think that's a good idea."

I had succeeded in confusing her and reducing her resistance, but something still held her back.

"Oh, for pity's sake," Mr. Bixby said. "*I'll* close this deal."

I turned in time to see him lunge at the ghost dog. She leapt right over him and charged directly at me. The jaunty angle of her tail told me it was a joyous romp, not an attack. Still, I stepped quickly aside as my short dog gave chase to the taller one. "Whoa! Did you feel that cold breeze?"

Laverne gasped and closed the door abruptly. Then she opened it just enough to shove her hand back in. The keys dangled between her thumb and index finger.

I grabbed it before she could change her mind, and she set off toward the Beanstalk Café on her jet-propelled rubber soles to inject some new life into the rumor mill.

CHAPTER EIGHT

Mr. Bixby clicked back to me over the hardwood floor with his skinny tail lashing in apparent pride. "I got rid of that mutt." His dark eyes had a slightly eerie glow I hadn't noticed before. "It is a girl, right?"

"I believe so, yes," I said. "She has a sweet way about her."

"Sweet? She acts like she owns the place."

I laughed. "She probably *has* owned the place for longer than I've been on the planet. The ghost stories were already circulating when I was a kid. So, I'd say we're guests on her turf, Mr. Bixby, and should behave as such."

He looked around for the playful poodle and then gave a disgruntled snort. "I'm higher in the pecking order than she is, now."

"Two days ago, you were exactly where she is. Maybe the same fate awaits her."

His muzzle swiveled back to me. "You're not bringing her back over, too, are you? Three's a crowd, Miss Brighton."

"I notice I'm always Miss Brighton when you disapprove of me," I said. "You sound like Boswell. All uppity butler, without the posh accent."

"If you're trying to insult me, I'd thank you to recall I just closed the deal on this dump for you."

"That you did. Laverne would not take a telling with my feeble powers, I'm afraid. Some silver fox dude has a bigger hold on her mind than I do." I strolled around the store, grinning. "The place is ours, Mr. Bixby. What a score!"

"You're welcome," he said. "I'll have my work cut out for me keeping that flighty poodle in check. She'll scare away your customers with her erratic, explosive maneuvers."

"How about you leave her alone and see what happens? She probably has something to tell us, and it won't happen till we gain her trust." I slipped behind the old oak counter and peered over at him. "Both of us."

He strutted around the open area between the door, window and counter. "I don't trust other dogs. Most are imbeciles, with the possible exception of Keats, the wonder dog."

"Our new ghost friend is no imbecile. She's managed to keep the place to herself for decades." I pulled out my phone. "Let's call Sinda and see what she thinks."

He circled back around. "Good idea. Counter, please. I don't want any sudden ambushes during our conversation. So far, you two are the only people who can actually hear me and I want to enjoy it."

"I don't know about the counter, Mr. Bixby. The ghost dog is springy. What if she startles you and you fall off?"

"I'll brace for attack."

I ran my fingers over the oak. "And scratch the wood? I don't think so. Let me find her."

I didn't have far to look. As soon as I spoke, she materialized on the window seat again, paws demurely crossed. Walking over slowly, I knelt on both knees and offered my hand, which she pretended to sniff, as if it were the polite thing to do.

"I'm Janelle," I said. "Thank you for helping us get the lease on this place. It's kind of you to share your space with us." Her ears came forward and her mouth opened in a happy pant. She understood me, even if she couldn't or wouldn't speak. "My dachshund has a heart of gold under that bluster. In fact, he saved my life. So, I hope you'll cut him a break and maybe not knock him off the counter—or anything else—because I need him."

"She most certainly does," he said, from behind me.

The ghost dog gave what appeared to be an eyeroll, but I could feel her relenting.

"What's your name?" I asked.

"Hear that?" Mr. Bixby said. "A whole lot of nothing."

"Not nothing," I said. The ghost dog's voice was little more than a faint whisper in my mind, but it was something. "Unless I'm much mistaken, her name is Bijou."

"You didn't hear that," he said. "I'd have heard it."

I nodded at the dog's swishing tail. "Proof positive that you don't hear everything I do. That message was encrypted just for me."

"Whatever," he said. "Sinda can hear me."

That was true, and I could only assume it was because Sinda had magical powers herself. She claimed they were low grade, like mine, but neither of us had fully explored the genetic hand we'd been dealt.

Bijou turned on the seat to look out the window and I nearly screamed. Outside, four women stood on the sidewalk with their faces practically pressed to the glass. I recognized most of them as former friends of Gran's. In addition to Mitzy from the Beanstalk Café, Frida Dayne, Virginia Steiner, and Candace Riordan all stared down at me. It appeared that they'd been watching as I knelt by the window seat chatting to Bijou, the ghost poodle.

"Probably thought you were praying," Mr. Bixby said, with a snicker. "It could be worse."

Oh, it was worse. Some of the biggest gossips in town had

caught me with my psychic pants down. Mitzy had her phone in hand and was probably getting the word out about my eccentricities. Maybe even added a video.

There was nothing to do but embrace the situation. Rising, I gave them a merry wave, and after Bijou flitted off, I beckoned them to come inside. The women looked at each other, decided against joining me, and moved off as quickly as flustered hens.

"Well, that was awkward," I said, heading back to the counter. "Not the first impression I'd hoped to make."

"They'll be back," Mr. Bixby said, as I lifted him onto the counter. "You've piqued their curiosity now."

He strutted across the countertop leaving paw prints in the thick dust. Then he lifted a paw and blew on it, sending particles into the sunbeams and my nose. When Sinda picked up, I was sneezing.

"Janelle, what a relief to hear from you. If you're sneezing, you're alive."

"Very much so, thanks to you."

I set the phone down to grab a tissue, and Mr. Bixby took the liberty of pressing the speaker button with a dusty paw. "And me," he said, projecting louder than necessary. "I'm here, too, Sinda, and I'm not too humble to say I'm earning my keep."

"Humility isn't one of his virtues," I said.

"Flaws, you mean," Mr. Bixby said. "Humility is making you play small, Janelle. And that's going to get us both in deep water here."

Ignoring that, I paced back and forth behind the counter while I filled my friend in on all that had transpired since we left her jewelry store down south. Was it really only two days ago? Sinda listened without interruption, which couldn't be said of the dog, who continued to interject his version of events. It was annoying, but his self-aggrandizement also added a note of levity to what might have been a rather grim tale.

"In summary," I said, picking up the phone again, "I've got someone on my tail, a ghost butler with a memory problem, and a mother either kidnapped or on the run."

"That's a lot of bad news," Sinda said. "Why do you sound so happy?"

"Because there's some fabulous news, too. Mr. Bixby and I just landed the new Whimsy—if you'll give me permission to use the name."

"A store? How wonderful!"

"It's absolutely perfect, Sinda." I came around the counter and twirled again. This place made me feel as giddy as young Maria in *The Sound of Music*. When I stopped spinning, I saw a few women lined up outside the window, staring. I gave them a wave and they scurried away. Clearly, landing this place was only getting me up to bat. There were plenty of bases to run before I was accepted in this town. "I'll sell your jewelry and other gifts."

"Janelle has failed to mention a little problem," Mr. Bixby said. Shouted, really, since the phone was now too far away for his liking. "A big problem, actually. The place is haunted."

"That's how we were able to get it," I said. "It's been haunted for decades but Bixby and I are probably the only ones who can see the ghost. She's a poodle cross. Maybe thirty pounds of apricot fluff."

"There's no fluff on a ghost," he said. "And air weighs nothing at all."

I shook my finger at him. "For a dog who was a ghost until very recently, you're very intolerant."

Sinda laughed. "There's nothing like the zeal of the recently converted. Mr. Bixby, you be nice to that fluffy little lady. It seems like she's in need of rescue, too."

"That's exactly what I wanted to know," I said. "Is she among your jewels, Sinda? And how exactly do I get her to cross over?

She's full of life, which seems like a strange thing to say about a ghost, but it's true."

"You've spoken to her?" she asked.

"I've tried, but all she'd tell me was her name, and not out loud," I said. "I don't know where to go from here."

"Oh dear, I really have no idea how this works either," she said.

I walked over to a pile of cardboard boxes in a corner. There was plenty of cleaning to do before I could set up properly. "How about you send me a photo of your pieces and we'll see if our new friend is among them?"

"I have a better idea," she said. "I'll deliver the jewelry personally and help you get the place up and running."

"Really? You'd do that?" My voice got high and squeaky, like the kid who got chosen first for a schoolyard team. Reality set in just as fast. "Probably not a good idea, though, Sinda. Remember, we were chased home. I don't know how well we can protect ourselves, let alone you."

"You let me worry about me," she said. "I may be old but I refuse to be counted out. In fact, I was thinking about taking an online survivalist course your gran told me about."

"With Ivy's friend, Edna Evans?" I asked.

"That's the one. If I come up that way, I could do some training in person."

I couldn't help grinning. Edna was a quirky octogenarian prepper, but she had the life force of someone half her age.

"All right, then," I said. "There's plenty of room at the house and I could sure use your advice on setting up and running the store. And everything else. No matter where I step, I put my foot in it."

"Don't worry, we'll figure it out together," she said. "I'll just ask your handsome boyfriend to keep an eye on this place while I'm gone."

My face flushed with a volcanic burst. "If you mean Chief Gillock, we've never even had a date."

"When there's a strong connection, dating is just a formality," she said. "I've seen enough couples in my time who were destined to be together—including my own dear husband and me."

"Dashing Drew for the win," Mr. Bixby said.

"I'm not the marrying type," I said. "I used to be the *dating* type, but that's behind me now. I have other priorities."

"I'm sure your gran would agree there are certain timelines a woman needs to keep in mind."

I gathered some boxes with my free hand, wondering if there was a dumpster out back, where this refuse—and the conversation —could go.

"You don't have children," I said. "Why are you concerned about my ticking clock?"

"I *couldn't* have children," she said. "You can and will. I sense it."

"If she doesn't mess it up," Mr. Bixby said, signaling with one paw that he wanted to be lifted down. "And speaking of messes, if you saw her now you'd wonder about her chances with Dashing Drew."

"Mom's taste was certainly different from mine," I said. "Very, uh—"

"Dowdy," Mr. Bixby said. "Dated. And undatable. In my opinion."

"And you know so much about dating?" I said, as he led me into the back room.

"Actually, yes. Like Sinda, I spent decades observing couples in a jewelry store, remember? On top of that, Lexie enjoyed that reality show with the hunky bachelors."

Sinda's laugh sounded as rich as a young woman's. "You two sound like an old married couple. I suppose that's Drew's true competition."

"Dashing Drew cannot compete with me," Mr. Bixby said, coming to an abrupt stop.

"Especially since he is chief of police in a far-off district," I said. "There's little chance of our fulfilling this so-called destiny."

"Watch your step," the dog said. "There's a road hazard."

I shifted the cardboard boxes out of my sightline and found the ghost poodle barring the back door. A canine stop sign.

"Move it," Mr. Bixby told the ghost. "We've got important business."

"Bixby, let me do the talking," I said. "Sinda, I'm just going to slip the phone in my pocket and have a word with my new friend. I'd like you to listen in if you don't mind."

"Of course, dear friend," Sinda said.

Setting the boxes down, I knelt again to meet the ghost dog on her level. "Bijou, if something's bothering you, you can tell me. We mean you no harm."

"Speak for yourself," Mr. Bixby said.

"Bixby, stop that." The voice came from my pocket and he deflated a little. "The dog doth protest too much. I think you've got a crush on this poodle."

He lapsed into a huffy silence, which allowed me to continue negotiating an exit with the poodle. "I just want to see if there's a dumpster. It's time to start turning this place into a thing of beauty, which I'm sure you'll enjoy after so many years alone."

The weak light in the back room made it difficult to see the dog clearly, especially since she had faded considerably. When I leaned closer, however, I saw that her hackles were up and there was a circle of white around her eyes.

Uh-oh.

"Step back, Janelle," Mr. Bixby said. "She's vicious."

I shook my head. "She's scared. Either of us or something outside."

"Maybe you shouldn't push your luck," Sinda called out. "Take some time to win her over."

I sat back on my heels and studied the dog. "Are you trying to protect us, Bijou? Because if you are, don't worry. I can handle myself."

Mr. Bixby snorted. "Sometimes it's touch and go, but we're a good team."

The poodle moved reluctantly out of the doorway, hackles still raised.

"I have the feeling there's more out back than a dumpster," I said.

"Do be careful, dear," Sinda called, from my pocket.

Standing, I picked up the boxes again and slid the bar back in the lock. There were probably threats on every corner in Wyldwood Springs. I had better get used to facing them head on.

"Let me go ahead, Mr. Bixby," I said. "See if it's safe."

"That's noble of you, but I didn't come back to the side of the living to let you die first," he said, pushing through my feet.

"We're not going to die." I eased open the door a crack and peered out. "Like you said, I'd sense that, right?"

"I don't know how it all works yet." He sounded less confident. The poodle had us both a little spooked.

Opening the door a bit wider, I saw a large blue dumpster that was likely shared by several stores, judging by the flies and stench. It wasn't the garbage that caught my attention, however, but a pair of shoes on the pavement at the end of the dumpster. They were black and sensible—the type you'd see on many senior ladies.

"That doesn't seem right," I said. It brought an instant flashback of discovering feet akimbo behind the counter at Sinda's jewelry store.

"What doesn't seem right?" Sinda asked from my dress pocket.

"There's a pair of shoes behind the dumpster. At a very awkward angle. I'm going to guess—"

"There's feet still in them," Mr. Bixby concluded.

I dropped the boxes and started to run toward the shoes. Sinda's questions cut in and out as the phone flopped around. Mom's Mary-Janes were a size too large and slowed me down, so the dog got ahead of me quickly.

He stopped abruptly and barked a warning. "Bad news. Bad news."

It was very bad news indeed. For Laverne Billings, in particular.

"What's happened?" Sinda called out, as I peered around for threats.

"I'm afraid Laverne Billings has passed away rather suddenly."

"The real estate agent who just leased you the store?"

"That's the one," I said. "She must have come back here to toss the 'For Lease' sign into the trash. It was sticking out of the planter in front of the store earlier."

"And now," Mr. Bixby said, "It's sticking out of Laverne."

CHAPTER NINE

A t first, I kept my eyes on the sign itself. Most of its real estate was taken up by Laverne's face in happier times. In the photo, she was about 30 years younger. Her hair was still dark and she wore cat eyeglasses with blue frames and a matching bead chain in the same shade as the agency's logo. She was also wearing a smile I hadn't seen on her even once today.

My eyes drifted down to her now, lying face up on the asphalt. Her sightless eyes stared at the blue sky and one hand was raised permanently.

"She must have taken a terrible fall," I told Sinda. "I assume she climbed the ladder to put the sign into the dumpster and then fell on top of it."

"You mean the sign fell on top of her," Mr. Bixby said. "And with considerable velocity. You must be in shock if that seems feasible, Janelle. Wouldn't you say it's more likely that the sign has been posted quite deliberately to say that Laverne's body is now for lease?" He circled the body, sniffing. "I suppose it is, if you believe in a potential zombie apocalypse."

"You have a point," I said. "Her body is certainly vacant. I can feel it... without actually feeling it."

"Perhaps you should, dear," Sinda said. "Touch it. Her, I mean. Make sure she's actually dead. Just in case."

That unglued my shoes and I took a couple of steps backward. "I don't want to touch her, poor thing. It would feel like a total violation."

"She's definitely dead," Mr. Bixby said. "Laverne has left the building."

"No jokes, Bixby," I said. "This is a terrible tragedy."

"And for it to happen behind your new store makes it even more so," Sinda said. Her voice was still muffled by the fabric of the dress. I pulled out my phone and turned down the volume. The stores on either side were open and someone might be listening. Might in fact emerge at any time.

A sunbeam hit Mr. Bixby's shiny black fur as he strutted around, taking inventory. "Here's something strange. Laverne doesn't smell like herself anymore."

"Should she?" I asked. "I mean, after she's..."

"Left the building?" he asked, with a sly chuckle. "Yes. At least in my experience of encountering dead bodies in my former life."

"As a ghost, you mean? Could you smell anything?"

"The life before my former life," he said. "When I was actually alive. Regrettably, a few bodies came into range of my impressive sniffer."

"Oh, Bixby," Sinda said. "I'm sorry to hear you experienced that."

"We'll need to wait on the stories," I said. "Because if he's right, Laverne may have died of very unnatural causes."

He applied his impressive sniffer to the asphalt and started moving around the area. "Aha! Rotten eggs."

"Rotten eggs?" I said. "The bistro next door probably serves brunch."

Lifting his nose, he stared at me as if I'd lost my faculties. Maybe I had, temporarily. Discovering bodies was becoming more commonplace, but I was far from acclimated to it yet. I hoped I never would be.

"Miss Brighton," he said. "Use your noggin."

"Who says noggin anymore?" I asked.

"A dog that was around long before your time. I've got all the slang, old and new."

"Stop bickering," Sinda said. "It's not the time for it, especially if Mr. Bixby is saying what I think he's saying."

"I'm saying it," he said. "And I couldn't be more delighted to have that ability."

"I've noticed," I said. "You like hearing your own voice talking in riddles."

"Janelle." This time, Sinda's voice was both calm and severe. "Take a deep breath and focus. You may be in danger."

Now the dog cocked his head while staring at me in silence, and finally my brain made the right connections. About the wrong connections. "Oh. Okay. You're saying you smell—"

"Quiet," he interrupted. "There are likely spies everywhere."

I leaned down and whispered, "Magical flatulence?"

"Precisely."

"Did I hear flatulence?" Sinda asked, and then added quickly, "I mean, the word?"

I took the phone off speaker and described the dog's olfactory experience during our drive home. "It seems that he smells the same thing here."

"Sulphur," he said. "Fermented yard waste. Hint of roadkill."

I put her back on speaker and said, "Take a good sniff around, Bixby. See if you can't learn more."

The dog did just that while I stared down at Laverne.

"Hey," I said. "Where are her glasses? She was wearing red-framed cat eyeglasses on a beaded string when she visited earlier."

"Let the police find them," Sinda said. "It's time to call this in,

Janelle. The longer you wait, the stranger this whole thing will look."

"But which police?" I said. "If it's the kind of problem we theorize, I might need the underground variety. But Gran told me you don't call them. They call you."

"Then just go with the regular type," Sinda said. "I do wish Chief Gillock were there to help get to the bottom of this."

"Me too." Something tightened in my heart. I had tried very hard to suppress any feelings I had for Drew Gillock and now they were leaking out of my pit of buried emotions. With Mom gone, it had become too full to hold everything in, apparently. "But we'll manage this ourselves. Right, Bixby?"

The dog didn't answer. He was on the other side of the dumpster using his special skills to follow the magical villain's flatulence trail.

I couldn't bear to be alone, so I kept Sinda on the line and slipped the phone back in my pocket. Then I went over to the ladder on the side of the tall dumpster.

"What are you doing?" she called out. "I don't need special senses to know you're up to something."

"Just poking around." I puffed a bit as I climbed the ladder. Panic had apparently given me the heart and lungs of someone far older than my septuagenarian friend. When I reached the top, I looked into the trash, tried not to gag and failed. It was nearly full of what appeared to be mostly bistro castoffs with a lot of decaying foliage from the flower store on the other side of my store. There was a scrabbling noise as a couple of rats emerged from the pile to clamber up and over the side. A sharp bark below told me my dachshund's natural prey drive kicked in at the sight of them.

"Focus, Bixby," I said. "You've traded in your old calling for a new one."

The dog followed his nose down an alley on the far side of the bistro.

Clinging to the dumpster handle with my left hand, I pulled out the phone with my right and snapped a few photos. "I see Laverne's glasses in the trash. She got this far. Or someone got her this far. I can reach them."

"Wouldn't they be evidence?" Sinda asked. "Better not to touch them, Janelle."

"You're right." I took another step up anyway. Now I was at the very top and balanced rather precariously on Mom's sensible heels. Honestly, I fared far better in stilettos than these supposedly less hazardous shoes. "But those beads could be real stones. I might be able to get a sense of who's behind this in a way the cops can't."

"It's their job to figure it out." Sinda was very much the voice of reason. "Your gran told me the two police forces have been giving each other checks and balances for more than a century."

"It *is* their job, but will they?" I asked. "Can they? The problem is I don't know who's on my side, Sinda. If anyone."

"Do you really think this is about you, dear?"

"Possibly, yes. We already know some people didn't want me to come home. Then Laverne leased the place to me and died within an hour. I feel like it's my fault."

"She didn't need to agree," Sinda said.

I popped the phone back into my pocket once more and leaned over to try to reach the eyeglasses. "That's the thing, Sinda. She tried to say no, and I may have given her a mental nudge when regular persuasion failed."

The fabric muffled the sigh that followed. "Happens to the best of us, dear."

"You, too?" I asked, stretching as far as I could.

"Once in a while. Lexie was so very difficult that I may have meddled with her mind sometimes. Never very successfully, I'm afraid. She was very stubborn and my gift is more a breeze than a heavy wind, like yours."

A chuckle drifted back from the alley at that, and I took note that Mr. Bixby's hearing was considerably better than the average dog's.

"And now that wind got her killed."

"You gave her a suggestion, that's all. She wanted you to have the store and you pushed her to agree."

I leaned over to snag the beads. "The least I can do is reunite her with her glasses."

In the end, nervous sweat was my undoing. My left hand slipped on the railing, and I fell forward into the garbage. I could hear Sinda shouting as I floundered to get a grip on something. Anything. Meanwhile the side of the dumpster pressed into my midriff, making it even harder to breathe among slimy peelings, rotting roses and a stripped chicken carcass.

Finally, I managed to push myself upright and found the beaded string of the glasses circling my wrist. All I had to do was pull it in like a life buoy.

Once I was upright, I leaned over again to part with the few bites of the delicious cupcake Renata had given me earlier.

It was a shame that I was still retching when a man stepped out the back door of the bistro next door. He was wearing chef whites and a hairnet over thick dark hair. Tilting his head at the noise, his eyes widened almost as much as Laverne's way down below.

"What in the blue blazes are you doing up there, lady?" he called. "Get out of my dumpster right now or I'm calling the cops."

CHAPTER TEN

"She's no lady," Bixby said, coming back out of the alley at a brisk trot.

"Be quiet," I said, forgetting in the moment that only Sinda and I could hear the dog. "This is important."

"Don't tell me to be quiet," the chef said, coming toward me, and snapping photos with his phone. "You're the one picking through my trash. Who are you and what do you want?"

He was still too far away to see Laverne's body. "Actually, I'd like you to call the police, if you don't mind."

"You *want* me to call the police?" He stopped walking. "Maybe I overreacted. Garbage picking is disgusting, but I'm not sure it's technically a crime." He couldn't help grinning. "I'd say you were punished enough."

I flicked back my hair and sent what appeared to be a slice of mango flying. "Very much so, yes. But it really would be best to call the police." Tipping my head toward the store, I added, "I'm the new tenant here and I've discovered something they'll want to see."

"You've leased Mabel's Fables?" His grin vanished in surprise. "It's haunted, you know. I hear strange noises all the time. You'll be gone in a month, like everyone is."

"Maybe," I said. "I'm the stubborn type."

"That much is true," Mr. Bixby said, staring up at me.

This time I had the sense not to answer back. Out loud, anyway. Mentally, I issued a request to drive the chef back into his restaurant before he could spot Laverne. There was something I wanted to do before the police came. Besides, I didn't care to become better acquainted with my new neighbor while trash hung off me like a junkyard Christmas tree.

Mr. Bixby got the message and sauntered in front of the chef to the open back door of the bistro. When the chef didn't turn, the dog shouted, "Dude. There's a mutt walking into your kitchen. I'm going to garnish your omelets with dog hair."

The stream of yapping didn't make the chef turn. Flicking another disgusting scrap aside, I pointed behind him. "I'm so sorry, but my dog is walking into your kitchen. He's a stray. Still has a few fleas, I'm afraid."

"Fleas!" Bixby was outraged. "I'm a pedigreed dachshund from a very distinguished lineage. We do not get fleas."

The man turned and the dog shot into the kitchen ahead of him.

"Mouthy one, isn't he?" the chef said, following him.

"You have no idea." I climbed down as fast as I could with both hands covered in garbage slime. When my shoes hit the asphalt, I shoved Laverne's glasses into my left pocket, the one without the phone.

"Are you okay, dear?" Sinda called. "That was quite an introduction."

"I'll get him to send you the photos he took," I said. "Words cannot do this justice."

"But you got the eyeglasses?" she asked, as I hurried over to Laverne.

"Yeah, but it was a bum lead. Plastic. I got slimed for nothing."

I was down, but not out.

Not yet.

Dropping to one knee, I reached for Laverne's big green ring. That stone had delivered earlier, and it might again. Wiping my hand on Mom's dress, I reached out.

My worries about garbage slime interfering with my reading were unwarranted. The moment I touched the stone, it literally fell out of its setting and into the palm of my hand.

With it came a rush of dreadful impressions. It was as if I was *in* Laverne's body before she passed, looking up in utter terror as someone—or something—leaned over her. If there was a face, I couldn't see it, because the writhing of the snakes I'd felt near the picnic ground had filled my soul.

There was no doubt in my mind now that Laverne had been murdered in magical cold blood. And unless I was much mistaken, the stone was sending me a powerful message, too. Specifically, to run... before I was run over.

My legs gave out and my butt hit the pavement just as Mr. Bixby careened around the dumpster. "I heard you screaming," he said. "Came as fast as I could."

The green stone dropped from my fingers to land beside Laverne's hand and instantly the images receded.

"I didn't scream. At least, I don't think so."

"Yeah, you did," the dog said. "It was like the devil himself was after you."

"Bixby," I whispered, "I think he might be."

CHAPTER ELEVEN

"Then, you'd better get moving," Bixby said. "You don't want the devil finding you on your backside, do you?"

"No," I said, pushing myself up. "I most definitely do not."

My fingers were still splayed on the ground and my butt in the air when I heard footsteps. Shiny black boots stood directly behind me.

"Ma'am? Are you all right?"

I pushed up the rest of the way and turned. It wasn't the devil, unless he looked like a man far too young to be in a police uniform. First, he stared, and then he winced. Finally, he wiped his nose with the back of his hand and moved a little further away.

"I'm fine," I said. "Thank you for coming."

"You were mumbling to yourself, ma'am. Did you fall and hit your head?"

"I did fall." I directed my thumb to the dumpster. "Inside, not out. I'm so sorry for the smell."

"There's no apology big enough for that." The voice came from down around my ankles, and inside my head. Sometimes it was like hearing in stereo. I'd have to get a handle on my brain-to-dog transmission because it could be very disorienting.

The police officer was so riveted by my stench or appearance that he probably didn't notice the dog and he definitely didn't notice Laverne. "Ethan Bogart next door said you needed a hand. I was doing security at pothole repair and—whoa! You staked Laverne Billings."

"She most certainly did not!"

Two voices overlapped. One was Sinda, indignant and shrill in my pocket. The other no doubt sounded like snarling, as Mr. Bixby expressed his indignation in regular dog language.

"Who was that?" the young cop asked.

"My friend Sinda Joffrey," I said, pulling the phone out of my pocket. "I've had her on the line since Laverne Billings left me with the key to the store about an hour ago. Sinda will be able to vouch for me."

"I most certainly will." Sinda sounded like a prim school mistress. "I can tell you're barely out of short pants, young man. Be careful about casually casting aspersions on someone of good character."

The tone worked to clear the shock from his pale eyes, and he brushed wispy blond hair off his sweaty forehead. Maybe it was his first time seeing a body. It was most certainly his first time seeing a body staked with a real estate sign. He pressed a button on his uniform jacket and requested backup. Then he turned to me and said, "Please go inside and wait. What's your name, ma'am?"

"Janelle Brighton," I said. "I just arrived in town after a long time away. You might know my mother, Shelley."

His mouth worked before he answered. "Yes, I've taken your mom down to the station a couple of times."

The blank mask of my hospitality training slipped into place despite my shock. "Oh dear. It sounds like Mom's had her share of conflicts in the community."

"Always managed to talk herself out of charges," he said. "I don't know how she did it because she was caught red-handed a few times."

"Red-handed?"

"Red-footed, I guess. She liked trespassing. A regular peeping Shelley." He gestured to my outfit. "The dresses were a giveaway. Didn't try very hard to hide what she was doing."

"Peeping Shelley," Mr. Bixby said, with a chuckle. "He may be a callow youth but he's not without humor."

"Mom is a character," I said. "No question about that."

"I suppose that's why you came home? To handle her affairs? The calls were getting more frequent. We left her at the hospital twice and I guess they probably tracked you down. She always asked us not to."

That shot a dart into my heart. If Mom was in such a bad way that she was getting hauled into the station or dropped at the hospital, why wouldn't she let them call me? She always had my number. Surely she knew I would come if she wanted me. But I guess that was just it: she didn't want help from me.

"You don't know what she was thinking," Bixby said. "Or if she was capable of thinking at all. Reserve judgment... of her and yourself."

I ran my hands over my dress, leaving smudges behind. "I didn't know about all this, Officer...?"

"Barrow. James Barrow. We respected your mother's wishes and just tried to keep her from getting hurt."

"Officer Barrow, when I got home this morning, my mother was gone. How long ago did you see her?"

"Few weeks, I guess. I'd have to check."

I tried to hold his gaze but his eyes kept dropping to Laverne and I could hardly blame him for being distracted.

"Laverne was an old friend of my grandmother's," I said. "That's why she agreed to lease me the place. I'm going to turn Mabel's Fables into a jewelry and gift store."

"A jewelry store?" Officer Barrow said. "Is that why you tried to steal the ring off Mrs. Billings? I saw you drop it when I came around the corner."

"Young man," Sinda piped up. "You really should wait till a senior officer arrives to start questioning my dear friend. You're only embarrassing yourself."

"I'm not the one covered in garbage and standing by a dead body," he said. "That's an awfully big emerald. Probably get your boutique off to a nice start."

He pronounced the word bow-tique, possibly deliberately.

"It's a green sapphire," I said. "Not as valuable, and not the sort of thing I'll be selling in my store. Oh, but I do need to surrender these." I reached into my pocket and pulled out the eyeglasses. "She was wearing them when we met earlier, so I climbed up to see if they were in the bin."

He shook his head. "Ma'am, you don't just go digging around a crime scene. Unless you *caused* the crime scene."

"Can you please stop calling me ma'am?" I said. "Just because I'm wearing my mother's dress doesn't make me—"

"Matronly," Mr. Bixby said. "And it kind of does."

I pressed my lips together, knowing that slipping up with Mr. Bixby would put me squarely in range of my supposedly addled mother in the young officer's opinion.

"My mother," I concluded, instead. "But you're right that I shouldn't have gone after the glasses. Officer Barrow, I was in shock and still am. I'm sure you can understand that. Why else would I tumble into a dumpster?"

"You should probably stop talking till my backup arrives. And your lawyer. Do you have one?"

"She doesn't need one," Sinda said. "I'm her alibi."

"We'll let the chief be the judge of that," he said.

The sirens were screaming down Main Street now, and I imagined people were pouring onto the sidewalk to see what terrible luck had befallen Mabel's Fables this time. Perhaps they'd blame the whole sordid affair on the legendary ghost and leave me out of it.

"Fat chance," Mr. Bixby said, reading my mind. "But chin up, Janelle. This will all work out just fine. I've got a good feeling about it."

I watched the cops pour down the alley beside the bistro, with my neighbor, the chef, in their midst.

"It'll be fine," Sinda echoed out loud. "Just another bump in the highway."

"I guess," I said. "The truth always comes out in the wash."

"You sure do need a wash," Mr. Bixby said, wanting the last word, as always. "But I have to admit, you do know how to make a splash."

CHAPTER TWELVE

I t seemed like half the town had gathered around the dumpster before the police managed to barricade the crime scene and chase everyone back to the street. The people who could tear their eyes away from Laverne stared at me and muttered things Mr. Bixby could no doubt hear but had the decency not to pass on. I hadn't expected a homecoming parade, but it was a tough way to make my local debut.

Given my trash perfume, the police probably would have liked to question me outside, but the persistent trickle of onlookers through the alley drove us into the store. Since there was nowhere to sit, the chief of police, Warren Dredger, a bald, rosy-cheeked man in his fifties, directed me to stand with my back to the wooden counter. Some of the officers peered around the store, possibly searching for the ghost. Unbeknownst to them, Bijou, the apricot poodle mix, lounged on the window seat with her tongue hanging out. She may have been the only one enjoying the commotion. I suppose when you've been alone for decades, even a murder investigation is a pleasant diversion.

Officer Barrow brought his boss up to speed quickly, dwelling longer than seemed necessary on my mother and her supposedly deteriorating mental state.

Sinda cleared her throat in my pocket and I pulled out the phone. "Officer Barrow," she said, "you neglected to mention that Janelle has a very sound alibi. Namely me. We've been on the phone since the real estate agent left the store and I'm sure your technology can verify that. She called to tell me the good news about leasing the store. I'm excited to be launching with her and will book the next flight."

"You will?" I said. "Oh Sinda, that's wonderful."

"Of course, dear friend. I can't have you dealing with all this alone. And I have half a mind to bring Chief Gillock with me."

"Andrew Gillock?" Chief Dredger said. "How do you know him?"

"I live in Strathmore County, where he's the chief of police," Sinda said. "How do *you* know him?"

"Drew and I did some special training together a few years ago," Chief Dredger said. "He's a good man."

"A wonderful man, who can also vouch for Janelle's character." Sinda had obviously designated herself my spokeswoman, which was better than a spokesdog.

"I could have stickhandled this fine," Mr. Bixby told me. "The problem is that you forget how this works and blather out loud. It makes you look as crazy as your mother."

My mother was not crazy. Combustible, yes, crazy no. At least, she never had been. Who knows what had happened since I left?

"Chief Dredger," I said, "do you have any idea where my mother is? My gran spoke to her about six weeks ago and didn't raise any concerns. But I came home to find her gone."

"We can discuss your mother another time," he said. "There's a more pressing matter today." He glared at me over his glasses, not unlike the way Laverne had earlier. The thought sent a shiver down my back. "Isn't there, young lady? Now hang up the phone and I'll contact your alibi later."

At least I was a "young lady" now and not a ma'am. That helped to bolster my flagging confidence somewhat as I reluctantly disconnected Sinda. I had always relied heavily on my looks and wardrobe—particularly my shoes—as my armor in the world. In this garbage-splattered frock I felt worse than naked. I didn't know who I was anymore.

"You never did," Mr. Bixby said. "Complete denial of the obvious. This conversation would go much faster if you'd use your skills."

I glared at the dog and directed my thoughts toward him. "It's a police investigation. I want to handle this on the up and up. Once you start with magical lies, it's probably a slippery slope."

"I guess," he said. "Like a big pile of decomposing food scraps."

"So let me do it my way," I said. Or rather thought, digging my teeth into my lower lip to remind me to hold back my commentary.

"Only if you let me create a little diversion," he said. "Trust me."

I trusted him with my life, but not crime scene etiquette. There was no time to quibble, however, because he took off and charged through black boots to the window seat, where Bijou did just as he'd hoped. She took a big leap, passed right through Chief Dredger, and landed on the counter behind him. Like most poodles, she came wired with springs.

The chief gasped and turned quickly to look behind him. "I think—I think I'll just head out back for a second to talk to the team. Make sure the scene is secure."

His boots thudded briskly, and I sent a mental thank you to the ghost dog. She acknowledged me with a deep bow, and then bounded back to the window seat. It seemed to be her favorite spot, so I'd need to get that old floral cushion reupholstered with something more stylish. If I was allowed to keep the place, that is.

The front door opened and Renata Scott walked in. "Hi there. Did someone forget to send my invitation?"

"Miss Scott," Officer Barrow said. "You can't walk into the middle of a police investigation. We're questioning this lady."

In fact, he was the only officer left in the store. The other officers had quietly followed the chief, leaving James Barrow to deal with me alone.

"Jimmy, this 'lady' used to be my best friend," Renata said. "Even before the time I was your babysitter."

The young officer's face flushed instantly, including his rather prominent ears. "That's no excuse, Ren. And in case you hadn't noticed, I'm on duty. Respect, please."

"I don't need an excuse to support an old friend," she said. "She has no connections in town right now. Am I right, Janelle?"

I gave her a grateful smile. "No one. Even my mother is gone, after being taken in for trespassing a few times. Officer Barrow called her a peeping Shelley."

Ren's laugh had been musical when we were teens. It was even more so now, though it sang a sadder song. "Shelley also had plenty of trespassers at your house, too, based on what she said when she came into the Beanstalk Café. I expect she was returning the favor."

"Why would people trespass at our place?" I asked.

"That's a very good question for you, Jimmy," Ren said. "And what were the police doing about it? The poor woman was exhausted from stress and you treated her like she was—"

"Losing her marbles?" Jimmy said. "She was caught in Maisie Gledhill's greenhouse at midnight, Ren. After they'd had a public standoff at Sour Grapes."

Renata moved in front of me, trying to form a human barrier. "Maybe they'd been doing shooters at the bar and Maisie lost," she said. "Regardless, there are always feuds in Wyldwood. Yet you took Shelley Brighton into the station time and again, discrediting her publicly, while doing nothing about the prowlers at her place. Can you explain that, Jimmy?"

"I don't need to explain that... or anything," he said.

"Personally, I think you owe Janelle an apology," Ren said. "Imagine coming home after so many years only to find your mom missing in action while the police ignored it. That would send you into hysterics. You're so fond of your mom."

Jimmy backed away from Renata, his Adam's apple bobbing as he swallowed whatever he really wanted to say. "That's no reason for her to murder Laverne Billings."

Renata's dark eyes widened but then she shook her head so hard the tie came out of her ponytail and unleased a cascade of black hair. "Not a chance, Jimmy. Despite what you might hear, Janelle's one of the good guys. In fact, I might not be around today if she hadn't protected me."

"Oh Ren, that's not true," I said. "We don't know what would have happened."

"I know it wasn't looking good when you intervened, Janelle. And that's why I'm here as a character reference." She took a step toward Officer Barrow. "You know what I'm like, Jimmy. I don't put my rep on the line for just anyone, but I'm doing it for Janelle. I'd thank you to be the voice of reason with Chief Dredger. He might be swayed by outside pressure, but you've been raised to stand up for what's right, thanks in part to me."

My eyes filled with tears of gratitude for my old friend's support. I didn't really feel I'd earned it, but I was glad she remembered what happened on prom night a little differently than I did.

While I was distracted, Bijou, the ghost poodle, had come down from the window seat again to circle Officer Jimmy's shins. He shuddered and the color faded from his face rather suddenly. Turning to me, he said, "Don't move. I'm just going to check on the chief."

The poodle followed him for a few steps and then came back to prance around Renata, fanning tail suggesting she was flirting with my friend.

An odd expression crossed Ren's face. "There's one here, isn't there?" she said, sounding mildly unnerved. "All the stories about this place were true."

I glanced at Bijou to see if she showed any sign of discomfort over my revealing the truth. On the contrary, she was gazing up at my friend adoringly. "It's not what you think, Ren."

"I think it's a Boz situation, and that caused a bit of trouble, didn't it?"

"Aha," Mr. Bixby said. "I knew Sir Windbag was the one who got you chased out of town."

"It's not a Boz situation." I peered around to make sure the police were still gone. "It's a dog, and she's taken quite a shine to you."

"To me!" Ren stepped sideways right into—or, more accurately, through—the ghost dog. The poodle held no grudge and continued prancing for attention. "That I don't need."

Someone cleared his throat conspicuously. "Who doesn't need the love of a good dog?"

"I wouldn't be so sure about that," I told Ren. "This is my dog, Mr. Bixby. He's the best thing that's happened to me in a long time."

"Ever," he said.

"Maybe ever," I added. "And I bet you could use the love of a good dog too."

Renata was dubious. "I had a good dog and it broke my heart to lose her. Sometimes it felt like she was my..." Her voice caught in her throat. "My only friend in this town. If I planned on getting another dog, I'd probably choose one that's alive."

The poodle continued to fawn at Ren's feet. Maybe these two were destined to be companions, like Bixby and me. If so, I'd need to figure out how to bring them together.

"I promise I'll try," I muttered to the ghost dog.

"Is she talking to herself?" Officer Barrow said, joining us again. "Her mother—"

"Never mind, Jimmy," Ren said. "Everyone talks to their dog. You certainly did. That beagle was your very best friend, wasn't she? Princess Leia?"

After that, Officer Barrow dismissed us quickly, saying the chief would question me later at home.

Bidding Bijou adieu, I followed Mr. Bixby and Renata out into the late afternoon sunshine.

CHAPTER THIRTEEN

"Renata seems nice enough," Mr. Bixby said, as we sat waiting in the car for Ren to clock out at the café. "Can we trust her?"

"She was my best friend, second only to Jilly," I said. "Ren had my back from elementary school all the way through to graduation." I leaned across and rolled down his window. "Not that I made it to the graduation ceremony."

"You could trust her *then*," Mr. Bixby said. "Can you trust her now?"

I looked down at the white smock covering Mom's stained and stinky dress. Renata had literally given me the shirt off her back before going back to change into her street clothes. Whether or not I looked better with the chocolate-streaked chef's uniform was debatable, but I felt better. That counted for something.

Still, I sighed over the dog's implication.

"Can I trust anyone anymore, Bixby? Once magic comes into the equation, can I ever be completely sure someone's on the up and up?"

"Nope," he said. "Only me. At least, I hope I have immunity

from magical tampering because you brought me over with your power."

"I would hope so, but there's no one to ask. Sinda is the most informed person I know about these things and she seems to think we broke new ground."

"Then you'll need to assume that the people who didn't want you to come home—who basically hired a hit-woman to keep it from happening—are lying in wait for you here."

I nodded. "I expected that but hoped the underground police would keep things in check long enough for Mom and me to settle some feathers. I wouldn't have come home at all if I thought someone would die because of me."

"You don't know that's what happened to Laverne," he said. "There's probably more to the story."

"The real estate sign sent a graphic message," I said, with a shudder. "Seems like Laverne was promptly and thoroughly punished for leasing the store to me—public enemy number one."

"Hard to believe you earned that designation over a high school prank, but you still have that memory locked down." He glanced over at me. "As annoying as it is, you'll need to do more of that."

"I've had years of practice with repression, but you're going to hear all about that prank today."

The dog sat up a little straighter. "Really? Just when I thought things couldn't get more interesting."

Renata stepped out of the café and waved. She was in jeans and a fresh T-shirt and her long black hair flowed down her back. From that distance, she looked exactly as she had in school—regular girl-next-door with a slightly exotic air.

"Here's what I'm going to do," I explained quickly to Bixby. "I'll test Ren with a stroll down bad-memory lane and see if anyone's been influencing her thoughts. If she runs that gauntlet, we'll give her the benefit of the doubt."

"Your idea sounds as good as any, I suppose."

I scooped him off the passenger seat and put him in the back over his strident objections. "Please do your part, Bixby. Just act like a normal dog for a couple of hours."

"Impossible," he said, as the door opened and Renata slid into the car. "I don't even know what that means."

"It means be quiet for a change," I said, using my inside voice.

Renata ran her hand over the dashboard and grinned. "I can't believe you still have Elsa. She was young and sexy last time I caught a ride."

"Now she's a cougar," I said, laughing. "And doing very well for herself. She was my first pet, and my only pet till very recently. I took very good care of her."

"I loved riding around in Elsa," Ren said, "and I'm so glad to see both of you." Turning, she smiled into the back seat. "And you, too, Mr. Bixby. Wouldn't you prefer to ride up here with me?"

"I thought you'd never ask," he said.

"What adorable sounds he makes," Ren said. "All mumbles and moans."

"Adorable," I agreed, grinning.

Since she couldn't understand him, the dog pounded the blistered upholstery with his front paws. Ren took that as a yes and lifted him gently into her lap. "When my dog passed away two years ago, I took on a couple of side jobs outside town. I'm trying to up my game to have my own store someday. A bakery or café."

Turning the key in the ignition, I double-checked every mirror before pulling out. Who knew when I would be blindsided next?

"How is it that I never knew you loved baking?" I said, driving slowly along the strip.

"Baking wasn't a cool-kid thing to do back then so I kept my sweet ambitions to myself," Renata said. "Not that we were cool kids, really."

I laughed. "Not even close. I barely had a date till the end of senior year."

"It wasn't for lack of fans," she said. "No one dared make a play because of Sir Nigel. The guys couldn't see him but I'm sure they could feel him."

My fingers tightened on the wheel as Renata casually dropped the name. She had seen him a few times when he had the talisman and never been fazed. That gave her a distinct advantage over Jilly, who refused to accept the truth of our ancestry even with evidence right before her eyes.

I took my time cruising along Main Street, taking in all the changes. The storefronts were freshly painted in strong, vibrant colors with names in ornate lettering. Vines crawled up red brick walls and burst into bloom over doorways, and planters did the rest of the heavy lifting. Wyldwood Springs had always been quaint. Now, it was postcard-perfect.

On the surface.

"Once Boz figured out how to find the day pass, nothing was the same," I said. "He assigned himself chaperone and popped out when least expected."

"Remember when you played Juliet in eighth grade and Boz charged on stage just as Romeo was going to kiss you?" Ren said. "Priceless. No one had a clue who tossed Dylan Camp on his butt. Everyone thought it was improv and came back night after night through the run. There was never a more popular production."

"Mom clamped down on Boz, but Dylan was too terrified to land the kiss after that. As was everyone else."

"Until Tanner Jefferson." Ren's smile lit up the car. She had the whitest teeth I'd ever seen. "He was willing to take the risk."

"Poor Tanner," I said. "Mom approved of the Jefferson family and thought I needed to get out a little more. But Boz couldn't stand it. He didn't trust anyone."

Mr. Bixby cleared his throat in my mind. "Sir Windbag just went up in my estimation."

We drove out of town on a modern two-lane bridge, and headed toward the outskirts, where Maisie Gledhill lived. I left the conversation hanging, to see where Renata would take it. So far, her storyline was solid. I would have to touch her to dig any deeper and I wasn't inclined to be that intrusive. There were no rings on her fingers for easy access. No jewelry at all, actually. I guess bakers kept things simple.

After another two bridges and a turn into the suburbs, Renata sighed. "And then came prom."

"And then came prom," I said. "Quite the night."

"The worst night of my life. So far."

"Well, I hope it doesn't get worse than that," I said. "I felt terrible about it and still do. Just so you know."

She crossed her arms, unsettling Mr. Bixby, who let it slide for the sake of the trustworthiness test.

"I figured as much, or you would have answered my calls," she said. "And texts. Your Mom shared your deets whenever she had them, but maybe you didn't get my notes."

"Sometimes I did, and I'm sorry I didn't reply, Ren. I didn't want to put you in danger by staying in contact. My enemies could have hurt you to get to me." I braked at a stoplight and turned to her. "They still might. You're taking a big risk to stand up for me now. I've only been back in town a few hours and look what's happened."

"I still try to do what's right," she said. "You didn't kill Laverne Billings and I'm not going to let you get pegged for it. Not when you were brave enough to come back here to sort things out." She flashed her brilliant smile again. "Remember, I have proof you'll protect me."

"I'll do my very best, I promise." I raised my eyebrows questioningly. "Still no sign of your own weapons system?"

She shook her head. "I'm a dud. It was just wishful thinking on my part that I'd have any magic."

This time I couldn't resist squeezing her arm and she gasped as I passed into her mind. It was as it always had been—a serene garden filled with strange and beautiful flowers. At least, that's the image that always came to me. The only difference now was that dusk had fallen and the cheery sunshine of our youth had vanished.

"You felt something, didn't you?" I asked. "That means you're not a dud, old friend. Just a late bloomer. Even later than me. I've stalled exactly where I was in high school. Arrested magical development."

She shook her head. "It won't happen. I've tried and tried to bring it forth."

"Meanwhile, I've tried and tried to bury it. Mostly been successful, too." I pulled into Withrow Park, which had the most enchanting waterfall in the county, in my opinion. "Let's get some fresh air before we do this."

Mr. Bixby cleared his throat conspicuously. "Impossible, after your dumpster diving."

We got out of the car, and Ren set Mr. Bixby very gently on the grass. He liked that enough to offer her pant leg a little lick of thanks.

"He's the sweetest dog," she said. "How did you find him?"

"Long story," I said. "Maybe we should talk about my mom, first. So that I have my ducks in a row before seeing Maisie. Was Jimmy Barrow right?"

Ren fell into step beside me on the main path, which was strewn with sparkling gravel that still showed to good effect late in the day. All the parks maintained by the town got the glitter treatment. It was part of the façade.

"Your mom seemed to be struggling," Ren said. "She used to come into the café all the time and when she stopped, I dropped by now and then."

She spoke slowly, as if to avoid upsetting me.

"What was wrong with her?" I asked. "The last time we spoke she was still very much herself. Heavy on the lectures and guilt trips about coming home. That only made me want to keep running."

"Maybe three months ago, I saw a change," Ren said. "Shelley started to look harried. Normally she was meticulous about her appearance, yet she was letting herself go." She paused and waited till I turned. "Janelle, she stopped wearing makeup."

"What?" I couldn't have been more shocked if she'd told me Mom had walked through town naked. While I didn't share my mother's tastes, she took pride in her appearance. Before she came down for coffee in the morning, her makeup was always on point. "That's impossible. Was she ill?"

"Maybe. I wondered about that," Ren said. "I finally asked and of course she was offended."

"At least she was well enough to feel offended," I said, brightening. "What happened then?"

"Jimmy wasn't wrong about the trespassing. People showed me photos of your mom creeping in yards at night. Some didn't call it in because they felt sorry for her. They thought she might be having a breakdown, after being alone all this time. Even people who hated you thought you should come home to look after her."

"Wow," I said. "I had no idea. Gran had no idea."

Renata walked over to a bench that was perfectly situated to take in the waterfall. "That's how Shelley wanted it. But I texted the last number I had to let you know."

"I ditched phones so often I didn't get it," I said. "Something awful must have happened because there's no way Mom would leave the house and Boz unattended."

"We'll get to the bottom of it," Ren said. "I want to help because your mom was good to me. Probably better than I even know."

I nodded. "She would have tried to protect you, both because what happened was my fault, and because she loved you for your own sake."

"Aw... I loved her, too," she said. "And especially your gran. With my family being so weird, I felt welcome at your house."

Mr. Bixby declined my invitation to sit on the bench with us and muttered internally, "How about getting to the trust test? Seems like you're beating around the bush."

I sent what I intended to be a chilly mental blast. Its only impact was a classic Bixby wry chuckle.

"Ren. About prom night... I really am so sorry. If it was traumatic for me, it must have been a million times more so for you."

"You didn't know that would happen, and I never blamed you. Especially when it was my idea."

"*Your* idea? How so?"

"Well, not the prank, obviously. But joining those kids. Jared Knight and his crew. They were the elite, and for that one night—our final high school hurrah—I wanted to feel like I belonged in their midst."

I glanced over my shoulder to make sure we were truly alone. The beautiful, peaceful park was empty and the rush of the waterfall drowned out any noise.

"We had high hopes for that night," I said.

"Remember the dresses we picked out together? Your mom paid to have mine altered because my mom wouldn't. It would have been frumpy instead of sultry without Shelley."

I laughed. "Meanwhile, she had mine altered to be frumpy to deter Tanner Jefferson."

"Which it didn't, probably because we were both drenched in Angel Tears."

That brought a heartier laugh. Angel Tears was *the* perfume of its day for teens. I couldn't get a whiff of it now without being whisked back to high school, for good or ill.

"Isn't it stupid that everyone wanted to smell exactly the same?" I asked.

"Right? But Tanner was all over you during the last dance—that tearjerker rock ballad. 'Love Hurts.' Strange way to close off prom."

"Not really," I said. "That song never gets old, because of its universal truth. Playing it last was supposed to drill it home that we'd never end up with our high school crushes."

It was Ren's turn to laugh. "That's been my experience, I'm afraid. I've had no success since, either."

"How can that be?" I said. "You're stunning and talented and... nice."

Mr. Bixby gave a sharp yap intended to move the conversation along. "There's time for girl bonding later," he said. "After we figure out who killed Laverne Billings and potentially absconded with your mother."

"Nice?" Ren said. "That's the kiss of death in romance."

"Please. The kiss of making the right choice." I shook my head. "Steve Fiatt was nowhere good enough for you."

"I know that now, but I was so thrilled he asked me to prom— even though I was his fallback after the popular girls turned him down." She leaned over and plucked a handful of clover from the grass. "That's why I said it was my fault. I should have had a little pride and said no. Steve was on the fringes of Jared's circle and wanted to prove himself. That's how we got sucked into egging Reggie Corby's Corvette."

"How were we to know egg yolk destroys a car's finish?" I said. "It seemed harmless. Nothing a run through the carwash couldn't fix."

"But Reggie caught us in the act and knew it would take a full paint job and cost thousands. That was his midlife crisis sports car."

"The guys were jealous of that car," I said. "It was a rare model."

"Plus, Reggie had turned them in to the police earlier for tagging his hardware store with graffiti. And for shoplifting the very paint to do it. They had an ongoing battle."

"Which you and I knew nothing about, as Jared pulled out the eggs from his trunk."

"But Tanner knew," she said. "That's why he refused to throw any, and the rest of the guys started pressuring him."

I pressed my lips together, picturing that night on Reggie Corby's long, heavily treed driveway. Tanner had tried to do the right thing, whereas Ren and I were on a high from our brief brush with popularity.

"Poor Tanner," I said. "I hope I get a chance to apologize to him one day."

"The guys totally framed him," Ren said. "Since he was the only one left holding the eggs, they pushed him forward into the beam of Reggie's flashlight. We didn't see the belt in Reggie's other hand."

A shiver ran down my spine as we faced the moment all over again. "No matter what happened to the car, Reggie shouldn't have tried to whip anyone. Especially Tanner."

"You did a brave thing by stepping right in front of him," she said.

"More stupid than brave. I didn't think Reggie would hit a girl."

"Me, either." Ren didn't seem to notice Mr. Bixby leaning into her lower leg. I wasn't sure if he was offering support or trying to tap into her feelings, but I rather suspected the former. He might be more of a softie than he let on.

"Reggie was aiming for my face," I said. "So I got lucky when he missed and smacked my shoulder instead. My purse strap took the brunt of it."

"He moved fast for a guy his age. Got around you to smack Tanner. And then me." Renata held out her arm to show me a shiny white scar about three inches long. "Hurt like stink and drew blood, but it was the shock that sent me reeling. I still remember the smell of the dirt when my face hit the lawn. Despite what happened, I was so worried about my dress being ruined." She shook her head. "Crazy what goes through your mind."

"I couldn't see where the belt struck, so I thought he'd killed you," I said. "My heart was pounding so hard when he turned back to me again. But I didn't mean to..."

"All you did was try to stop him," Ren said. "Push him away."

That *wasn't* all I'd tried to do, though. I had tried to focus my rarely used and never-dependable firepower on Reggie because he'd struck my best friend and an innocent bystander. For once, it worked on command but I wasn't able to calibrate it. Reggie went down hard, clutching his chest where I'd shoved him with both hands.

"He was so strong," I said. "So angry. I didn't know what he'd do next."

What he'd do next was move into the intensive care unit at our local hospital. Jared and his crew tried to take off but the police blocked the lane after I called 911.

Most people said it was a near-fatal heart attack, and Reggie wasn't conscious to say otherwise. His family stayed silent, as did his many powerful allies. Turned out the inconspicuous hardware store owner had criminal ties.

Renata leaned down and stroked Mr. Bixby's ears. I half expected him to recoil, but he took it like a champ.

"I was never so happy to see Boswell," she said. "The way he swept in to collect you, wearing his tuxedo... That was the stuff of movies."

"Horror movies," I said, smiling as Mr. Bixby moved away from her fingers. The dog wasn't ready to share hero status with the family ghost yet. "Mom was beside herself over what happened. I'd unknowingly crossed the most dangerous faction in town."

"Jared Knight knew it though. We were duped."

"Naïve," I said. "I'm so sorry you and Tanner got taken to the station with the riffraff. Boswell came back for you, but there was too much commotion with the police and ambulance to risk his being seen again."

She brightened. "He came back for me? It would have been so

cool to be rescued by your ghostly hero. Instead, my dad picked me up and grounded me for months. By then you were long gone."

I nodded. "We had a huge fight that night, and while Mom, Gran and Boz were trying to figure out the best move, I climbed out the window, push-started Elsa down the drive and took off. I figured these people wouldn't come after you and Tanner if I was out of the picture."

"And they didn't," Ren said, patting my arm. "Things simmered down fast and only bubbled up again when Reggie's memory started coming back. He'd been moved to a rehab facility and everyone said he was recovering."

"I was sorry to hear he died suddenly." And surprised, since I didn't believe the shock I'd given Reggie that night was anywhere near strong enough to kill him. Reggie's energy still felt strong so I'd always assumed he had a weak heart that got worse over time. Either way, I got pegged with the murder, both in my own mind and nearly everyone else's.

I was so lost in memory that Mr. Bixby pressed a paw into my shoe to bring me back to the present, where Ren was putting a positive spin on everything.

"The tension dissipated eventually, at least for me," she said. "Your mom had plenty of skirmishes that seemed fairly minor until recently."

With her hand still patting my arm, I could sense that even today, Ren lived in fear that the criminal faction would come after her again. Reggie Corby had apparently been a dearly missed player in their syndicate.

"Now that I'm back, I'm going to try to make this up to you, Ren. I'm sure you've felt like there's a target on your back."

"Maybe a little. I'm sure you have, too."

"Definitely." I glanced at the dog and then stood up. "I doubt it's an accident that Laverne got killed right after renting me the store. Someone's sending me a message."

"Or it's just a terrible coincidence," Renata said, as Mr. Bixby set off to the car ahead of us. "Laverne had detractors. At the café, people were always complaining she wouldn't lease to them. Or that she gave the magical side the better deals. Maybe she enjoyed her power too much."

"I didn't see that today, but it was probably different for Mabel's Fables. The poor orphan store."

"No longer motherless," Ren said. She smiled and then it faded. "Sorry. I firmly believe Shelley will turn up."

"I do, too. I'll need to unravel this mess before anyone else gets hurt." I picked up speed as we got closer to Elsa. "Starting with finding Mom. She'll help me deal with the rest."

Ren nearly had to run to keep up with me. "I hope so, but I honestly think she needs your help more than you need hers."

"Then I might be in even bigger trouble than I thought," I said. "Because she's the family strategist."

"It'll work out just fine," Renata said, letting me open the passenger door for her. "Otherwise, you wouldn't have landed the store, and something about that feels right. Meant to be."

"I think so, too," I said. "It's the only good thing to happen since I got home. Other than reconnecting with an old friend and finding she isn't holding a grudge."

"Far from it," she said, swinging her legs in. "I'm so glad you're back."

Mr. Bixby trotted around the car ahead of me. "At least your friend passed the trust test with flying colors," he said. "No one could plant all those vivid sensory memories so well."

I nodded but it made me sad to realize all that Ren had suffered since that long-ago night. The worst of it, in my view, was that she felt her best friend had abandoned her at the scene of the crime. The incident had stolen her innocence—our innocence—and blighted her mental garden. All I could do now was make sure she never felt abandoned like that again.

"It's good to have another ally," I told the dog. "Someone who knows this town inside and out."

"Ren's proven she's a good egg," Mr. Bixby said. "At least for now."

"It's too soon for egg puns, Bixby," I said. "Timing is everything."

"Too soon? It's been fifteen years. You should have started punning ages ago."

I glared at him with my hand on the door. "This was the defining incident of my life."

"Until this week, when your life got redefined... by me." He gave a fetching head tilt. "Now, I'll take that lift into the car. I can do it, but I'm too vain to let your friend see me scrabble. And please see to ordering that staircase, will you?"

Sighing, I opened the door and lifted the dog inside, where he moved into Ren's lap.

"Were you talking to him?" she asked. "Your lips were moving."

"Yeah," I said. "As long as he doesn't talk back, right?"

CHAPTER FOURTEEN

M aisie Gledhill crossed her arms on the other side of her screen door. She was nearly Gran's age but looked older, with deeply etched lines around her small pale eyes. Her gray hair was buzzed so short I suspected she'd used her husband's electric shaver. It sent a strong message that she wasn't the kind of woman to waste valuable time on personal grooming.

"Janelle Brighton," she said, her mouth puckering tighter than the elastic waistband on her pants.

"Hi, Mrs. Gledhill," I said. "You're looking well."

It wasn't a lie. She looked in good health and must be if she'd gone a round or two with my mom in a fistfight. Mom was two decades her junior and wiry.

The house was nearly as spacious as the Brighton manor, but without the Tudor and gothic touches. Many of the homes in Wyldwood Springs had a similar design to this one, as if town council had issued a memo to keep things cohesive as part of the façade that all was as quaint as it seemed. Regardless, our quirky house just stood out even more.

"I heard you were home," Maisie said, eyeing the white baker's smock, stained skirt and drab shoes. "People said you hadn't changed a bit, but you're not the girl I remember."

Reaching into the drawers of my hospitality file cabinet, I pulled out some conflict management skills. I had been wrong to think my best years were wasted sucking up to guests. It was all leading to this moment.

"I'm not the girl *I* remember, either, Mrs. Gledhill," I said. "But whoever I am now... I'm home."

Her eyes ran over me. "You were such a pretty thing. Just like your grandmother, only more stylish. She dressed like a beatnik."

I laughed. "She still does. Peasant dresses and hair down to there. Gran sure hasn't lost her zest for life."

"That's good," Maisie said. "Maybe your mother should follow her example and move into a gated community. To protect *her* zest for life. Or just her life."

"What a strange thing to say, Mrs. Gledhill. I heard you'd had words with Mom and came to ask you what happened. She isn't home, you see, and I haven't heard from her in a while."

Six months, in fact, but there was no need to get into the weeds here.

"Shelley and I had words, all right," Mrs. Gledhill said. "She thought she could sashay onto my property at midnight. Triggered both the sprinkler system and security. I found her out back drenched and defiant."

"That really doesn't sound like my mom." Defiant, sure, but she was smart enough not to get drenched while trespassing.

"It wasn't her first yard invasion," Maisie said. "I'm the only one who's dared to confront her. I care about my home and property and I don't need the likes of her poking around."

"Do you mind if I ask what she was doing? When you came upon her, I mean?"

"Yes, I do mind," Maisie said. "I've given a full statement to the police. Talk to them if you're so curious."

Renata stepped forward with a sweet smile that looked as guileless as a schoolgirl's. "Maisie, you know Shelley hadn't been herself. We're just worried about her."

"You should be worried," Maisie said. "That woman fought like a wolverine. Slipped out of my grip because she was wet, snapped the lock on my greenhouse and ran inside."

My eyebrows rose despite my efforts to contain them. "Why on earth would she do that?"

Maisie's pucker deepened. "Just for thrills, I suppose. Your family's known for daring pranks, right?"

It was another reminder of the old egging incident, and it wouldn't be the last. Ren and I exchanged glances and Mr. Bixby gave an exasperated yap from down below.

"Can I bite her?" he asked. "Just a little nip? Put a run in those support hose?"

"No," I said. The word was meant for the dog but it worked as a response for Maisie. "At least I don't think so. One high school prank doesn't need to define my family for a lifetime, does it?"

"Didn't I just say that?" Mr. Bixby said. "Are you going to steal my best material and call it your own?"

Maisie spoke over the dog. "It does when it's a prank like that. Poor Reggie. I can tell you, it took guts for me to confront Shelley when I knew what the fallout could be. And now here you are, threatening me."

"Threatening you? What are you talking about?"

"I heard that dog growl," she said. "You can never trust a wiener dog. They're unpredictable and vicious."

Mr. Bixby gave a great belly laugh that made Maisie step back. Even Ren looked startled.

"Unpredictable and vicious? I like that," the dog said. "When you're height-challenged, it's good to have a big reputation."

"I don't think your shoelaces are in any peril, Mrs. Gledhill," I said. "My dog is charming when you get to know him."

"I doubt you'll be around long enough for that to happen," she said. "At least, I hope not."

"Maisie, come now," Ren said. "As a mother yourself, you must understand how Janelle feels coming home to find the house empty."

"That house is never empty," Maisie said. "I've heard the stories. You two were as thick as thieves in high school, Renata, and it's no surprise you're already in cahoots again."

"You know me pretty well, Maisie," Ren said. "We've chatted at the café countless times. Do you think I've suddenly lost my judgment?"

"I trust your judgment when it comes to baking brownies. That's about it."

"Well, that stings," Ren said, trying to smother a grin.

"Honestly," Maisie said, crossing her arms. "Do you think I'm going to share anything with you two after what happened to Laverne? Janelle was found standing over her body. Covered in blood, I heard, which explains that smock. Is it any wonder I'm scared?"

The grapevine had always worked with miraculous efficiency in Wyldwood Springs, but I was still surprised rumors were springing up like mushrooms that fast.

"I was the first to find her," I said. "It was a terrible shock."

"Like the terrible shock Reggie got when he crossed you?" she asked.

Now I drew on another old skill, which was breathing almost imperceptibly, so that annoying hotel guests wouldn't know they were getting to me.

Mr. Bixby cleared his throat below. "Keep the party going for a few minutes while I slip out back for a look around."

Meanwhile, Renata spoke for me. "I was there that night, and I know exactly what happened. In case you've forgotten, Maisie, your great-nephew, Steve, was my date that night. Did he mention he tossed a dozen eggs?"

The old woman opened the screen door with a bang to make sure we got the full force of her scalding glare. "Janelle was the instigator. My nephew told the police so and was freed the same night."

"Janelle was only there because I asked her to come," Ren said. "If you want to blame someone other than Steve and his friends, blame me. But don't expect to see your favorite strawberry mousse cake on the café's chalkboard anytime soon."

"This is bigger than mousse, young lady," Maisie said. "It's about a longstanding member of our community being murdered hours after Janelle Brighton chugged into town in a steaming heap of rust."

"That's the worst thing you've said to me so far, Mrs. Gledhill. My Elsa is a thing of beauty," I said. "Call me a murderer if you must, but don't insult my car."

Renata laughed. "She's not calling you a murderer."

"Oh, yes I—" Maisie began.

"Don't, then," Ren said. "Because that would remind me about all the stories I've heard over bottomless cups of coffee about you, Maisie."

"Are *you* threatening me now, Renata Scott?" She shook her index finger, a gesture that probably caused universal defiance. If she'd done that to Mom, if would explain a lot. "You girls might be able to get around some people in town but I'm sharper than most."

Maybe she was, but her vision wasn't sharp enough to notice the unpredictable, vicious wiener dog return to her ankles. He gave a deep, booming bark and she jumped.

"Sorry," I said, as the dog chuckled. "We'll leave you to enjoy the rest of your evening, ma'am. If you think of anything more you can tell me about my mother, I'd truly appreciate hearing from you."

I took Ren's elbow and turned her to head down the walk.

"The only thing I can tell you about Shelley," Maisie called after me, "is that the apple doesn't fall far from the tree."

I wasn't sure whether that was an insult to Mom or me.

"Probably both," Mr. Bixby said. "Your mom must be a treat. I can't wait to meet her."

"Good seeing you," I called back. "Come down to my jewelry store when it opens and I'll hook you up with a lovely choker."

"They're not in style again, are they?" Ren said, as she climbed into the car.

"Chokers never went out of style for a certain kind of lady. There are plenty of them in this town so it's a good thing I have the right supplier."

"This is going to be fun," Ren said, stroking Mr. Bixby as the car rolled down the road. Elsa did sound a bit rough since our adventure on the way home. I'd need to get her in for servicing soon.

"See?" Mr. Bixby said. "Even Ren thinks this is going to be fun."

"Fun like those amusement park rides that toss you around till you throw up," I said.

"I've always loved those," Ren said.

"Hard pass for me," Mr. Bixby said. "Riding around in this junker gives me all the cheap thrills I need."

CHAPTER FIFTEEN

That evening, I rounded up my two charges in the manor's living room, put my hands on my hips and delivered a lecture on propriety around police officers.

Staring from the current ghost to the former one, I said, "Am I understood, gentlemen?"

Mr. Bixby lifted his pointy nose and gave an ostentatious sniff. "You look better, but frankly, I can still smell dumpster clinging to you like a bad reputation."

I squinted at him. "Never mind your red herrings, Mr. Bixby. I want your word that you won't embarrass me in front of the police when they get here. If I get put away, you two will need to work together to find Mom and get me out."

His sniff turned into a snort. "I'm not working with the stiff. We can't even communicate."

I walked across the living room, picked up the remote and switched off the TV. "Sir Nigel, you'll need to go without *Survivor* till the police leave. Please stay very quiet. I need to look normal."

"That dress hasn't been normal since the Beverly Hillbillies went off the air," Mr. Bixby said. "It's a good thing you didn't inherit your style sense from your mother. Or your grandmother, from the sounds of it. You dressed rather well when we met. Otherwise, I probably wouldn't have crossed over for you."

"Red herring," I said. "I have no time to shop and this town was never known for its style, anyway." I set the remote down again and put my hands back on my hips. "Gentlemen. Promise me, please. We want those cops in and out of here quickly so they can direct their investigative powers elsewhere."

The dog strutted across the living room and then scrambled onto an ottoman in front of the window. It hadn't been there earlier. He must have shoved it over when I was detoxing in the shower. That would have taken some effort for a dachshund.

"You're dang right it took effort," he said. "But someone needs to guard this house."

"Guarding the house is Sir Nigel's job," I said to the tuxedoed man lounging on the couch. "But it appears he's abdicated his duties."

"Not at all, Miss Brighton," he said, sitting upright. "I've just been a trifle distracted."

"Distracted? Sir Nigel, you used to patrol this house like a one-man platoon. What's happened?"

He stared around the room with oddly vacant eyes. It was a myth that ghosts didn't have a full range of expressions, at least in my limited experience. Boswell had always been animated in the extreme. He'd reminded me of a jack-in-the-box, simmering below the surface and ready to explode into action.

But not now.

Since I got home, there hadn't been a glimmer of his old personality. It was like our family ghost had actually died.

Mr. Bixby chuckled from his perch by the window. "Use it or lose it, I guess," he said. "I intend to wring out every bit of extra time I've been given. A vaudeville cane could come out and hook me back into obscurity at any moment."

"I hate it when he yips like that," Sir Nigel said, covering his ears. "If he's trying to talk he must be very annoying."

"Another red herring," I said. "Although in your case, it might be unintentional. Look, I'm not asking much, here..."

"You want us to let the cops drag you away and then find your mother?" the dog said. "And by us, I mean me, because Sir Windbag is a dud. Like Ren said. Although she isn't, of course."

That was a red herring I actually wanted to chase, but if Bixby knew something about Ren having magic powers, it would need to wait.

"Sir Nigel is ill," I said. "You don't know him like I know him."

"I'm perfectly fine," the butler said. "Please don't give me another second's thought, Miss Brighton."

"Ghosts don't get sick," Mr. Bixby said. "Do they?"

I sighed. "I don't know. He never did before. I can't help thinking he's been hexed."

"Ghosts don't get hexed either." The dog nudged the heavy brocade curtain aside and peered out. "But I suppose someone might have wanted him silenced."

Boswell reached for the remote control and I snatched it out of reach. "Boswell, please. *Survivor* will wait for the police to leave. Got it?"

"Of course, Miss Brighton. I think I've seen this episode anyway." He actually smiled and that startled me more than anything else. I had never seen his teeth before, at least not framed by a big false grin. The ghost butler I knew took life very seriously indeed.

"They're here," Mr. Bixby said, jumping down. "I'll abide by your wishes and stay silent, but I bet you'll regret that decision. I could be your Cyrano de Bergerac feeding you lines."

I slipped the TV remote into my pocket and walked with the dog to the front door. "It won't help if they think I'm even crazier than my mother." I smoothed her dress—another frumpy full-skirted number—and sighed. "Hearing people say she's unstable hurts, Mr. Bixby. Mom may be volatile but she's brilliant."

"Perhaps she's going senile," he said.

"She's not even sixty," I said.

"It happens. Or maybe the same person who hexed Sir Windbag fired a double at your Mom."

"Oh gosh, that's another can of worms. How would I fix that?"

"For the moment, you need to turn on the Brighton charm at full volume," he said. "It worked wonders on Chief Gillock and these two combined aren't half the cop he is."

"You barely know Drew," I said.

"I know enough." He gave a full body shake. "I thought you were going to pretend we were normal."

I followed his example and gave myself a shake. "Right." Opening the door, I offered Officer Barrow and Chief Dredger my most winsome smile as they came up the front steps. That smile hadn't gotten much use lately, but Jimmy nearly stumbled on the top step so I assumed it still worked. The chief was too busy casing out the property, now shrouded in the shadows of dusk, to notice or even greet me. His eyes darted around the front hall, which I'd restored to order, and when I invited them into the kitchen, it was Jimmy who thanked me.

They turned down my offer of coffee but I put on a pot anyway because I needed it. Plus it gave me something to do with my hands. I took great pride in my skilled nonchalance, but stress and sleep deprivation were taking their toll. I'd need to be extra vigilant.

The officers also declined my offer of a seat at the kitchen island. Perhaps it was beneath their dignity to sit on bar stools during a professional call, but I couldn't risk taking them into the living room in case Boswell and Bixby provoked each other—and me. Instead, I leaned against the marble counter and waited for the coffee to drip through. Mom had renovated the kitchen at some point and done a nice job of it. The rest of the house seemed dated in comparison.

The chief cleared his throat and spoke first. "Ms. Brighton, how is it that you've caused such a kerfuffle since arriving in town only today?"

"Kerfuffle?" I turned up the wattage on my smile. "That's a strange term, Chief."

"I don't know what else to call it. Everyone's atwitter." He took out his notepad and flipped through it. "And they have plenty to say."

"Little of it true, I'm sure." The coffee machine gave a beep and I turned. Pulling a mug out of the cupboard, I poured the first cup and slid it toward the men. Jimmy folded and took it, looking guiltily over the brim at his boss as he sipped.

After pouring two more mugs, I went to the fridge looking for cream. Big mistake. There was little food inside, but some of it had gone rotten. Hopefully, there were staples in the cupboard because I'd only shopped for the dog's needs.

Mr. Bixby offered a loud choking sound but kept his smart aleck remarks to himself.

The chief tapped his notepad. "Please tell us again how you managed to convince Laverne Billings to lease you the store. There hasn't been a tenant there in years and the owner intended to keep it that way."

I pressed my back against the fridge, hoping to engage the seal fully and contain the smell. "Chief, you've probably heard the stories about the store being haunted. And you've probably heard the stories about this house being haunted. It's something I'm used to, so I figured I'd be the perfect tenant and I guess Laverne did, too."

The chief's gray eyebrows rose. "You're used to ghosts?"

"Who could ever get used to ghosts?" I said, with what I hoped was a charming giggle. "What I'm used to is gossip and tall tales. I hoped I could get the store for a good deal because it's sat empty so long. I want to bring it new life." The dog gave a little whine and I added, "Poor choice of words after what happened to poor Laverne. I assume you've confirmed she wasn't actually in the store with me?"

"There was no evidence she came inside," the chief said. "What I'd like to know is how you could miss hearing what happened out back if you were supposedly still in the store."

"As you know, I was on the phone with my friend Sinda the whole time," I said. "We were brainstorming. She's going to supply me with merchandise, you see."

"If you get to keep the place," Jimmy said. "The owner isn't happy about it."

"Laverne and I have an agreement in writing," I said. "Anyway, how could anyone object to finally getting that place leased?"

The two men glanced at each other and then the chief twirled his pen. "Some reputations are too far gone to salvage."

I suspected he was talking about mine, as well as the store's. There was no question both were circling the drain, but I was still full of hope and determination.

Mr. Bixby couldn't resist a faint cheer. *Atta girl.*

"Chief, I'm sure you'll find no evidence that I touched the... the murder weapon. All I did was collect Laverne's glasses from the dumpster."

"Would you mind explaining why you did that?" he asked.

I sighed. "It doesn't really make sense, but they seemed like part of her identity and I wanted her to have them back. I was in shock. Wouldn't you be?"

"I'm pretty sure I'd be calling the police before I reunited a dead woman with her glasses," the chief said.

"I asked my new neighbor to call you the very moment I found them," I said.

"And that's when you tried to steal her ring?" Officer Jimmy said. "When Ethan Bogart was distracted?"

"Nice try, Jimmy," I said. "I mean, Officer Barrow. The stone had fallen out of Laverne's ring and I tried to put it back into its setting. It belonged with her, just like the glasses."

"You are aware you can't touch anything at a crime scene, Ms. Brighton? Don't you watch TV?"

"Actually, I don't, Chief, no," I said. "I've been very career focused."

There was a raucous shriek from the living room as the TV came on. We all jumped, even the dog, who muttered, "Idiot!"

I reached into my pocket for the remote and switched off the TV again.

"I hope watching TV is the only thing you're lying about, Ms. Brighton," Chief Dredger said. "I certainly aim to find out."

"I have nothing to hide," I said.

"Except a fridge full of rotting food?" he asked.

"I'm not hiding that," I said. "I was protecting you from the smell."

"And how about your missing mother? You told Mitzy Lennox at the Beanstalk Café that your mom was in Strathmore County with your grandmother."

"I hoped she was. It made sense she would go there, but it didn't turn out that way."

The chief twirled the pen again. "You're as evasive as your mother."

"You know more about my mom than I do right now, Chief. It sounds like you harassed her to the point of a nervous breakdown."

Both men took a step back and I realized my charm had stalled out.

The chief opened his mouth, but before he could say anything, the TV came back on. There was a loud round of applause, as someone got voted off the show. Apparently, Boswell couldn't resist seeing it happen again. Or perhaps he was punctuating our conversation.

"How strange," I said. "If you'll excuse me for a second, gentlemen, my television appears to be malfunctioning."

I walked into the living room and found the butler standing right in front of the TV, utterly transfixed. There was barely room to slip between him and the screen to block the image. Only then could I get his attention without speaking. I shooed him back to the couch, turned off the TV and returned to the kitchen, where Mr. Bixby was staring up at the police. They didn't seem to notice him.

"You can see how a place could earn a reputation," I said, with a light laugh. "One faulty TV and the crowd says you've got a haunted house."

"Maybe you'll have more time to catch up on TV while we finish our investigation," Jimmy said.

"I've got a store to set up," I said. "No time to waste since I spent most of my savings on rent."

The two men glanced at each other again.

"Mr. Knight will probably refund your cash," Jimmy said. "He's a great guy. A pillar of our community."

A chill raced from the roots of my hair to the tips of my toes. "Jared Knight?"

"His father," Jimmy said. "Oscar Knight owns most of the property on Main Street, now, including the store you just tried to lease."

Suddenly I had a really bad feeling about all of this.

"Me too," said Mr. Bixby. "Or maybe it's just your bad feeling killing my buzz."

"You must know the family," the chief said. "Judging from your expression."

"I went to school with Jared," I said. "I don't believe I ever met his father."

Survivor blared from the living room once again. My hand was still in my pocket and I switched it off.

Mr. Bixby could contain himself no more. "My word, that ghost needs to—"

The men flinched as the yapping began and then backed to the kitchen door. "Could I ask where you worked last?" the chief said. "I'd like to do some checking around."

"The Squire Hotel in Tennessee," I said. "I was assistant manager."

They were at the front door now, and Jimmy fumbled with the knob, anxious to leave.

The chief waggled his eyebrows. "Was that right before your job at the Briar Estates?"

"Oops," the dog said. "He already knows about what happened down south."

I found my smile again. "I just helped out at the Briars when I was visiting with my gran. She's the one who asked me to come back here. This house is still in her name, of course."

He opened his mouth, perhaps to end the conversation with a veiled threat, but he didn't get the chance before *Survivor* cut him off once more.

"Don't let the door hit you on the way out," Mr. Bixby shouted after them as they left.

It was strangely satisfying to see two grown men hightail it down the stairs.

I had to savor the moment, because I sensed I wasn't likely to get many of them.

CHAPTER SIXTEEN

I covered the manor from bottom to top three times the next day looking for clues about Mom's whereabouts before Mr. Bixby started complaining.

"You're the one who's always telling me that stairs are bad for my back, and yet here we are in the attic again."

"They're not bad for your back when I'm the one carrying you," I said. "They're bad for mine."

"Semantics," he said. "The point is, we've combed the place and there's nothing."

It certainly seemed that way. Other than the obvious disruption in the front hall when we arrived, everything was in its proper place. Mom wasn't that neat, but Boswell was... or he used to be. That's why his leaving the front hall in disarray made no sense. It should have offended his sense of order.

"I can't help thinking Mom's deliberately left me a puzzle to solve," I said. "It wouldn't have killed her to leave a few more clues."

"Or maybe it would," the dog said. "That's probably the point, right? You're going to have to think harder."

"My brain's already working overtime." I stared around the room. It wasn't creepy in the way some attics were because Boswell had cleaned every day—at least until about a month ago. For the first time in my memory, there was a film of dust on the bookshelves and the round oak table that sat between the two small windows. It was stuffy and would soon be very hot. September in Wyldwood Springs could be sweltering by day and crisp by night. "This is where Mom would hide clues. She loved it up here. Sometimes I'd hear her pacing overhead all night long."

"That doesn't sound like peace of mind," he said, stretching out in a beam of sunlight. Dust motes drifted up around him and he looked almost ghostly again. "What troubled her?"

"Politics, mostly," I said. "Even when I was a kid there were petty disputes all over town. Back then, she wasn't causing them but trying to sidestep them, like landmines."

"So that *you* could have peace of mind," he suggested. "And come of age to help."

Another dart of pain shot into my heart. "Maybe. She didn't have many friends, and I never knew her to have a date, although she had admirers. My dad left before I can remember."

"It sounds like a lonely life. With your grandmother, aunt and cousin all being defenseless," he said. "She probably felt responsible for protecting everyone."

I walked over to the bookshelf and ran my index finger through the dust. "Sure, take her side."

"I'm on your side, which is also her side," he said. "My job is to present another point of view when I can." He rolled onto his side and sighed. "It's the least strenuous of my many duties."

I looked over my shoulder at him and smiled. "Don't wear yourself out on my account."

"Oh, I won't. I have no idea what this role holds so I need to pace myself. I may be the first of my kind."

"You may indeed," I said. "I've never heard of a dog—or any other animal for that matter—crossing back over."

He stretched his short legs like a cat and licked his lips. "Then maybe cut me some slack. I can't do all the mental heavy lifting. How are you going to grow into the—"

"Don't say it. Bixby. Do not use the w-word."

"*Woman* your mother wanted you to become if you don't flex your muscles?"

I stared at the spot on the floor where I'd concealed the spell book after I got home. Mom's cubbyhole probably wouldn't keep others with magical powers from finding it. It probably gave off a certain vibe, or even a smell.

"What does the spell book smell like?" I asked, suddenly curious. "Rotten eggs?"

Mr. Bixby let out a small groan of contentment as the sun warmed his sleek sides. "It smells like any of these books. Just paper with hints of must and dust. It's like the words themselves are neutral and it's the user who creates an odor. Or at least the intent of the user." Lifting his head, he cast one brown eye on me. "And before you ask, you smell like moss."

"Moss! What a terrible thing to say."

He chuckled. "I calls 'em like I smells 'em. Want to know my theory?"

"About moss? Not really, no."

"Let's pretend you said yes. It's more fun that way. I believe you smell of thick damp greenery because you've let your innate gifts lie dormant." Satisfied, he let his head drop again. "I fully expect as you get moving, the moss will give way to something more fragrant. Wildflowers, perhaps. Or a clear, running stream. Sound better?"

"I said no for a reason. Now that image—that smell—is in my head."

"Do you even know what moss smells like?" he asked.

"It ain't Angel Tears perfume," I said, with a smirk.

"Renata may be nostalgic for her high school days, but I doubt you are. Certainly not for a perfume every girl wore." He rolled over onto his stomach again. "Moss is better. Unique is better. Do you remember exactly when you discovered you were a—"

"Bixby," I interrupted.

"A blessing to your poor lonely and overburdened mother?" he continued.

I didn't have to dig deep in my mental library. "Jared Knight. Back when he was just a bully in the elementary school playground. He lifted my skirt once too often and Mom said it was okay to fight back." Walking over, I slid back the false floor that concealed the cubbyhole holding *Everyday Spells for Everyday Magic*. "I don't think Mom expected me to knock him out."

The dog sat right up. "You stunned this Jared with your taser move?"

"Actually, I hit him in the head with a rock. It was barely a tap but he went down hard and came up dazed. The principal suspended me for two days. On the way out, Mom made me find the rock. I put it in the palm of her hand, and a smile like I'd never seen lit up her face. You'd think it was the most exotic pink diamond instead of a lump of quartz."

"She felt the charge?" he asked, tilting his head.

I nodded. "She said it's like a fingerprint some magical people can read and I'd have to be very careful until I could control it." Lifting the big book, which was still wrapped in my slinky silver dress, I walked over to the round table and set it down. "I never have learned to control it, though. Not fully."

"So when you touched Laverne's ring, someone might know about it?"

"Possibly. Mom also said we don't leave actual fingerprints, like ordinary people." I sighed as I pulled out a chair and sat down. "I don't know how it all works."

"Because you didn't want to know?" He heaved himself up and followed me to the table.

"Partly. You don't want to be different as a kid, Mr. Bixby. After

I got suspended, all my friends except Renata turned their backs. And that's another reason I couldn't get a date later. All the Brighton charm couldn't counter clunking a guy on the head, it seems."

"I suppose not. Boys are stupid till they're thirty anyway. At least, so I observed with all the young men who came into Sinda's store to buy gifts for their ladies." A swishing motion with his muzzle told me he wanted to be lifted. "I could always tell who'd last." He waited till all four beefy paws were on the table before adding, "Chief Gillock is the lasting type. In case you were wondering. For some reason the smell of moss is like catnip to him."

I threw the dog a look. "That was a past life, Bixby."

"A past life when you remembered to use 'mister.'"

"I don't want to think about Drew, right now. If Chief Dredger has reached out, Drew knows about what happened here. Meanwhile, Drew's still figuring out what happened in Sinda's store before we ran."

The dog sat on his haunches and fixed me with both eyes. "I would imagine you're right. That's why I figure you should light a fire under your moss. Blow that greenery right off."

"Your metaphors could use work," I said.

"Probably. I went decades without being able to exchange witticisms, remember?" He scraped his claws lightly over the book to pull back the silver dress. "My point is, that thing probably fell into your paws for a reason. You might as well figure out how to use it."

"And do what, exactly?"

"Start flipping, for starters. See if anything jumps out at you."

My throat tightened and a groan slipped out. "It's a tacit admission, Mr. Bixby. Of being a... whatever."

"Only if it works. I assume spells wouldn't have much oomph if the caster didn't have the force of magic behind them. Who knows, maybe all you can do is read minds and stun people." He examined his paw. "Not to throw stones, but..."

"Very clever, Bixby-without-the-mister. I can do more than throw stones, but even Mom didn't know how much. She said it was unknowable, until maturity and practical use revealed the extent of it."

"Less talk, more flip," he said.

Sighing, I stared at the big spell book. I had only examined it once before, when I found it in a killer's house at the Briar Estates. The book had been open to a spell called, "How to Exterminate Everyday Pests." As I had obviously been the pest in question, I'd simply grabbed the book and the supposed ingredients and fled. I'd had no desire to touch it again, other than to keep other people from doing just that. I wasn't convinced you needed much natural ability to use it.

"I'm sure it works better if you do," Mr. Bixby said, not bothering to wait for me to speak aloud.

"Can you stop doing that?" I asked. "If I want you in my head, I'll invite you."

"Understood," he said, agreeing a little too easily. "Sorry."

"You're just being nice because you want me to—"

"No flies on that moss." He stretched out on his belly on the tabletop. "I have a ringside seat for this great adventure. Please make it worth my while."

I ran my fingers across the cover and gave a little gasp. The book was full of percolating energy. Just like I was, I supposed. Normally I repelled with my energy but in this case, I attracted. When I lifted my fingers, the cover flipped open and pages came along for the ride.

"Oh my," I said. "That feels very strange."

"Saves work, no?" the dog said. "Maybe it even shows you what you want. Like book and TV recommendations online."

"That'd be super handy." I laughed as the pages flipped under my fingers. "But unless our pipes are plugged here, I don't think this spell's going to help."

The pages had stopped on a spell called, "Blow Out Everyday Blocks in Three Easy Moves."

"A little pre-emptive plumbing never hurt," he said. "Do you have what it takes?"

I ran one hand after another through my hair—a nervous gesture I'd tried hard to lose. "I'm sure this stuff can totally backfire, Bixby. Who knows what could be unblocked if I tried it? It could leave me even more vulnerable."

"Find another one, then. Something that looks user-friendly for beginners. Take your time and decide. You've got plenty of problems to solve."

"Yeah. Like how I can get past the police tape and into my store. I need to establish myself before Oscar Knight throws me out." My sigh lifted the page and it settled rather slowly. "That place is meant to be mine, Mr. Bixby."

His hackles lifted suddenly. "Did you feel that?"

"Feel what?" I said, closing the book. "All I can feel is the thrumming of energy between these covers. It's making my ears ring."

"That's probably not all it's done. I felt a whoosh of magic just then."

"Really? Well, maybe the pipes are clear." I got up to put the book away and my phone rang. "Hey Ren," I said, putting the phone on speaker. "What's up?"

"More like what's down," she said. "I was just walking out of the Beanstalk when there was this... I don't know... huffing sound, is the best way to describe it. I looked across the street and saw the door to Mabel's Fables fall off."

"Fall off?" My voice was loud enough to make Bixby jump.

"More like blow off. It lifted right off its hinges, flew over the sidewalk and crashed in the street."

"Told you so," the dog said. "You blew it up good."

"Was anyone hurt?" I asked Ren.

"No, but if the store's in your name you're probably on the hook for cleanup, Janelle."

"I'll be right there," I said, grabbing the dog and setting him on the floor.

"Check the spell," he said, after I hung up. "Before you put the book away."

Under "Blow Out Everyday Blocks in Three Easy Moves," it read:

One pressing care...
One strand of hair...
One gust of air...
One less block to bear.

CHAPTER SEVENTEEN

"Satisfied?" I said, racing toward town with Mr. Bixby in the passenger seat. "Looks like one stray hair and a sigh blew the door off my store. It could have killed someone."

"So, it's my fault?" he said. "I distinctly recall suggesting you make a thoughtful decision about using the spell. Instead, you just let it go, like an involuntary sneeze or—"

"Never mind," I said. "The point is someone could have been crushed, decapitated or slashed to bits."

"It didn't happen. I suppose there's more order to the universe than that."

"If that were true, Laverne wouldn't be dead and my mom wouldn't be MIA."

"We have to assume that's exactly what the universe intended," he said. "At least in Laverne's case. Your mom may have had more choice in the matter. That feels deliberate to me."

"What makes you such an expert on these things?" I asked.

He stood up and tapped the glass. "Window please. I haven't been reanimated long enough to forfeit the simple joys of a car ride. Besides, I don't care to be contained with your wrath."

"Evasion duly noted," I said. "If you're withholding information that could stop me from hurting people, I might second-guess my decision to animate you."

"It wasn't a decision," he said. "That was a magical sneeze, too. All I was saying is that you might want to be more intentional about what you do." Some of his words were faint as they drifted away on the breeze. "But if you must know, I once had the opportunity to study a talentless hack try casting many a spell to no avail. You have more magic in a simple sigh than any—"

"Don't say the w-word or I'll use the w-word," I said. "The ones we removed from our lexicon."

He turned a baleful eye on me. "I'll excuse the pettiness because I know you're fretting about the flying glass. Just remember we learned something valuable today. Very valuable indeed."

"Something terrifying," I said. "You're not far off with your sneeze analogy. If I happened to sneeze over that spell book, the whole town could blow up."

That made him laugh. "Good thing you opened this window so there's room for your ego. If Wyldwood Springs were that easy to blow off the map, it would have happened already. There are probably magical protections in place on the municipal level."

I turned onto Main Street and looked for a parking spot. "Something else to ask Mom when she turns up."

"Just try to relax," he said. "You wanted to get into the store and now the blocks are removed, just like you asked."

"It's a crime scene," I said. "I'll get tossed out by Chief By-the-Book."

"You've got your own book now," the dog said, as I maneuvered into a tight spot half a block from Mabel's Fables. "And yours wins, as long as you can hold your wind."

"Enough with the wind jokes," I said. "Enough jokes, period. We're likely to have company and I need my wits about me."

"Exactly. Be intentional, and I'll do my best to keep that poodle thing corralled."

I grabbed my purse and got out of the car. "Good luck with that. Bijou doesn't strike me as the type who's easily held down."

"I was bred for predatory stubbornness. Leave me to it."

He stepped onto the driver's seat and I reached in for him. It was amazing how quickly that act had become second nature. Now if the dog wasn't tucked under my arm, I felt somehow naked.

"Ew," he said. "Spare me your unseemly thoughts."

"Spare me your unseemly comments."

"Pardon me?" A woman on the sidewalk ahead of us turned suddenly. "Why, Janelle Brighton, I could barely believe my eyes yesterday. It really is you."

It was Candace Riordan, one of Gran's old frenemies. She'd been at the Brighton manor many times for book club or euchre night, or whatever event Gran concocted to keep the ladies of town in good moods and the gossip somewhat in check.

"In the flesh, Mrs. Riordan," I said.

"Ew," the dog repeated, inside my head this time. "Warning number two."

Candace reached for my arm, and I sidestepped her easily. One touch could sweep me under the wave of her thoughts and I really didn't want to know what Candace Riordan was thinking about me. It was crucial to keep a clear head.

"My dear, you're the spitting image of your grandmother," Candace said. "It's funny how genes can skip a generation, isn't it?"

"Gran would be so thrilled to hear you say that." I was less thrilled to be compared to a senior citizen, but I knew it was mainly a dig at Mom, since all the Brighton women had similar features, including our green eyes. Jilly and I were practically twins, other than hair color.

Candace picked up her pace to stay in step with me. "How is Bridie? I felt so terrible that she had to be packed up and moved like an old piano that didn't get played anymore."

"An old piano?" I said. "Well, a grand piano, possibly. At any rate, it was Gran's idea to retire early to the Briar Estates and she was having the time of her life when I left." That was closer to being true than when I had arrived, anyway. I'd even managed to send her on two dates with men from other gated communities. A little dancing went a long way to creating some music in Gran's life. "It's Mom I'm worried about now, Mrs. Riordan. There are all kinds of stories circulating but I don't know who to believe."

"No one, dear," she said. "Trust no one, including the police. It's a wise code to live by here."

She tried to grab my arm again to slow me down. I sidestepped once more and made a mental note to find shoes my size as soon as possible. Mom's floppy Mary-janes were going to trip me up and send me into a gutter with the glass I could see glittering outside my store. Renata was using a dustpan and whisk broom to sweep up the shards.

"I expect you're right," I said. "You and Mom had a meeting of minds there."

I turned in time to see Mrs. Riordan frown over the idea of sharing anything with Shelley Brighton. Mom really had made enemies in the time I was gone. Legit enemies, unlike Gran, who always managed to smooth the waters.

"Renata Scott, you get away from that glass," Mrs. Riordan called out. "You'll slice your wrist and where will that leave us? Without a star baker, that's where."

Ren smiled as she straightened. "Play your cards right and I'll share the recipe to your favorite oat fudge bars before I bleed out, Mrs. Riordan."

"Don't even joke about that, Ren," I said. "I don't have insurance to cover the glass, let alone a hospital stay. That screaming you hear is my bank account dying."

"Girls, you can call me Candace," Mrs. Riordan said. "You're all grown up and formalities make me feel old. You're in and out of my store all the time, Renata, and I expect Janelle will be, too. No one can resist my truffles."

"They are addictive," Ren said, with a smile. "The Nutty Chocolatier is the most popular place in town. Always has been."

"You're a doll to say so," Candace said. "Now, step inside and let the street crew take care of that mess. I called them the minute I heard the explosion."

"Explosion?" I asked. "What exactly happened here?"

Candace shrugged chubby shoulders under a red-striped cardigan that was a size too small. "Who knows? A gas leak, perhaps?"

Mr. Bixby made an odd rattling sound to disguise his chuckle. This dog really enjoyed his flatulence jokes. But at least he was keeping quiet.

"Maybe we shouldn't go in," I said. "Who knows what might happen next?"

"If there's a gas leak, the open doorway will let it out," Candace said. "I called an inspector, just in case, as well as Main Street's most reliable contractor to install a new door. I've got you covered, Janelle."

The kindness was enough to ease one of the many knots in my stomach. It had been in short supply since my return, and was particularly unexpected from any of the women who'd witnessed my animated conversation with Bijou, the ghost dog.

"Thank you so much, Candace," I said, peering around. "It looks like the police tape is gone. I guess we can go in."

"Jimmy Barrow came by and then left to respond to a more urgent call," Ren said. "He'll circle back but he said they're done for now."

A white van with the city logo pulled up and the maintenance workers assured us they had cleanup in hand. That left us free to follow Candace Riordan inside. She took a good look around and then walked over to the counter, took off her jacket and opened her big purse to get her phone. After a few moments of texting, she dropped the phone back into her purse and pulled out a striped tin that matched her sweater. "Champagne truffle, Janelle?"

"Oh, I couldn't, Candace, but thanks," I said. "I'm flustered over the door. It's made me a little queasy."

"I'll take one," Ren said. She started to move forward and stopped.

Bijou, the ghost dog, was circling Ren's feet, and Mr. Bixby was hot on the poodle's heels. Ren looked from Bixby to me questioningly and I shrugged.

"What an odd little dog you have, Janelle," Candace said. "I would have expected you to choose something bigger. Like a police dog. Girls like you need protection."

I decided not to question what she meant about protection. "Mr. Bixby is a very big dog in his own mind. He's alert in ways other dogs aren't, and I was lucky to find him."

The dachshund stopped chasing Bijou and looked up at me. "Thank you. I feel the same, although I could do without the specters you attract. You're a ghost magnet."

I pressed my lips together to cut off the conversation, inside and out, and decided to try a new strategy for blocking him. Choosing a tune from the boy band Ren and I had once loved, I started humming mentally. Maybe if I filled my head with inane songs, I could block the dog's mental "signal."

"Are you all right, dear?" Candace asked, pressing the striped tin on me again. "You're a little pale. Let's give that blood sugar a boost."

I shook my head and Ren reached out instead, saying, "I'll have hers."

Candace pulled the container away from Ren. "These are a brand new flavor, designed especially for Janelle. Champagne is appropriate to launch her new venture. We can't crack a bottle over the bow, but we can have a truffle with real bubbly inside."

Having just cracked a door over the street, I wasn't hungry for sweets. I was starved for support, however, so I plucked a chocolate from the tin and popped it into my mouth whole. "Delicious," I mumbled, as the rich bonbon melted in my mouth. "Is that a hint of lavender?"

Candace clapped with delight. "You have a refined palate. I thought that might be the case, with your work in fine hotels. Please, have another."

There were five, so I took another and pushed the tin toward Ren. I had a sweet tooth, but Ren's was even sweeter and she didn't hesitate to grab the rest.

I went behind the counter to call a locksmith, and when I looked up, two women of similar vintage to Candace walked through the open doorway and joined us. Each carried a cardboard tray. One held what appeared to be juice samples, and the other ice cream.

"Meet the Main Street Welcome Committee," Candace called out to me, and I waved. "We're happy to have you in our midst, Janelle."

Virginia Steiner and Frida Dayne looked pretty much as they had when I left town. Like Candace, they'd aged very well. Hopefully it was something in the water because it would be nice to slide into old age that easily, too. Their cheeks were rosy and relatively unlined, and all had meticulously colored and highlighted hair. Virginia had a slash of magenta in her sleek bob, and Frida had royal blue strands throughout her crazy curls. Candace had chosen a more subdued blonde with glints of auburn. It was nice to know there was a good stylist in town.

Ren drew the women into conversation while I finished my call. It gave me a moment to watch Bijou repeatedly try to separate my friend from the older ladies and herd her to the window seat. Ren didn't seem at all aware that she was responding to the poodle's energy, gradually moving closer to the window. Mr. Bixby's tail lashed proudly when he finally drove Bijou away. I didn't hear him gloat because my mental humming was working rather well at blocking him out.

Finally, I came back around the counter and joined the group. "It's so good to see you, Mrs. Steiner and Mrs. Dayne. You look wonderful." I pretended to be distracted by the bustle on the sidewalk outside to avoid shaking the hands they offered. There was enough going on in my mental space without a deluge of thoughts and memories from women who barely tolerated Gran, let alone my mother.

"Call me Ginny," Mrs. Steiner said. "My word, you've grown up to be the most stunning of all the Brighton women."

"Isn't she?" Candace said. "I told her she was the very image of Bridie."

"Oh Candace, no girl her age wants to be told she looks like an old lady," Ginny said. "Right, Frida?"

"I can't believe you girls are single," Frida said. "We'll have to change that. Between us, we know all the eligible men in town and can present detailed dossiers."

That made me laugh. "Dating is the least of my worries right now, Frida. But thank you for thinking of me."

"I see the problem," Candace said, gesturing from Ren to me and back. "They're both far too thin. Men like some meat on a woman's bones, so we'll need to fatten you up."

"I've got just the thing," Frida said, offering me a cup with a plastic spoon sticking out of it. "Maybe you've heard I run Frida's Froyo down the street. I've brought you a sample of one of my biggest hits. It's called Tropical Storm. A piña colada in a cup."

"My favorite," Ren said, reaching for a sample.

Shrugging, I joined her. I was in no position to turn down a warm welcome in frozen yogurt.

"Now mine," Virginia said. "Come by Ginny's Juice Bar when you get settled and choose your own favorite. Today, I brought Ginny's Ginger Zinger. It'll put some color in those cheeks."

The collision of flavors numbed my tongue and made my head throb. Or maybe that was just the hangover from casting my first spell.

"Delicious, all of it," I told the women. "I truly appreciate your welcome to Main Street." Glancing around the dusty store, I smiled. "I hope you'll come to my grand opening."

"What exactly do you intend to do with the place?" Candace asked. "I'm sure you know the stories."

"Yes, and I felt bad for this store every time I passed it as a kid," I said. "It seemed unfair that it couldn't have the right owner. Someone who loved it for what it was."

"How cute," Ginny said. "You talk like it's a stray cat."

I glanced down and met Mr. Bixby's big brown eyes, and then Bijou's. "More like a rescue dog. It's my latest passion."

"You're going to run a dog rescue out of here?" Frida's brow furrowed. "Or a pet store? I'm not sure the landlord will approve of that."

"I'm sure he won't," Ginny said. "Mr. Knight has a vision for Main Street. Frida and I were given a short list of businesses to choose from. I'll admit a juice bar wasn't on my radar, but it was a condition of the lease."

"I'd never liked frozen yogurt before but I've developed a fondness for it," Frida said. "It's a foot in the door on Main."

"My store's been around for decades, as you know," Candace said. "But now I have to run my recipes by Mr. Knight. He's very hands-on, and he'll want a say in your plans."

"Really?" I said. "Well, I look forward to meeting him."

Mr. Bixby snorted over that lie. I had no desire to meet Jared Knight's father and I didn't care to have him weigh in on my vision for Whimsy. The only person whose opinion mattered was Sinda Joffrey's, and she'd be here soon to help bring it to life.

Candace pressed forward a little, clearly the leader of the trio. "What exactly will you be selling here, dear?"

"Jewelry and gifts," I said. "I'm calling the store Whimsy, to honor a friend who had a store of the same name."

"Whimsy? Mr. Knight might find that too fanciful," Ginny said. "How about Janny's Gems?"

Ren fought a smirk, but the other women were too busy endorsing the idea to notice.

"That's a great idea, but I've already ordered the sign, ladies," I said. "I'm sure Mr. Knight will love it when he sees the line of fine jewelry my friend makes. I'll introduce them when she visits."

"I just hope customers will visit," Candace said. "People are nervous about this place."

"Not us, of course," Frida said. "I've always thought the ghost stories were hogwash."

Ginny nodded. "Me, too. We'll do what we can by dropping in often and coming out alive. That's the best way to dispel silly rumors."

The contractor's pickup truck pulled right onto the curb out front and Ren ushered the trio to the door.

"Thank you so much for the welcome and the treats," I said, as they left.

"You're welcome," Frida said. "Your mother loved my Tropical Storm, by the way."

"And my Ginger Zinger," Ginny said. "It seems you had a lot in common."

Had. Past tense. Did they all believe Mom was dead? I didn't want to go down that road, so I decided to keep it light.

Making a little circle with my right foot, I said, "Everything except shoe size. "She won't be happy to find out I've pillaged her wardrobe when she gets home."

"*If* she gets home," Ginny said, brushing past the contractor on her way out.

"Don't scare the girl," Candace said. "Shelley may not be popular around here but she's still Janny's mother."

"I didn't mean anything by it," Ginny said. "Shelley's probably off joyriding in that red Mustang she loves. You Brightons get very attached to your cars."

"We do," I said, laughing. "And Mom will turn up eventually. I think the township plants a homing device in us at birth. We always come back." They turned on the sidewalk and I gave them a big smile. "I tried hard to stay away and look what happened."

"My dear, you're delightful," Candace said. "It's good to have you home where you belong."

"Don't you worry, Janny," Frida added. "You got off to a rocky start here, but things can turn around. There's no need to walk in your mother's footsteps."

"Good," I said, "because these are big shoes to fill."

Mr. Bixby stood in the doorway and yapped insults after them. "I don't like them," he said. "They smell bad."

"Like magical flatulence?" I asked, silently.

"Nah. Just your regular phonies."

That we could handle, I figured. Even a fake welcome was better than none at all.

CHAPTER EIGHTEEN

The next day, I went over the manor one more time looking for clues to Mom's whereabouts and made sure the spell book was securely hidden. Then I tried interrogating Sir Nigel again to no avail, before finally heading out to collect Sinda Joffrey from the airstrip a few towns up the hill country range.

Sinda disembarked the small plane looking as I'd left her a few days earlier, minus the housecoat. In other words, an ordinary 70-something woman with gray hair and enough lines to etch character into her pink cheeks. Would her visit to Wyldwood Springs reverse her natural aging process, as it seemed to have done with Candace, Ginny and Frida? Or perhaps intensify it, as it had with grumpy Maisie Gledhill?

I took a video of Mr. Bixby abasing himself before Sinda in a frenzy of greeting. My cocky doxy had grown very fond of her during the time he'd inhabited her store and the apartment above as a ghost. While she hadn't been able to see or hear him till he crossed back over, she had a mental vision of him that inspired the dachshund pendant I wore.

I got her settled into Elsa's passenger seat with the dog on her lap. "Are you ready for Wyldwood Springs? It probably won't be a restful getaway."

Sinda unbuttoned her light wool jacket. "Who needs restful? It was plenty quiet after my husband died and Lexie took over my store. Without Mr. Bixby to keep me company, I've become very lonely."

"You said another ghost would take my place in a second." His tone was a little snippy. "It was rude."

She laughed and ran her fingers over his sleek back. "That was only to make you leave with Janelle. You know you're irreplaceable."

"I do." He turned a few times and collapsed. Normally he liked to look out the window, but out of respect to our guest, he curled up like the placid lapdog he wasn't. "It's a relief to have someone to talk to, Sinda. Janelle's been trying to shut me out with incessant mental humming. The boy band she's chosen would drive any dog mad. It wasn't a real band and it isn't real music."

I laughed. "Sorry, Mr. Bixby, but there's a method to this madness. Every time I answer you out loud or even in my head, I risk exposing my crazy to local citizens. I need to keep that under wraps for the sake of Whimsy, among other things."

"I'll need to do the same, dear dog," Sinda said. "I'm not half the witch Janelle is, and there are powerful forces at play in that town."

The word sent a chill up my spine, but with Sinda claiming the label, I couldn't object without insulting her.

Mr. Bixby didn't hold back. "Janelle doesn't like that word. She's in denial."

"We've banished it from our lexicon, along with wiener dog," I said. "No offence, Sinda."

"None taken." She stared around as we left the airport. "I understand the word has negative connotations for some. For me, it's just a convenience. What other term applies?"

"I don't know. Gran didn't use labels, and Mom didn't, either. They just called it 'the gift.' As in, he has the gift, or she has the gift." I turned south, toward Wyldwood. "The tone always suggested it was more of a curse than a gift. Even for Mom, who was extremely gifted."

"*Is* extremely gifted," Sinda corrected. "Present tense. I refuse to believe she's passed without your feeling it. The bond between mother and daughter is so strong, and never more so than when both are... well, gifted."

Mr. Bixby gave a snide chuckle. "Janelle doesn't like hearing that, either. This one's super touchy."

"I am not touchy." In fact, I prided myself on being tolerant. Easygoing. Unflappable. If there was a disturbance under the hood, as it were, I could always hide it.

"You two bicker like siblings," Sinda said. "Speaking of family, how is Jillian doing?"

"Fine, I guess. I haven't reached out since I came home."

Sinda turned to stare at the side of my head. "Why not? You're just hours apart and surely she'd want to know her aunt is missing."

I eased off the gas so that Sinda could admire the gorgeous scenery. Instead, she kept staring till Mr. Bixby answered for me.

"There was no love lost between Jilly and Shelley, apparently," he said. "Despite being kin."

"Sad but true," I said. "For Mom, if you didn't have the gift, you were a liability. Someone else to protect with scarce resources. That's why she packed Gran off to the Briars, where she'd be safe. And probably why she picked a fight with Aunt Eva. To chase her out of town for good."

"Oh my. The poor thing must have been very lonely," Sinda said. "Speaking from experience. Perhaps she hoped when you came of age you could protect them together and the family could reunite."

"Possibly, but she burned the sister bridge thoroughly. I doubt a relationship could be rebuilt with Eva. Jilly... maybe."

"Then why don't we run up and visit?" Sinda said. "I'd love to see Runaway Farm. It sounds charming."

"It *is* charming, but this isn't the best time to be away from either the manor or the store. When things settle down, we'll visit Jilly."

She reached over and patted my arm. "Things may never settle down enough for you to feel comfortable leaving town. But knowing you have family behind you will give you strength."

"You're my family now," I said. "You and Mr. Bixby and Sir Nigel."

"Replace the ghost butler with Renata and you've got a deal," the dog said.

I sighed. "I'm starting to understand Mom's perspective now. If people are coming after me, I don't want others to become collateral damage."

"This Renata... does she have the gift?" Sinda asked.

"I've always suspected so, but it hasn't really materialized," I said.

"Rudimentary," Mr. Bixby said. "But it's there."

My spirits lifted knowing Ren had at least a hint of the magic she'd always wanted. "I worry about her spending time with me. She'll be tainted by association."

"You need Renata to help negotiate the politics of that town," Sinda said. "She knows how things work. And if you can get to the bottom of this trouble, everyone will be safer."

"I hope you're right," I said. "It might be a bottomless pit."

The dog cleared his throat. "Turn this heap around and head up to Runaway Farm. You know Jilly wants you at the party."

"Party!" Sinda said. "You didn't mention a party."

"It's a bridal shower," I said. "And like I said, now is a bad time."

She made a circle with her index finger. "About face to Clover Grove. It will mean a lot to Jilly that you were there for this special event." Shaking her head, she looked at the dog. "Thank goodness I have you to run interference, Bixby."

"I told you she was difficult, and yet you assigned me to her."

"You're giving me too much credit," she said. "I'm just the messenger."

I turned the car around. "Sorry, my smart aleck friend. If you weren't meant to be with me, you'd still be hiding behind a potted plant at Haute Baubles."

"I've closed the store for good," Sinda said. "Lexie's murder created a black cloud overhead that may never disperse. The chief can't resolve it to his satisfaction."

"He knows who killed Lexie. There's a recorded confession."

"But he doesn't know why. The killer's memory was wiped clean, either from the shock you gave her or the people who came afterward."

I turned my head so fast the car nearly went off the road. "What people?"

"The two men who came in by the front door as I was seeing you and Bixby out the back. They were trying to cart the killer out but she was as slippery as a fish."

"Sinda! You didn't tell me that. It must have been the magical police from Wyldwood. Did they have neon insignias on their lapels?"

"Plain clothes," she said. "When they saw me they dropped her. The local police were already pulling up."

"Why didn't you say so earlier?" I asked.

She raised elegant silvery eyebrows. "Because of precisely this reaction. I'm fine, you're fine, and Drew Gillock is fine, too. In case you're wondering."

"Oh, she's wondering," Mr. Bixby said. "I can hear that through the boy band love songs she's humming."

I ignored him. "This is exactly what I was talking about, Sinda. Who knows what those men could have done to you?"

"Like I said, we're all fine except for the killer, who made her own bed. If her faculties never return, it might be for the best."

We continued to analyze all the implications during the long drive to Runaway Farm, and my heart was lighter than it had been in ages by the time we turned into the lane. I had only visited once before, to attend Jilly's engagement party, and found the property had a distinctly welcoming vibe. We passed under the rusted out iron sign that was missing the "m" on "farm." It made me smile, because that's exactly what I wanted to do: runaway "far" from my life of... running away.

My doubts about coming vanished when Jilly ran down the front stairs of the large farmhouse and inn. My cousin had never looked more radiant, and the large group of women who spilled out the door behind her were all beaming, too.

"They look like..." Sinda's voice trailed off as she stared through the windshield.

"Russian nesting dolls?" I asked, laughing. "That's what Ivy always says. She's the youngest and tallest, and her mom is the petite one dressed in red."

Mr. Bixby was on his feet now, struggling to see out the window. "Where is he? Keats the wonder dog?"

"He's got nothing on you, my friend," I said. "Sure, he has some crime-solving chops, but can he talk?" I lifted him off Sinda's lap and opened my door. "Of course, your tongue is a double-edged sword."

"You're no sweet Ivy yourself," he said as we got out of the car. "We're the opposite of that pair."

"Nonsense," Sinda called after us. "You two are delightful in your own way. But I suggest putting a lid on it while we're here."

"Normal as we can be," I muttered, just before Jilly swept me into a hug.

There was squirming and grumbling between us as Mr. Bixby tried to escape the embrace. "Would you mind?" he said. "I detest public displays of affection, even if I'm the filling in a cousin sandwich."

"Oh, chill out, dude. It's a family reunion." I looked up at the others and grinned. "Meet Mr. Bixby, my new dog."

Jilly stepped back beside Ivy and they tilted their heads in unison. They spent so much time together that they'd developed the same mannerisms. Ivy's dark, straight hair and hazel eyes were a great counterbalance for my cousin's fair curls.

Ivy spoke first. "You're talking to that dog like he understands you. We like it."

"Speak for yourself," Jilly said.

"I am speaking for myself. And Keats," Ivy said. "You're free to have your own opinions."

Jilly scowled. "I think someone's stolen my cousin and replaced her with a…"

"Hillbilly?" I suggested.

"I would never have used that term," Jilly said. "But that dress, Janny. Those shoes."

"Mom's," I said, simply. "I came home without packing."

"Without packing? Do you mean you—?"

"Fled? Bolted? Vamoosed? Yes. The less you know the better, really and truly. The point is, I went home and now I'm here for your wedding shower. I'm afraid we can't stay long." I turned and beckoned Sinda. "I told you about my friend, Sinda Joffrey, from Clarington. She's come to visit and help me open the store."

"The store?" I'd developed an echo that wasn't Bixby, and he laughed as I set him on his paws. His witty rejoinders had to wait, because Keats had sunk to his belly, either in greeting or ambush. Finally, the sheepdog's bum came up into a play pose.

"I don't really play, per se," Mr. Bixby advised Keats. "But I'd appreciate a tour of the place. No manure please."

Keats may or may not have understood the dachshund's words,

but he let Bixby trot ahead of him down to the barn, and raced in big arcs behind him.

"Be careful," I called after them. "Don't let him get squished, Keats."

Bixby stopped and turned so quickly Keats nearly plowed into him. "Respect, please."

"That's a cheeky yap," Ivy said.

"You have no idea." I shook my head as the two dogs went into the barn. "He's not the dog I imagined, Ivy."

Mr. Bixby came back to the doorway and yelled, "You're no cream puff, either."

Ivy laughed out loud. "Oh my, oh my. He is exactly the dog I imagined for you, Janelle. Remember I said long, low and opinionated?"

Dahlia, Ivy's mom, came forward to draw Sinda and Jilly into conversation. It meant I could speak more freely because my cousin hated hearing anything that smacked of woo-woo. Ivy was more open minded.

"Ivy, is this the dog you saw in the jewelry store?" I whispered.

"The dog I *thought* I saw. Just for a moment," she said, beckoning for me to follow the dogs. "It was like dust gathering in a sunbeam. After that, I couldn't imagine you with any other dog. I'd love to hear how you met."

"It's a story for our next visit," I said. "Suffice to say Jilly wouldn't like it at all."

"She'll come around. With you back in hill country we can get together often."

"I hope so," I said. "There's a little matter I need to clear up at home, first. I don't want to put any of you at risk."

"Don't worry about us," Ivy said, heading into the barn. "We can handle ourselves."

"With typical killers, yes," I said. "I don't know what we're dealing with, yet. Remember the limo that chased you?"

Ivy shuddered. "I'll never forget it. But that means you *really* need our help."

"I can handle it. Honestly. I've got more friends than I thought in Wyldwood."

Ivy paused and then nodded. "Call if you need us. Know that we'll come, no matter what."

"Thank you." My voice quavered a little. "That means a lot."

Staring around at the livestock, I blinked to dissolve the tears that gathered. This wasn't how I wanted to celebrate Jilly's upcoming wedding.

Ivy turned into a human sheepdog, nudging me through the barn. "How about we put everything aside for tonight and just enjoy the party?"

"I would love to pretend like everything's normal. And safe."

"That's mostly what I do all the time," Ivy said. "Pretend. Because it's often not normal or safe around here."

I paused beside the empty stall that once held Clippers, the miniature horse, and Bocelli, the donkey. "Oh dear. It looks like I was right about Clippers being called to service."

Ivy nodded. "I'm getting used to the idea now. But I can't fill the stall just yet."

"He's happy, I'm sure of it," I said. Behind Ivy's sadness, I could sense a rightness to the change. "Bocelli is happy, too."

"That's all we can ask for our animals," she said, as we joined the dogs beside the pig pasture.

Keats seemed to be introducing the dachshund to Byron, the huge Caucasian shepherd that kept Wilma the pig happy. I was impressed by Mr. Bixby's poise in the presence of these larger animals. He was small but mighty.

"That's what I keep telling you, lady." His voice was in my head, but Keats' ears came forward as if picking up on our frequency.

"Keats is quite taken with Mr. Bixby," Ivy said. "Normally he doesn't waste time on other dogs, and he's never given one the grand tour. I do worry about wayward hooves."

"I still worry about wayward hooves, myself," Jilly said, joining us.

"Good thing I wore sensible shoes," I said.

"About that," Jilly said. "I've packed a few things for you. You can't open a store in Wyldwood Springs looking like a—"

"Hillbillies aren't so rare there," I interrupted. Jilly was less than two years older than me but she had a certain air of superiority. It was like she thought being non-magical was better than the reverse. Perhaps she was right, if you never wanted to survive in Wyldwood, which she didn't. "Mom's clothes make me look innocuous."

"Exactly what kind of store are you opening?" Jilly asked.

"Jewelry and gifts. Probably some crystals and other paraphernalia for those inclined to such things."

"You've always liked pretty stones," Jilly said. There was no edge in her voice because she didn't know what the pretty stones could do for me.

"And the jewelry will be Sinda's original designs." I lifted the dog pendant and dangled it for them. "She made this."

Ivy and Jilly cooed over it admiringly.

"Can I commission one of Keats?" Ivy asked.

"And I want one of Percy," Jilly said.

No matter how superior my cousin might sound, she really had changed. The Jilly Blackwood of old would have poo-pooed cute pet-themed jewelry.

"Ask her later," I said. "Pour some champagne. She deserves it for saving my life."

Their mouths dropped open, and again, Ivy recovered first. "Tell us what happened."

"There was a murder in Sinda's store in Clarington and I got caught in the middle of it. Sinda's niece died. Remember Lexie?"

"Lexie!" Ivy said. "I can see how she might provoke someone to violence. She refused to let me buy that ring for Jilly."

Jilly angled her left hand till the sunlight bounced off the emeralds. "I'm glad you found it. This ring is perfect for me."

Since my pendant from Sinda felt like a talisman, I hoped the ring would bring Jilly a measure of protection. There was no telling what Sinda baked into her designs, deliberately or otherwise.

"Who killed Lexie?" Ivy asked.

Their gasp when I revealed the killer's name was pretty satisfying, I had to admit.

"That's impossible," Jilly said. "She was one of the nicer women at the Briars."

"Aside from the tawdry affair, you mean," I said.

"True," Ivy said. "But still, why would she kill Lexie?"

"It was part of a convoluted plot to keep me from coming home to Wyldwood Springs. I'll only say that Sinda intervened just in time."

The dogs appeared to be in deep discussion but Mr. Bixby turned and yapped, "Don't forget the part about me saving the day."

Ivy laughed. "Color commentary. I love this dog."

His thin tale whipped back and forth, and he panted happily.

"Mr. Bixby attacked the killer, just as Keats has saved you, Ivy," I said. "Then we beat it home. No way I'd risk bringing trouble on Gran."

Jilly's hand was at her throat and there was no light flashing off the ring now. "This is awful. You jumped out of the frying pan and into the fire."

"Tell me about it. But I managed to lease Mabel's Fables, Jilly. Remember how quaint it is? It's going to be wonderful when it's fixed up."

"The haunted store?" she asked, and then added quickly, "Never mind."

"It's not what you think and it'll all work out great." I took a deep breath and then spit out the bad news. "After I find Mom, that is."

"Find Aunt Shelley?" Jilly's voice turned raspy. "What's happened?"

I gave a little shrug. "She was gone when I arrived and there are crazy stories circulating. The police took her in for trespassing several times, I'm afraid."

"Oh no," Jilly said. "She's having a breakdown of some sort."

"Possibly. It's unclear."

"What do *you* think happened?" Ivy asked me, pointedly.

"I'm guessing that she's either been kidnapped or gone into hiding," I said.

"We need to come and help you find her. Right now," Jilly said, turning. "Let's postpone the shower and get moving."

This time I couldn't stop the tears welling up. I loved my mom but she hadn't treated Jilly well and didn't deserve this sacrifice.

"You can't do that," I said, catching her arm.

"I have to do that," Jilly said. "She's my aunt. My mom's sister. My gran's daughter. And your mom."

"Family," Ivy said. "That's what we do, and you're part of our family now, Janelle."

The tears spilled down my cheeks. "That means so much to me, really it does. And if it were safe, I'd welcome you with open arms. But it's not safe."

"Yet you'd bring Sinda into the Brighton manor?" Jilly asked. "She's a senior citizen."

"A senior with a little extra," I said. "Rather like Edna, with a different defense system."

"Let's talk more over cocktails," Ivy said, pulling Jilly along. "I'm sure Janelle will invite us down just as soon as she thinks the time is right."

I nodded and wiped my eyes on the sleeve of Mom's dowdy frock.

Jilly's gaze told me she was as startled to see me cry as I was to shed the tears. The Brighton women had stiff upper lips and stitched tear ducts. We didn't cry easily.

"It's enough that you're lending me clothes," I said. "And hopefully nice shoes. There are some occasions I just—" I looked down at the outfit and then laughed. "I just can't. I'd rather be kidnapped with Mom."

"I've got you covered till Gran sends your things," Jilly said. "Plus I'll send you home with good meals. I bet there isn't a thing in that fridge."

"Oh, there is," I said. "But I'll need a hazmat suit to clean it out."

"So, she's been gone awhile," Ivy said.

"A month at least. Renata, my old friend, tried to let me know but I ditched my last phone before going to the Briars."

"The police should have called," Jilly said. "Are they corrupt or just useless?"

"Still to be determined," I said. "Everyone knows where Gran lives and no one contacted her."

"All right." Jilly clapped her hands briskly. "So you trust no one except Sinda, Mr. Bixby and possibly Renata, with all due caution."

I nodded and the dogs came back to sit at our feet.

"You'll stay the night, and we'll send you home fully stocked. Then, just as soon as the imminent threat you're not mentioning dies down, we're coming to find Aunt Shelley." Jilly herded us out of the barn. "We practically have an army, Janelle."

On the front lawn, Sinda was talking to Ivy's friends Edna Evans and Gertie Rhodes, the octogenarian preppers I'd met before. Both women were wearing fatigues, and Gertie's outfit was topped by a ratty brown poncho that concealed a rifle. I suspected Edna was trying to recruit Sinda into her online apocalyptic prepper course. My new friend didn't seem like the type, but in hill country... you became the type. It just made sense to take all due precautions.

We all went into the backyard, where a couple of dozen women gathered around Jilly in the time-honored way of supporting a bride-to-be. I hadn't planned to come, but I wasn't empty-handed. While picking through Mom's things in search of clues, I'd checked her jewelry to see if anything of value was missing. There was an old cuff bracelet studded with small emeralds that looked like something Wonder Woman might wear. It had once belonged to Gran's grandmother, one of our longest-lived magical ancestors. I didn't know if it would offer any protection to Jilly, but I had tucked it into a velvet bag and kept it in my purse awaiting the right moment.

My cousin lit up when she saw it. As kids, we'd loved lying on Gran's bed playing with the jewels and amulets. This bracelet had been Jilly's first choice every time and I knew Gran would be thrilled to see her clipping it in place. It was like a hug from afar.

Afterward, I circulated with Sinda, tasting the gourmet food and avoiding the champagne entirely. I'd never had a head for alcohol, which served me well. Booze made people affectionate and lowered my defenses to mental incursions. The rare occasions I got tipsy, I ended up with a different kind of hangover—a head full of other people's woes.

Keats and Mr. Bixby circulated, too, along with Percy. They made a curious and cute security team, but I didn't underestimate their abilities.

Despite all my worries, I enjoyed chitchatting with Ivy's family and Jilly's new friends. It all felt surprisingly easy and comfortable, and for a blissful few hours, I pretended I belonged here in Clover Grove. This town certainly had its share of secrets and a distinct undercurrent of crime, but Wyldwood Springs took trouble to a whole new level.

It was well past midnight when the dachshund wound through the ladies' feet and led me aside.

"Keats has a bad feeling," he said. "I only pick up about half of what he's thinking, unfortunately. Dog is a curious language—a mix of words and sensory experiences."

"Maybe Ivy's in for more trouble. There's always something going on around here."

Mr. Bixby's sigh had an exasperated note. "I wouldn't bother you with a sheepdog's farm worries. His bad feeling was about *you*. It was a full hackles moment and it pains me to say he may be more intuitive than I am."

"He's had more practice," I said. "But we'd best be on the alert."

"Here I thought we might have one night off," the dog said. The chuckle that followed said he didn't mind at all. Like Keats, Mr. Bixby enjoyed staying busy.

"I knew it was too good to be true," I said. "Maybe when the wedding comes, we can take a vacation."

"Don't count your chickens before they're hatched," he said. "They're very silly birds, by the way. I don't really see the point of them."

My phone rang and when I saw it was Renata, Mr. Bixby and I walked around the side of the house.

"You'd better come home, Janelle," Ren said, getting straight to the point. "The store's door is gone. Again. This time it was blown in."

I had nothing to do with it, I was sure. Once I'd realized how little it took to cast a spell, I'd been paying attention. That odd sensation of humming magical energy was unmistakable, and I hadn't felt it again.

"Why would someone break into the store?" I said. "There was nothing of value."

Mr. Bixby pressed one beefy paw on my foot. "Nothing of value to *you*. We need to take a closer look."

Ren sounded like she was on the move at the other end. "I'll keep you posted. I called the police and I'm heading down there."

"Thanks, my friend. It's too bad we didn't get the new security feed set up in time."

"That's the good news," Ren said. "I'm not half bad with technology and I stayed up late to work on it. The feed was live when the burglar arrived."

"Could you see anything? Was it magic?" I was heading for the parking area, but Keats joined us and circled gently to herd me back to the party. Of course. I'd forgotten Sinda. I'd also forgotten to say goodbye to Jilly and Ivy. With the life I led currently, I couldn't afford to skip a hug with a loved one, because it might be my last.

"Positive thinking in action," Mr. Bixby said with a snicker. "You're an inspiration."

"It looked like a brick or rock," Ren continued, on the phone. "We'll check the footage together later, but I doubt we can get an ID. The person was wearing a hoodie."

Hanging up, I let Keats herd me to my cousin and smiled despite my worry. The break-in might very well be a break in my case.

Keats looked up at me and panted a ha-ha-ha that seemed like confirmation. Then he circled to draw me into a hug with Jilly.

I looked over at Bixby and mentally muttered, "Watch and learn."

Then Keats dove in to deliver a sharp nip on my bare leg.

The time for hugs was over.

"Got it," Bixby said, taking a dive at my other leg. "Now, get hopping."

CHAPTER NINETEEN

S inda drifted off to sleep 10 minutes into the drive, leaving me alone with my thoughts.

Well, one was never alone when a nosy former ghost dog was able to dive in and out, pretty much at whim. He was so pleased with the skills he'd picked up from Keats that he was trying to herd my thoughts around, as he chillaxed on his blanket in the back seat. The only good thing was that with Sinda resting, the dog and I were forced to rely on mental communication. I regretted pulling her into this mess, now.

"Don't," Mr. Bixby said. "She came willingly, and she was ready for a fresh start. Lexie kept her on a tight lead and Sinda isn't ready to retire from life. From what you've told me, she's like Edna Evans, only without the explosives." He fell quiet for a second and then added, "Or with a different type of explosives. There's more magic in Sinda than she probably realizes."

"You can smell that, too?" I asked.

"Yep. Like that smell you give off. Only hers is zesty, like spearmint."

"What about Renata?" I asked. "How does she smell?"

"Like a tulip bulb," he said. "Buried, with a faint whiff of promise."

I couldn't help smiling. "Something needs to happen to make Ren realize it's possible, I guess."

"Exactly. That may be true of your cousin, too. As for Ivy, she smells like a magical meadow at dawn."

"Really? I suspected as much with her connection to animals."

"It's pretty basic, from what I can tell," Bixby said. "Or smell. There have always been people whose magic starts and ends with animals. She may be one of them. You're meant for other things. Equally dangerous, if not more so."

"I wish there were training classes," I said. "Where I could get some answers."

"That would imply there are patterns and rules. Maybe it doesn't work that way."

"The spell book suggests rules," I said. "Look what happens when you don't follow them."

He got up and turned around a few times on the blanket, creating a nest. "Try to see the humor in it and cut yourself some slack. It probably won't be your last misfire. We're all learning, here."

I appreciated his kindness. In fact, it was a balm for my soul. The stakes seemed so high and I'd never expected to be alone in this. Seeing Jilly with her newfound family made me realize just how much I missed Mom.

"I thought you hated your mother." The dog's voice in my head was a sleepy murmur now. "That's what you told me."

"I never said 'hate.' What a terrible word! She grates on me, no question. Grates on everyone, it seems." The car ahead of me turned off the highway and I flicked on the high beams. They sliced through the deep back country darkness and seemed to shed a little light on my situation. "I feel sorry for Mom, now. Everyone wanted her gone, and that's at least partly because of what I did on prom night."

"That's what mothers do," he said. "Carry the burdens of their pups, until the pups learn to bite for themselves."

I started to laugh out loud, and he growled to remind me to keep it down.

"Am I really ready to bite?" I mused mentally.

"You tell me. How many decades does it take for you humans to mature?"

"Some never do," I said. "But I don't want that to be me."

"How about I leave you to ruminate over it while I catch some shuteye? Cataloguing those farm smells tired me right out."

"Okay. And thanks, buddy."

There was a faint mental chuckle and then, "It's *Mr.* buddy. And apparently, that's what I'm here for."

My mind felt strangely empty as he drifted into slumber. I was rarely alone in my thoughts even before he arrived. It was a constant battle to shield myself from emotions wafting off others. That's why I'd always loved road trips. I could zip past towns and take in a flurry of images that blew away as fast as they came. Keeping Elsa chugging forward meant most things slid off me like Teflon.

There would be few road trips ahead now. I couldn't just pack up and leave when I had a store to run. A mother to find. A murder to solve. A ghost butler to heal. Good friends to protect and support. A reputation to live down.

The key to all of it likely resided in *Everyday Spells for Everyday Magic.*

That name... Honestly. Maybe there was another book with more gravitas. Mine was a spell book for hacks.

Well, that's what I was right now. A hack. A rank amateur.

The winding road unfurled in the high beams and I bit my lip to stay alert. It was an old trick that had kept Elsa and me out of the ditch.

After another mile or two I realized it wasn't the spell book I needed to embrace, but magic itself. I needed to understand my abilities and limitations so that I knew when I was batting out of my league. If I couldn't flee like I used to, I needed to get off the bench and into the game. Mr. Bixby was right. I was too old to shrug off responsibility. Whatever gifts I had were almost certainly in place. Time to take them for a test drive. With Mr. Bixby and Sinda riding shotgun, I was better off than I had ever been, despite feeling more in peril.

That feeling only grew as I took the exit to Wyldwood Springs. The horizon was beginning to brighten after another sleepless night. Maybe I could grab a nap later, after checking things out at the store.

Finding parking at that early hour was easy, and I thought about leaving the car running in hopes that my passengers would sleep a little longer. A police car was parked out front so I could afford to be without bodyguards.

"Hold on a hot minute." Mr. Bixby's voice was prickly with irritation and woke Sinda. "No way am I missing this."

"Missing what?" I said, turning off the car and opening the door. "It's just another investigation."

"Maybe, but it's an entirely new investigator." The dog climbed between the seats and into my lap. "Unless my nose deceives me, things are about to take a dramatic turn for the better."

"Oh yeah?" I scooped him up and got out of the car. "That's good news."

The dog struggled to get down. "You might faint and fall on me," he said.

"I don't faint, Bixby. That's insulting."

Sinda got out and because she was closer to the storefront, she was the first to see the so-called dramatic turn. "Oh my," she said. "That is a surprise."

I didn't faint, but the world did spin for a second when I saw a uniformed officer leaning on the counter of my store with his arms crossed talking to Renata. It wasn't Jimmy Barrow or Warren Dredger, or any of the other Wyldwood cops I knew.

Instead, it was tall, auburn and handsome Drew Gillock.

"Consider your world officially rocked," Mr. Bixby said.

My shoes started to turn of their own volition.

Mom's shoes.

Why hadn't I changed into Jilly's clothes at the farm?

"Let's do this later," I said.

"He's already seen you, dear," Sinda said. "And I would imagine that's Renata, who's been waiting, too."

Mr. Bixby circled to give me a sheepdog poke in the back of my leg. "Next it'll be a nip. Get moving."

Scooping up the dog, I walked through the empty doorway and plastered on the biggest smile I could muster. Drew straightened abruptly and Renata gasped. Did I really look that bad? Dowdy, yes, but hardly worth the look of dismay on a man who'd found me rather fetching a few days ago.

"Less teeth," Bixby said. "Less teeth."

"What?" I said. The word was directed at the dog, but Drew answered.

"Your mouth is covered in blood," he said. "Have you been struck?"

I clawed in my pockets for a tissue and Sinda pulled out an embroidered handkerchief. "Sinda, I can't. It will stain."

"There are more in my suitcase," she said. "And I may be done with hankies, anyway. No place for them in a bunker, I'm sure Edna Evans would say."

I tried not to laugh, knowing I'd just split my lip even more. "Chief Gillock, I'm fine," I said. "We had a long drive down from Clover Grove and I guess I was biting my lip to stay awake at the wheel."

"Oh Janelle, you should have told me," Sinda said. "I'm still a capable driver."

"It's okay. You needed your sleep." I glanced around for Bijou and found her perched on the window seat, watching Renata. At least the resident ghost was okay after the break-in.

"And you needed sleep even more," Sinda said. "Now you have to deal with Chief Gillock's questions when you're exhausted." She gave him an entreating smile. "Unless he'd consider having the conversation later."

Drew gave one shake of his head. Normally, he wouldn't meet my eyes, instead looking above, below or off to the side. It was as if he were trying to avoid being transfixed—or bewitched, as Ivy said. Today, however, his brown eyes came in for a landing. The bloody lip must have undermined my allure. Stepping forward, he offered me a bottle of water, and gestured to the side of his mouth.

"You look like a clown," Mr. Bixby said. "In case you're wondering."

I moved around Drew and set the dog on the counter to protect his paws from broken glass.

"Hush, now," Sinda told Mr. Bixby.

Drew looked at her curiously and apparently decided she was speaking to me. "I'd prefer that she speak up, actually," he said. "A split lip shouldn't keep her from explaining herself."

I dampened the hankie and dabbed at my lips and teeth while staring around the store. The brick Ren had mentioned was still on the floor among the shards of glass.

"I've sent messages for the contractor and locksmith who came before," Ren said. "I expect they'll be here before too long."

I nodded my thanks and then looked back at Drew. "What would you like me to explain, Chief? I wasn't here when the break-in occurred. Luckily, Renata happened to be downtown late and saw the smashed glass."

He shook his head and nearly smiled. "If only that was all that needed explaining, Miss Brighton."

Ah, so we were on formal terms again. Well, I supposed he had almost always called me that, even when his visits to the Briar Estates were casual. The formality was meant to keep me at arm's length, like avoiding my eyes.

"He did ask you out on a date," Mr. Bixby said. "At least according to your memories, which I'm examining with great interest right now. Plus, he gave you a potted plant, which, alas, did not survive. I hope you'll take better care of me. If not, I'll request a transfer to Ivy Galloway. She knows how to treat a dog right."

I glared at the dog as he strutted across the counter but resisted his taunt.

"Fine," Bixby said. "I do believe this man is smitten with you. But he doesn't trust you either."

Why would he? Drew very nearly caught me in a couple of magically compromising positions down south. I had stunned a man at the Briars, for starters—took the guy right out of commission for trying to kill Ivy. He hadn't regained his memories after months of incarceration. Then I did the same to the woman who attacked me in Sinda's store, leaving her addled, perhaps permanently, with bite wounds on her hands from the pedigree dachshund snickering beside me.

"Did you get a dog?" Drew asked. He was across the store now, with his back to the window and his eyes on Bixby. I didn't need to be a mind-reader to sense the churn as he made connections.

"A dog got me," I said, around the handkerchief. "He's a rescue who turned up at Sinda's store."

"As I told you myself, Chief," Sinda said. "When that woman attacked Janelle, the dog protected her. Mr. Bixby is a true hero."

"I see," Drew said. "Although I'm anxious to hear the rest of the story. Directly from Janelle's cracked lips."

"Excuse me, Chief," Renata said. "You're not being very kind to Janelle. She's been through a lot, lately."

"It's okay, Ren," I said. "But thanks. I know I left some question marks behind when I left Clarington."

"Plenty," Drew said, but his tone warmed a touch after Ren's reproof.

"Whatever Sinda told you is true," I said. "I was ambushed in her jewelry store and it turned into what seemed like a duel to the death. I'm sure you found the weapon the attacker used. She was quite adept with it."

"What I don't understand is how she went down without a mark on her, aside from the dog bites." He pushed off the counter and circled me. "Or what grudge she had to pick with you."

"I tripped her and threw her off balance," I said, turning to face him. "As for the grudge, I guessed it was sudden onset of dementia. I'm sure you found some evidence of that in her home?"

He gave a curt nod. "Indeed. There were a number of items belonging to you. I hope that doesn't upset you."

It upset me all right. I'd managed to scoop up some of them, including a significant amount of my purloined hair, not to mention the spell book, before Lexie's killer could use them against me. Turns out I'd always valued my hair without knowing its true power.

"Of course it does, but many people at the Briars hold strange beliefs. There are tarot cards, crystal balls and other curiosities. Maybe she was trying to create a voodoo doll with my name on it."

"Why would she take such a loathing to you?" he asked. He circled the store again and his boots crunched over broken glass. "You were very well liked by the other Briars residents, according to my conversations."

"I made a lot of changes in my short time managing the property," I said. "Change is difficult for some people."

Drew stopped with his back to the window again, noticing neither the ghost poodle nor the town's early risers gathering outside to see what was going on. "I'd also like to know why you ran. Without so much as a word of explanation."

"Red alert," Bixby said. "Wounded man feelings. Tread carefully in those frumpy shoes."

"Chief, I was scared." My words had the ring of truth and he nodded. "I wanted to come home to my mother. That's not easy to admit at my age, but it's true."

"And you found her gone," he said.

I nodded and the hankie drifted to my side. "I'm afraid so. Chief Dredger hasn't bothered with a search, either."

"Chief Dredger said your mom showed signs of mental instability," Drew said. "They assumed she went down to the Briars to see your grandmother."

"No one even bothered to call Gran and check," I said. "I had to tell her, and I've just been up to break the news to Jilly. Finding my mom is my first priority."

"It's the first priority of the police here, too. For different reasons... She's a suspect in the murder of Laverne Billings."

"Mom? That's ridiculous. Why would she hide from me and then kill Laverne?"

"I know Shelley Brighton very well," Renata said. "She'd never do something like that."

"She was behaving erratically and had disputes with plenty of people, or so I've heard," Drew said. "Not from Miss Brighton, of course."

Sensing my temper rising, Sinda reached over and touched my arm. It infused me with calm.

"You seem to have learned a lot in a short time in Wyldwood Springs, Chief Gillock," I said.

"I learned a lot even before coming," he said. "Chief Dredger was intrigued to hear about your activities in Strathmore County. It made him wonder if you might be responsible for the murder, perhaps in conjunction with your mother."

I shook my head sadly. "I figured you'd know me better than that by now."

He shrugged. "There are so many loose ends that don't make

sense. I decided to make the trip and check things out firsthand."

"Good," I said. "I'd sure appreciate it if you'd help the local police investigate. Including finding out who broke into my store and why."

"We're on it," he said. "There were no witnesses."

I gestured to the people on the sidewalk. "There are always witnesses in Wyldwood. You mean there are none who will talk."

"I'm sure we'll get to the bottom of it in due course," he said. "With your cooperation."

"There's nothing here to steal," I said. The single display case had been tipped over and empty boxes moved. "It looks like someone just threw things around for the sake of being destructive."

"Is there anyone who'd want to keep you from opening a business?" Drew asked.

I started walking around and he followed. "Sure. There are grudges here, too. Very old ones. I assume you know about what happened when I was a teen."

"I heard the story, but I'm hard pressed to believe a prank like that ended in murder."

"Exactly, but I was a convenient scapegoat." Bijou jumped down from the window seat and led me to the top of the basement stairs. Her tail drifted down but it was clear she wanted me to follow. "Chief, would you mind joining me? I've only been into the basement once before and it gives me the creeps. I'd like to check it out."

"I'll stay here with Sinda and Renata and keep them safe," Mr. Bixby shouted after me.

I covered my mouth with the handkerchief to hide my smile. The former ghost dog wasn't too comfortable being trapped in the basement with the current one. Maybe he was worried being undead was contagious.

Drew opened the door and turned on the basement light. For good measure, he added a flashlight. I appreciated it, but the ghost poodle had a glow of her own and I was confident she wouldn't lead me directly into trouble.

The basement was unfinished—just one big room with a cement floor and bare rafters. Drew had to duck his head because the ceiling was so low.

"Nothing to see here," he said.

The ghost dog disagreed. She pranced over to the wall near the back of the store and circled on the spot.

"Huh," I said. "Does it strike you that the basement seems shorter than the main floor?" I walked over to the dog and stared at the red bricks in the light of the flashlight. "Any chance this is a false wall?"

Drew examined it closely, from one side of the building to the other, unconsciously walking around Bijou. "Possibly. But if so, there's no way inside."

Bijou made scratching motions at the midpoint. "Here," I said. "Try here."

He pushed on the brick and then started prying at the mortar. "Not getting anywhere, Janelle."

I was happy to hear my given name again. "Let me try," I said, as the ghost dog swung her muzzle from me to the wall and back. "My fingers are smaller and my nails longer." I stared at them, clenched around the bloody handkerchief, and sighed. There were few good nails left out of 10. My last manicure at the Briars had taken a deadly beating.

Luckily, it didn't take any prying at all. I felt my way gently over the bricks, casting glances at Bijou for direction. Finally, I pressed the right spot and the bricks basically folded back to reveal a small room.

"Well," Drew said. "It looks like your intruder may have missed something."

I nodded, as Bijou walked inside ahead of us. "Something important. But what?"

CHAPTER TWENTY

The room was empty, except for a circle of 10 folding chairs. It looked innocent enough, but there was a decidedly eerie feeling. If Mr. Bixby were downstairs with us, he'd say—

"Magical flatulence." I jumped at the sound of the dog's voice, but luckily Drew didn't hear anything. "Even you can smell it now, can't you?"

I didn't answer because I didn't trust myself to use our internal line efficiently. Drew had plenty of suspicions about me already without adding snarky one-sided conversations with dogs into the mix.

"It looks like a meeting room," I said. "For a secret club."

"What kind of club wants to meet in the basement of an abandoned store on folding chairs?" Drew asked. "There's nothing else here except a few candles in the corner. Unnecessary when there's a light." He gestured to the single bulb dangling from the ceiling. "Such as it is."

"I doubt it's a quilting club," I said, walking around the perimeter with Bijou ahead and Bixby behind. "The store is rumored to be haunted and most people don't want to come inside upstairs, let alone down here with the cobwebs and creep factor."

"A paranormal club," Drew suggested. "Ghostbusters. There are plenty of those around, even in Strathmore County."

"That makes sense," I said, watching Bijou closely. Her hackles were up and her tail tucked, so I knew the visitors didn't have her blessing. It was an invasion of her safe space.

If she knew more, however, she wasn't saying. Judging by the wide berth she gave Drew as she went back to the stairs, it had something to do with him. There were probably very few people Bijou trusted, and I was honored to be one of them.

Her tail rose again and gave a feeble flicker. We couldn't communicate well—not yet, anyway—but I felt her loneliness and sorrow. Life in-between was difficult for Bijou and I hoped I could find a way to fix that.

"What are you staring at?" Drew asked.

"Nothing. Just lost in thought." I turned before heading upstairs and looked back at the secret room. "Trying to figure out why someone would break into the store for this."

"Not to mention blowing the door into the street yesterday," Drew said. "That was bizarre."

"Totally bizarre," I said, over canine laughter Drew couldn't hear. "You'd almost think someone wanted me out of the place."

"I suppose Laverne's murder was the first indication," he said.

I patted my lips to make sure the blood had dried before answering. "You don't really think I had anything to do with that, do you?"

He shook his head. "I know you're not telling us everything, but no DNA evidence has been found yet so we can't link anyone to the crime. Regardless, I don't believe you're capable of running a stake through a real estate agent."

"Especially when she'd already given me what I wanted, which was a lease on the store. Seems more likely the people who use this room for their so-called meetings didn't care to share the space with fine jewelry and gifts."

"Or a psychic with a bad reputation," Mr. Bixby said. I glared at the dog and he added, "What? Just trying to be helpful."

Just trying to bait me into snapping back and embarrassing myself in front of Drew, more like.

The dog snickered. "That would definitely be a bonus."

"I'm going to stick around Wyldwood Springs for a few days," Drew said. "Lend Warren a hand. He's a good guy, really."

"What about Strathmore County?" I asked. "Who's watching over the Briar Estates? I worry about Gran."

He smiled openly for the first time. "Bridie's doing fine. Asked me to come, actually."

"She did?" I was surprised Gran would knowingly send a human cop into this dangerous cesspool.

"After she heard about your mother, yes. She was worried about your being alone here, and suspected things wouldn't go as well as you hoped with the store."

"I haven't told her about Laverne's passing," I said. "I didn't want to upset her even more."

"Keeping secrets from your own grandmother? I guess I feel better about being cut out of the loop."

"Told ya," Mr. Bixby said. "Mantrum."

"Well, I'm very grateful you're here, Chief, but I'm not completely alone. I have Sinda and Renata. And Mr. Bixby."

His smile verged on a smirk, which told me he underestimated all of us.

"I just docked him a few points for that smirk," Mr. Bixby said. "I bet he's dismissed me as a wiener dog, when I'm a fierce badger-hunting dachshund."

Oblivious to the canine snit, Drew spoke up again. "With the way things are going, it seems like you could use even more rein-forcements."

I knew that Drew was conflicted. Part of him probably wanted to be my hero. The other part wanted to figure out exactly what happened in his own county and whether or not it overlapped with trouble here. He was likely doomed to disappointment on both fronts. A regular guy like Drew didn't have the capacity to understand my current predicament.

"Don't underestimate him even if he underestimated me," Bixby said. "There's more to Dashing Drew than meets the eye. My nose is an accurate judge of character and he smells rather nice. Like a cedar hope chest." The dog strutted to the bottom of the stairs and waited to be picked up. "Cedar and moss make a healthy blend."

I forced myself to ignore the dog and trained my eyes on Drew. "That's wonderful, Chief. You've left someone reliable in charge?"

"My second in command is a good cop," he said. "And the chief of the neighboring county is even better. Between them, they'll keep the Briars and Clarington safe until we get things sorted out here."

"Where do we start?" I asked.

He smiled again. "By 'we,' I meant the police. Chief Dredger, his officers and me."

"You know I can't sit around waiting for the police to get to the bottom of this," I said. "There's a lot at stake for me. On top of my missing mother, I invested most of my savings in rent here."

"Leave it in our capable hands while you plan your new business and integrate into the community," he said. "So you'll be ready to launch when this is all behind you."

"Docked another point for being patronizing," Mr. Bixby said. "Dashing Drew just turned back into Big Red. But I suggest you agree with him. It's probably easier that way."

"That will keep me plenty busy, I suppose," I told Drew, digging up a compliant smile.

I had no intention of stepping back, of course. I'd find my own way through this mess, and probably faster than the authorities. While they dallied, my enemies rallied.

"That's what your gran was afraid of," Mr. Bixby said. "You're proving her right."

"I need to flush those losers," I said.

Out loud. I said it out loud.

Drew's eyebrows rose like copper swallows. "Pardon me?"

I let Mr. Bixby enjoy a full-throated chortle before answering. "The people using this place for meetings, I mean. They can't just trespass."

At the bottom of the basement stairs, he stood aside to let me pass. "I suppose every old place comes with unwelcome visitors."

"I wish it were just rats," I said. "My dog is bred to handle those."

"I relish that," Bixby said, as I lifted him and walked upstairs. "No relish required."

The dog and I exchanged an inner smile. While I appreciated Drew's support, I had more faith in my original team, now sweeping up the glass. Sinda and Renata were chatting as if they were friends already, while Bijou looked on from the window seat, with her front paws elegantly crossed.

The contractor arrived moments later, although it was just past six a.m. He was still setting up as the Main Street Welcome Committee crunched in over the last bits of glass.

"Oh, Janelle, you poor dear," Candace said. "The rumors are true. You've had two accidents in just two days."

"Once is an accident, twice is a pattern," Drew said.

Candace, Frida and Ginny glanced at each other before scanning Drew from his auburn hair to his police issue boots.

"Are you new to the force?" Frida asked. "We know all the officers here."

Drew nodded. "I'm a friend of Chief Dredger's and an acquaintance of Miss Brighton and her grandmother."

Aha. So he was a friend of Warren Dredger's and an acquaintance of mine. It was good to know where I stood.

"Docked again," Mr. Bixby said. "Big Red better up his game."

The Welcome Committee stared at him, waiting for more. It didn't come. Not from Drew and not from me.

Sinda stepped forward to break the awkward silence and shook each woman's hand in turn. "I'm Janelle's friend, Sinda Joffrey. I've come to help her set up the store."

"She's the jewelry designer I told you about, ladies," I said, dangling the dachshund pendant. "She made this and I absolutely love it."

"Adorable," Candace said. "Although we're not pet fanciers. They just tie you down."

"True," I said, hugging Bixby tighter than he liked. "I'm looking to be tied down here. I won't be going anywhere anytime soon."

Ginny stepped forward and offered a cardboard tray holding four cups of juice. "That's wonderful because we need your fine palate. After hearing what happened, I brought you a pick-me-up. It's called Sassy Sunshine."

"Sass in a glass," I said. "All for it."

"I could use it, too," Ren said, reaching for a cup. "What a night."

Bijou jumped down from the window seat and circled Renata, once again showing her fondness for my old friend.

Gently batting Ren's hand away, Ginny said, "Guests first, Renata. I'm sure Sinda and Officer..."

She trailed off strategically and Drew supplied, "Chief Andrew Gillock, ma'am."

"Chief Gillock, it's lovely to meet you. I run Ginny's Juice Bar down the street. Please try a sample."

He shook his head and smiled. "I never drink sunshine on duty, but thank you."

The trio tittered and Mr. Bixby muttered, "Oh, brother."

The tittering got even louder when Ethan Bogart, the chef from the bistro next door, wove around the workers to join us. He was carrying a plate of freshly baked croissants that smelled heavenly and a pot of coffee that smelled even better. In the pocket of his chef's apron was a stack of paper cups, creamers and sugar packets.

I wanted to hug him.

"Join the line," Mr. Bixby said.

Indeed, all eyes had shifted from the chief to the chef, with one notable exception. Renata's dark eyes had dropped to the floor and she ran her fingers through her long, tangled hair, twisting it into a knot. There was something more appealing here than hot croissants.

Bijou must have agreed, because she started romping back and forth between Ethan and Renata, although neither could see her.

"Maybe they can double date with you and Big Red," Mr. Bixby said. "If he can redeem himself."

Ethan set the plate of croissants on the window seat so that he could shake Drew's hand, and offered him a cup of coffee.

Drew declined and stepped behind the counter to respond to the ping of a text.

Sinda, Ren and I ate a croissant and then chased it with Ginny's liquid sunshine. Ethan circulated with the coffee and I downed mine black and scalding, wincing as it touched my cracked lip.

Candace followed him with her striped tin of truffles. It was a little early for chocolate but I appreciated that the women were trying to lift our spirits. The richness of the filling did offer a certain comfort. How bad could life be when truffles arrived daily?

Frida finished off our breakfast with frozen yogurt that was already half melted. Her face fell when I tried to pass, so I changed my mind. I couldn't afford to alienate the friendly people in town.

"You're all so kind," I said, holding out my paper cup for more coffee. "Thank you for making us feel welcome."

"You got dealt a bad hand here," Ethan said. "Although I admit I had doubts when I saw you in that dumpster."

"In the dumpster?" The question came from Drew. "That doesn't sound like you, Janelle. You're normally so..."

His voice drifted off. I hoped he wanted to say poised, or polished. When he met me, I flattered myself that I'd been both of those things. Now I was wearing my mother's cast-off frump wear with a whiff of garbage about me, I supposed.

"It's not that bad," Mr. Bixby said. "Only I can smell it, probably."

"I was looking for Laverne's glasses," I said. "They seemed part of her identity."

"Oh, they were," Candace said. "Those beaded strings were definitely part of her image."

"Back when she used to visit Gran at the manor, I always wanted to touch those beads," I said. "I finally got my chance, but it was such a shame how it happened."

"The police will figure it out," Ethan said, offering the last croissant to Drew.

Drew shook his head, keeping up the formal front.

By the time the contractor had installed the new door, and the locksmith offered new keys for the front and back doors, our little crowd had dispersed. Drew lingered, but finally succumbed to persuasion from Bijou, who pressed him toward the door with her energy.

Once everyone was out of sight, Ren led Sinda and me behind the counter and pulled her laptop out of her bag. "There's something from the security footage you need to see," she said.

"Didn't the police ask for it?" Sinda said.

"They don't know about it," Ren said. "I hid the camera well and no one's noticed. I wanted Janelle to see this first. She can decide whether to share it."

A grainy image appeared on the screen. As Ren had said on the phone, the person peering into the store was wearing an oversized hoodie. It could have been either a man or a woman. The baggy pants and running shoes gave nothing away.

"Give me a lift," Mr. Bixby said. I set him on the counter so that he could see. "A young thug, I suppose? A hired hand to do some dirty work downstairs?"

"Probably," I said out loud. When Ren looked at me questioningly, I continued, "Probably some kid hired to do some dirty work downstairs in the secret room we just discovered. I couldn't mention it in front of the Welcome Committee, or it would have been all over town. Candace and crew are probably collecting information in exchange for sweet treats."

"For sure," Ren said. "That's the only reason they were here before their stores even opened. They would have doubled our servings if they got a chance to see this."

"Maybe they'd have known who it is," I said.

"We don't need them," Ren said. "I bet we can figure it out between us."

"Really? I'd better watch it again."

I hit replay seconds before a black paw did it for me. Then I watched it a couple more times for good measure, each replay revealing more detail in the short clip.

"What do you see?" Ren prompted me.

The intruder was only on screen a few seconds. They paused outside the door to look around, and then broke the glass and came inside in a hurry. But something must have happened because they turned and ran in just a few minutes. Had they heard the sirens? Or did something else happen?

Ren hit replay again, pressing the key to advance the video frame by frame. Then she paused strategically.

"Hey," I said. "The brick didn't even smack the glass. It basically just crumbled."

"Exactly," Ren said. "Looks like it was just a prop."

"Magic," Sinda said. "That's a problem."

"Not as big as you think," Mr. Bixby said. "There wasn't the faintest whiff of sulphur upstairs. The basement was another story."

"Maybe it's good magic," I said. "But it was still a break-in."

"Watch again," Ren said. There was a little smile on her face as if waiting for me to catch onto a joke. "Doesn't the person's posture and gait look familiar?"

I shook my head. "Not really."

"Look at her hand when she drops the brick," Ren said, blowing up the image for me.

I gasped. "That ring is my mother's. It's been in our family for generations."

Sinda touched my arm and I felt the sensation of cool calm water flowing through me. "I think she's suggesting it still is, dear friend."

Mr. Bixby was less refined. "Duh."

"That's *Mom*?" I grabbed the counter, as relief and confusion sent tremors through my legs.

"I hope you're not always the last to clue in," he said. "I may need to switch allegiance to the smart girls."

"It is your mom, I'm quite sure of it," Ren said, grinning. "She's alive and well."

She was alive, and I was incredibly happy about that. But if Mom was breaking into a very recent crime scene, she probably wasn't well at all.

CHAPTER TWENTY-ONE

W e met again at noon in Tingle Square, which got its name from the original founder of Wyldwood Springs. The town's official center had always been well maintained and decorated with seasonally appropriate floral displays. Now there were dozens of raised beds filled with fall blooms in rust, yellow and maroon. Artfully arranged decorative gourds were inspected daily and swapped out if a squirrel dared to take a bite. And tall urns with feathery grasses graced every nook and cranny.

It was all pretty and soothing for those with jangled nerves, like mine.

The hordes of people? Not so much.

The square was nearly full when we arrived for the Founder's Day ceremony. This was always a major event on the Wyldwood Springs social calendar.

No one knew exactly when Orville Tingle had unhitched his horse and wagon and decided to set down roots, but this was as good a day as any. It doubled as the kickoff to the harvest festival, which ran a full month with small daily celebrations and bigger family events on weekends.

I had loved the fall fair as a kid. Back when Mom and I got

along. And Gran and Mom got along. Aunt Eva and Mom never really did get along, according to Gran. It was a shame and one reason I was committed to making and keeping peace with Jilly. There was nothing like a brush with death to make one appreciate family.

"Isn't this wonderful?" Sinda said, gazing around the square. She was wearing a simple, stylish dress in muted orange with a matching jacket that suited the occasion perfectly. "I missed the seasons down south."

I wore a gray dress with a green wool jacket and a sharp pair of faux alligator stilettos. The entire ensemble belonged to Jilly, yet I felt like myself again. Exhausted and a little dazed, but far more comfortable in my own skin. I hoped my cousin wouldn't mind black and tan dog hair penetrating the fibers of her coat, because there was no way I was setting Mr. Bixby down among this sea of feet. I switched him from one arm to the other and back, clutching him a little tighter each time.

"Dare I remind you that I'm not a handbag?" he said. "You're squeezing me till I'm queasy."

"I feel queasy in this crowd," I said, as much to Ren as Bixby. "So many eyes on us, and none of them friendly."

"They're just curious," Ren said. "And cautious. No one knows which side you're on."

"There are sides?" I asked.

"For sure, although I don't know the dividing lines. The big players don't trust me enough to tell me."

"We're in this together, girls," Sinda said. "I expect we can acquit ourselves quite well."

"It's no wonder you're feeling queasy," Bixby said. "Good magic and bad are colliding in a cloud overhead and it's going to rain trouble."

"Fabulous," I said. I tried to use one-word answers that wouldn't confuse Ren. Since Sinda and I could both hear Mr. Bixby, he spoke aloud when he wanted to include her. It did make things tricky.

"Isn't it great news that your mom's fine and breaking into stores?" Ren asked.

Her voice was so upbeat, I couldn't help smiling even though the image replaying in my mind made me anxious.

"If Mom is running around town looking like a common thug and breaking into places, it's probably not great news, Ren. The Shelley Brighton I know wouldn't be caught dead in a hoodie and sneakers. I bet she wasn't even wearing makeup."

"Where there's life, there's hope, right?" Ren said.

I nodded. Seeing Mom alive had stirred hope in my heart, along with plenty of other emotions. Maybe we'd get our chance to heal the old rift after all. "I'll do anything in my power to set things right with her," I said.

It would probably help if I knew just where my power began and ended. Not knowing wasn't serving me terribly well right now.

"So, all that blather about hating your mom was poppycock," Mr. Bixby said. "I didn't cross back over to indulge your angst, you know. I came back for action."

"You'll get your chance," Sinda said, either to the dog or me, or both. "I'm sure we'll be seeing your mother again soon, Janelle. But before the story ends, there may be rough water here in Wyldwood Springs."

"No doubt," I said. "I wonder if she was planning to meet someone in that secret basement lair. It's the perfect place for illicit magical business."

"Or maybe she just wanted to chase you out of that store," Sinda said. "If she knows what happened to Laverne, she'll be worried."

"Unless she *is* what happened to Laverne," I said. "Drew said there was no DNA evidence yet. It could be a magical assailant."

"Did Shelley have bad blood with Laverne?" Sinda turned curiously to Ren, expecting her to have more current information.

"I don't know," Ren said, as we wove through the crowd toward the stage. "She fell out with a lot of people, but I refuse to believe she'd kill anyone. Like I said before, Janny, your mom was kind to me."

"I can't help wondering if she's been hexed," I whispered, as the throngs closed in around us. "It's the most logical explanation for her erratic behavior."

"I should have waited before calling the police," Ren said. "Then we could have gotten a better idea of what she was doing. I didn't recognize her and my fingers got itchy."

"Probably for the best," I said. "Otherwise, she might be in custody right now."

"But she'd be safe," Ren said.

"Not necessarily. The good cops aren't always equal to the bad ones," I said. "If she's wanted by the other side, she might have vanished from her cell."

We easily found a spot near the stage because people automatically gave us space. Being a pariah had its perks, it turned out. That didn't stop me from looking forward to the ceremony, which always delivered the same rallying cry—a yearly reminder that we were all in this together.

In a way, we were. Everyone wanted the town to thrive. There were just differing ideas of how to achieve success.

The Welcoming Committee forced their way through the crowd, elbowing people aside while somehow shielding their samples.

"I don't know if I can handle any more sweets," I said. "I haven't had a square meal since I got home."

"Not with a fridge full of putrid garbage," Bixby said.

"You are looking a bit pale and worn, Janelle," Sinda said.

We all were, and it was understandable. Sinda and I had eaten some delicious finger foods at Runaway Farm but we'd had to "Runaway Far" before Jilly packed up the leftovers she'd promised. She'd used her last moments with me to hurl clothes into the trunk. The Brighton women generally valued presentation over food.

I made a mental note to schedule meals while Sinda was staying with me. Not only was I a terrible host but a negligent friend, since she was not a young woman.

This time, Ginny served a Harvest Surprise vegetable juice along with some banana bread. "Gluten free and full of flax and good fats," she said. "You girls need beefing up."

"There's an entire serving of fruit in my cinnamon apple cheesecake special," Frida said. "Not to mention calcium in the dairy."

I managed to juggle the dog and the frozen yogurt, which really was delicious, and almost worth his grumbles.

Candace grinned as she tipped coffee from a thermos into little cups to cleanse our palates before serving white chocolate pumpkin spice truffles.

"You ladies spoil us," I said. "I think some people are giving you the evil eye."

"Let them," Candace said. "No one understands the politics of this town better than we do, Janelle. We're hoping our warm welcome will smooth some feathers your mother ruffled."

"I ruffled some on my own before that, remember." I handed back the paper cup and the truffle wrapper. "Mom was the one stuck trying to live that down."

"Young people get into trouble," Candace said. "Although you and your cousin were well-mannered kids. I still remember you staring over my counter at the candy with big green eyes. The two prettiest girls in town, I daresay. Such a shame the family fell apart."

My inner hackles rose but Sinda squeezed my arm and infused calm. I was rapidly coming to depend on that. It was so much easier than calming myself.

"We ran up to see Jilly in Clover Grove yesterday," Sinda said. "She's getting married next month."

"I'm a bridesmaid," I said. "As long as we can get everything here sorted out by then. I won't be much use to her if I'm in jail."

"Don't be silly," Frida said. "That isn't going to happen."

"You need to get out of this crowd," Candace said, tapping me gently with her empty truffle tin. "Come over and visit our stores."

"But I'm looking forward to hearing—"

My words got swallowed up in the din as Candace beat a path through the crowd to the sidewalk. Frida towed Sinda, and Ginny pushed Ren ahead of her, like a human shield.

I tried to follow but seemed to get shoved back with every step and fell far behind my friends.

Mr. Bixby threw back his long nose and then growled. "Keep moving. There's a decided stench around here and—hey! Do NOT touch me, you viper."

A big hand with an enormous ruby-studded ring had probably targeted my sleeve and landed on the dog instead.

Stepping aside quickly, I stared up at a very tall, gray-haired man I recognized instantly, though we'd never met. Oscar Knight was an older, classier version of my schoolyard nemesis, Jared, whose leering face was etched forever in my memory.

"I'm sorry, sir," I said, tucking Mr. Bixby more firmly under my arm. The dog's teeth bared, and his growled insults verged on profanity. "My dog isn't used to crowds and strangers."

"Strangers who take liberties and smell like rotting roadkill," the dog said.

No doubt the words sounded like a snarl to Oscar Knight because he took a step backward. I doubted he was the type of man to yield easily to a wiener dog.

"Dachshund." Mr. Bixby wasn't too flustered to correct me.

"I hear you're my newest tenant," Oscar said. "You had some turbulence on landing."

"I'm afraid so." It seemed like he was receding but then I realized it was my feet that were moving. The dog's energy seemed to propel us apart. "I was happy to see Laverne after all these years, and sad to see her go. I'm sure you must feel the loss."

"Oh, yes." He closed the gap between us. "Laverne was my property manager for a decade and she's irreplaceable. I've always tried to have a direct relationship with my tenants, though, so I'll set up a meeting with you shortly. As you may have heard, I have a vision for Main Street and I'll want to shape your business, Janelle."

"Seriously?" Bixby said. "We have our own vision."

I didn't know whether to be more annoyed by Mr. Knight's meddling or his use of my first name. In this case, I actually preferred the formality of proper titles.

"I'd be happy to come by your office, Mr. Knight," I said. "How is Jared doing?"

He smiled and it struck me that his eye teeth were a little too long. "Very well indeed. I forgot you two were classmates."

"All through school," I said. "What's he up to these days?"

I kept backing away and he kept following until we reached the sidewalk, where I ended up pressed up against The Knuckle Sandwich deli. Now I was stuck, so I offered my biggest, fakest smile.

Mr. Bixby managed a chuckle. "Try not to split your lip."

"Jared's representing my business interests all over hill country," Mr. Knight said. "My wife and I miss him terribly. No doubt your mother felt the same when you left."

"Not really," I said, and unfortunately, my lip did split. I could feel the blood beading up before I tasted it. The sight seemed to startle Oscar and he finally gave me some breathing room. "After the prank on prom night, I'm afraid we all agreed it was best that I leave Wyldwood Springs."

Oscar had a commanding presence, but he blinked a few times before replying. He probably hadn't expected me to take that incident head on.

"It was a long time ago," he said, broad shoulders rising and falling. His suit was charcoal gray and beautifully tailored. The attire of the modern gentleman warlock.

"Feels like yesterday," I said, patting my lip with a tissue. "The prank was Jared's idea, you know. But I went along with it."

Oscar stepped forward again, and Mr. Bixby snapped at his sleeve. "Young lady, you're wrong about that. Memory problems must run in your family."

The dog squirmed under my arm. "Squeezing. Too. Tight. Remember this: she who loses her cool around vipers is lost."

I took a deep breath, relaxed my grip on the dog and changed the channel on the conversation. "I miss my mother, Mr. Knight. Things don't feel right here without her." I summoned an entreating smile. "Do you know anything about what's happened?"

"Much better," Bixby said. "Sucking up usually works on guys like him. They expect it."

Oscar stared down at the dog. "He's a chatty little fellow, isn't he? It's almost like he's weighing in on the conversation."

"Dachshunds," I said. "They're quite full of themselves."

The tall man laughed and some of the tension dissipated. But just as I started to let my guard down, someone came up beside me and knocked me right into Oscar. I grabbed his arm for balance and accidentally touched his watch.

My vision clouded instantly, and serpents stirred in the depths of my soul. I teetered on my heels and he reached out to steady me. His big ring might just finish the job the watch began.

A sharp nip on my wrist brought instant clarity. "Walk away," Mr. Bixby said. "Now."

I managed to sidle around Oscar, and an arm dropped over my shoulders. The serpents recoiled from the sunlight that flooded me and I looked up to see Drew Gillock.

"Are you all right, Miss Brighton?" he asked. "You look very pale."

"Just tired, Chief Gillock." My voice was faint and hoarse. "Thank you for asking."

While I collected my wits, another man appeared behind Oscar Knight. He was wearing a uniform that was similar to that of the local police, but with a small neon insignia over the left breast pocket. I'd never personally seen it but knew from Mom and Gran that this belonged to the underground, magical police.

Oscar apparently had his own security detail.

"As do you," Bixby said. "Good cop, bad cop. You can tell the bad one by all the gel in his hair."

I didn't leave Drew's sheltering arm. The infusion of sunshine and strength let me know I'd been running on empty. I was going to fuel right up if it didn't deplete Drew's own energy reserves.

The chief gripped my shoulder tighter, staring from one man to the other. "Are these men bothering you?" he asked.

"Not at all," I said. "Mr. Knight is my new landlord. We were discussing my store."

The older man tipped his head and the feral smile reappeared. "That's probably not going to work out, sweetheart. Don't get too invested in the idea."

"I'm already invested," I said. "I've ordered signage, shelving and flyers for my grand opening. Not to mention paying a year's rent."

"What a shame," he said, scanning me from head to foot. "But now that we've met in person, I see you're not Main Street material."

"I have an agreement in writing, Mr. Knight," I said. "What's more, I called a lawyer yesterday and was told it would be considered binding."

He waved his big ring and I suppressed a shudder. Maybe he sensed his advantage because his eyes fixed on mine and became almost hypnotic. If it weren't for the warmth coming from the dog and Drew, I might well have become entranced. It probably worked wonders on people with fewer resources.

"Leases need to work for both parties," he said. "If Laverne had checked in with me first, as she normally did, I'd have insisted on a sit-down to make sure we were a good fit. Your plans don't seem to align with mine."

"Bringing Whimsy to Main Street will only add to the town's charm, sir."

His gray eyebrows came together. "Whimsy?"

"Designer jewelry," I said. "And unique gifts. There's no offering like that in town and I think locals and tourists alike will respond very well."

His dismissive sniff said otherwise. "Doesn't fit with our folksy image. Sorry."

"Oh, it does," I said. "I'll prove it to you."

He shook his head and I marveled over his abundant silver hair. Maybe there was a spell for good hair. I'd be all over that.

"I don't think so, sweetheart," he said.

His condescending tone grated on me, but I forged on. "I can't wait to show you what I can do with the place, and we'll discuss our future together a year from now."

Meeting his eyes was getting harder and harder to do. The snakes coiled and writhed in my stomach, overpowering the good energy I drew from my companions.

"Sweetheart, you aren't listening," he said. "I said no to Whimsy."

Drew had let me fight my own battles, but now he spoke up. "Miss Brighton said a lawyer was of the mind that the agreement was sound."

"Lawyers. We have a special creek here just for them," he said. "They drink or drown when I say so. Like anyone else in Wyldwood."

"Excuse me?" Drew's voice and Bixby's overlapped.

"It's a joke. Loosen up, constable."

Oscar laughed and the snakes inside me unfurled and swayed. My vision clouded again and nausea washed over me. Was I going to lose everything in one fell swoop? My savings, my pride and my hopes for a fresh start?

"*Chief*," Drew said. "Chief Andrew Gillock. I must say, you sound rather threatening, Mr. Knight."

His heavily gelled counterpart made an almost imperceptible move forward, which wasn't lost on Drew, at least judging by his grip.

"I'd never threaten a lady," Oscar said. His tone lightened and the snakes inside me settled a little. "Janelle can ask to be released from her lease for a full refund. I would imagine every cent counts."

"I can't do that, sir," I said. "This store is my dream come true."

"Here in Wyldwood, the fit needs to be just right," he said. "Perhaps we can find you another storefront up the range. Jared will know just where to put you."

I might have expected a visceral reaction to that threat, but it didn't happen. Jared was far less intimidating than his father.

"Mr. Knight," Drew said. "With all your business holdings, I doubt you have time to worry about a jewelry boutique and an entrepreneur eager to contribute to this town."

"Constable, I don't know where you're from, but we do things differently here," Oscar said.

"I look forward to learning the local nuances of the law," Drew said. "In the meantime, do let Miss Brighton go about her business in peace. She has the best of intentions."

"You can't run a town on good intentions," the older man said. "Although I'm all about community. That's our great strength, of course." He signaled to his henchman that he was ready to move back into the crowd. "Still, I have a vision. A story I want Wyldwood Springs to tell the world. There's absolutely no room for Whimsy in it."

The throngs seemed to open and close on cue to absorb Oscar Knight, and despite being extremely tall, he vanished into it.

"Good riddance to bad garbage," Mr. Bixby said.

"Don't worry too much," Drew said, walking me away from the crowd and back toward my store. "Although it wouldn't hurt to get a second legal opinion."

"Good idea," I said, knowing it wouldn't matter how many lawyers I consulted. If Oscar Knight wanted me gone, drowning might be the easiest way out.

CHAPTER TWENTY-TWO

S inda and Renata sat across from me on high stools at the kitchen island at the Brighton manor. I'd suggested ordering takeout, but no one was hungry except Mr. Bixby.

"What's that smell?" Ren asked, wrinkling her nose.

"Magical flatulence," Mr. Bixby answered for me. Ren couldn't hear him, but Sinda smiled.

"Two options," I said. "It's either the rotting food Mom left in the fridge, or my dead ambitions."

Ren slid off the stool. "I can deal with the former right now. Rotting food offends my professional sensibilities."

I caught her arm and directed her back to the stool. "I'll do it later. It'll wait, whereas Oscar Knight might not."

"Tell us every detail," Sinda said, leaning on the island's granite surface.

It struck me how much she'd changed since we met in that park down south. Her cheeks had been pink that day, despite hearing bad news about her niece. In fact, I could have sworn they were pink when she got off the plane recently. Maybe I should prioritize that fridge in case the rot was making her ill.

For the moment, I decided to put on a pot of coffee to offset the fridge bouquet. Then I told them the story as it brewed.

"Wait," Ren said, when I got to the part about Drew joining me. "Dashing Drew put his arm around you? In plain sight of the entire town? While in uniform?"

"Don't look at me," Bixby said. "She can't hear me, so Sinda must have spilled the beans about your hottie."

Sinda smiled, which brightened her up. "I'm quite sure that dashing young man is Janelle's destined match."

"I beg to differ," I said. "My true match—if such a thing exists— also needs to be a match for people like Oscar Knight and his henchmen."

"Don't count Drew out," Sinda said. "You came away from the encounter with energy. I felt it."

"Not to mention fluttery feelings," Mr. Bixby said. "While you could have been strategizing, you were thinking about that hand on your shoulder."

"Dogs really don't belong on the counter," I said, reaching for him. "That probably offends Ren's professional sensibilities more than the fridge."

Ren laughed. "I'm not too concerned because that dog is airlifted practically everywhere we go."

"Which I don't enjoy," Mr. Bixby said. "Tell them about how I tried to bite Oscar Knight and forced him to back up."

"This dog is a hero," Sinda said, stroking his head. "A fool and a hero."

I poured three mugs of black coffee and continued with the story, highlighting Mr. Bixby's contributions. At the right moment, I lifted my sleeve to show them the imprint of his teeth. They gasped, but I said, "It was the right thing to do. Oscar was trying to use his magical mojo on me and very nearly succeeding."

When I was done, Sinda said, "Why would Oscar Knight care so much about a jewelry store? How is that a threat to him?"

"He wants absolute power," I said. "At least that was my take on it. He was annoyed Laverne hadn't consulted him about letting me lease the store and more annoyed that I wouldn't bow down to his folksy suggestions."

"You don't think he'd have killed Laverne over this?" Sinda asked. "Just how annoyed was he?"

I shrugged. "He's capable, no doubt in my mind. But it hardly seems worth so much trouble. His nails were manicured so I doubt he does any dirty work himself."

"I doubt Oscar would risk his hold over the town by doing it directly," Ren said. "But his security team might make problems go away for him."

"That cop looked slimy," I said. "And Mr. Bixby didn't like the smell of him."

Ren sighed and tapped her fingers on the counter, thinking. She looked utterly spent, which wasn't surprising after the past couple of days.

"Oscar Knight doesn't need to go to extremes to make life miserable," she said. "He's already drummed out a couple of other businesses. Ran them into the ground with bogus claims. The worst part was that he ruined their reputations and chances of doing well anywhere else."

"At least I got an offer of Jared's help up the range and out of the way," I said, smirking.

Ren shuddered. "I haven't seen Jared in years, but his help you don't need."

"We'll figure something out," Sinda said, making a circle with her index finger that included the dog. "Together."

"Thank you," I said. "The only good part about being here is spending time with you guys. After leaving Gran, I feared I'd never have a— well, a family, again."

There, I'd said it. My plans had been to send Mom off to Gran's and live a solitary life. Now I felt quite differently. I missed Mom in ways I hadn't anticipated. Meanwhile, I'd found friendships that felt deep and authentic.

Mr. Bixby cleared his throat to remind me to keep my guard up. No one was quite what she seemed, I supposed.

"I feel the same," Renata said. "With my family long gone, it's been hard and lonely."

Sinda nodded. "My husband's passing knocked my feet right out and left me prey to his conniving niece. All I had to keep me going was my imaginary friends." She smiled fondly at Mr. Bixby. "Some have become real."

We all clasped hands across the counter, and a silence fell over the kitchen that somehow made the stench of the fridge seem even worse.

"It's not just the fridge that stinks," Mr. Bixby said. "I don't wish to offend you—this time—but you're all giving off a strange smell. It's like the early signs of decay."

Sinda and I turned in unison to stare at him. His nose was high and his snorting anything but flattering.

"Mr. Bixby smells something unpleasant," I said, for Ren's benefit. "Beyond the rotting food."

The dog pawed at my right hand, which was still holding Ren's. "Do you feel anything strange?" he asked silently. "Use your other skills to take a temperature check."

I blinked at him a few times, trying to digest what he was implying. Why would any of us be giving off a smell that could be likened to decay? We were in a crowd earlier. Perhaps we'd rubbed up against the wrong people.

"Stop thinking," he said, "and start sensing."

He stayed in my head, probably to avoid upsetting Sinda.

I squeezed my friends' hands and they both squeezed back, unaware that I was trying to do more than thank them for being awesome. Neither wore a ring, so I had to dig deeper into my psychic toolkit than usual.

It was easier than I expected, probably because both were intuitive and aware. Those traits opened the door and let me slip into the entryway of their minds. I didn't want to go further without asking permission, and I didn't want to scare them if there was nothing to worry about.

There was something to worry about. That much was clear even from a cursory look. I'd already been here before and something in their mental landscapes had changed. Normally both Sinda and Ren had a relaxed and welcoming vibe, whether authentic or cultivated. They were the type of people it was safe for me to hug.

But not today.

"It reeks," Mr. Bixby said. "That's what's changed."

He was with me, of course, because it took too much focus to do a reading and block him out with humming at the same time.

I let go of their hands abruptly. Knowing something was wrong with them made the intrusion feel even worse.

"Newsflash: you smell the same," Bixby said. "Start your research at home."

Sinda watched as I picked up my coffee cup, tried to take a sip and then put it down. The fragrance—one of my all-time favorites—was off-putting.

"What's wrong?" she asked.

"I feel nauseated," I said. "Earlier I was lightheaded, and Drew said I was pale."

"You are pale," Sinda said. "Do you feel feverish?"

"Just tired. And my feet feel heavy." I scanned her and then Ren. "You both seem a little under the weather too, if you don't mind my saying."

Sinda nodded. "I thought I might have caught something on the plane. Maybe I passed it to both of you."

Ren touched her cheeks and then her forehead. "I've been super restless. My mind goes round and round in circles but if I try to rest, I can't."

"Same," I said. "I thought it was just stress."

"Do I need to spell this out for you?" Mr. Bixby said. He was still in my head, giving me the chance to break the news. "Because I will. It starts with a p."

I held up one finger to silence him and Renata blinked a few times. If she'd had any curiosity about my relationship with the dog earlier, it was gone now. Her big black eyes seemed oddly vacant. Whatever had overtaken us was getting worse, and rather quickly, too.

"Janelle," Sinda said. "I can sense there's bad news. Just tell us."

"Okay," I said. "I think we've all been poisoned."

CHAPTER TWENTY-THREE

"Poisoned?" Renata said. "What would give you that idea? I don't feel *that* sick."

"Poisoned," Sinda said. It was a statement. "That makes sense. The only other likely reason we'd all feel ill at the same time is a hex."

"Also possible," I said. "Either way, we have a problem on our hands."

"Why would anyone poison us?" Ren asked. "Or hex us, for that matter."

"If it's true, then the main target is probably me. You would both be collateral damage." I ran my fingers through my hair and sighed. "I'm so sorry."

"There's no need to apologize on my account," Sinda said. "I came willingly and was under no delusions about what I might find here."

Ren managed a faint smile. "I was on borrowed time anyway, Janny. People mostly turned a blind eye to me because I kept a low profile."

"You mean, when I wasn't around you were considered harmless."

Her shoulders rose and fell and then her lips pressed into a firm line. Finally, she said, "I don't want to be written off as harmless anymore. Even if I am. I feel like I've been living a…"

"Small life?" Mr. Bixby suggested.

"A small life," Ren concluded, although she showed no sign of actually hearing the dog.

Sinda and I exchanged a smile and the dog gave a delighted chuckle. "I know exactly how Renata feels," he said. "I was trapped in a small life for ages until I crossed back over. It's no way to live, especially if you're actually living."

"I want to do more with my life," Ren said. "I want to run my own bakery. Volunteer. Have a dog. Maybe have a relationship. But it's felt like everyone wanted me stuck in the back room of that café. Every time I raised a hope or dream, someone would squelch it."

"It was the same for me, even before my beloved husband died," Sinda said. "He wanted to protect me from the slings and arrows of the world, and even my business. So he got Lexie to take over and left me to vegetate. I felt like a prisoner in my own home." She patted her skirt and Mr. Bixby stepped off the counter and curled up on her lap. "Without this dog, I'd have gone insane."

"You owned Mr. Bixby before?" Ren asked.

"He's a rescue, and it's an interesting story for another day," I said. "But we have more pressing issues. Namely, figuring out how we got sick, and finding a remedy."

"I can think of three people who had easy access," Sinda said.

"The Welcome Committee." Four voices overlapped and echoed in the kitchen.

"Exactly," I said. "Someone's probably spiking our tasty treats with toxins. Today we gobbled a double dose at breakfast and lunch."

Renata slid off the stool and then clutched the counter to stay upright. "Let's go from store to store and get samples to test."

"Good idea, but that'll take time," I said. "Time and energy we may not have if Mr. Bixby's nose is as sharp as I think it is."

"What do you mean?" Ren asked, looking down at the dog. "Are you able to read him, too?"

I thought about dropping the façade with Ren. If we were dying, I didn't want to leave the world lying to my oldest friend. "In a manner of speaking, yes," I said. "He's suggested that we smell like... well, decay."

"Decay!" Ren's voice was painfully shrill.

The dog sat up and stared at her. "You're in the early stages of decomp. If it continues, you'll—"

"Bixby, enough!" My voice was so loud it startled Ren and she knocked her purse off the counter. A few tubes of lipstick rolled out.

The mug in Sinda's hand rattled on the counter. "Mr. Bixby, dear friend, please don't say such things to an old lady. I'll be the first to go, you know."

Ren bent over to collect the lipstick and then sat on the floor, looking up at us. "You're both talking to him. So he must be talking back."

"We understand our friend very well, that's all," Sinda said. "I've known him a long time."

I shook my head. "I'm not going to dance around this anymore. Not when we're all sick and need the dog's help more than ever. So yes, Renata, we can understand the dog. And I have every reason to think you could too. But that's also a story for another day."

"Why do all the stories about me have to wait?" Mr. Bixby said. "You're not dying today. Particularly if you stop taking the poison your so-called Welcome Committee offers. It might even start reversing itself."

"He's talking now, isn't he?" Renata said. "I've noticed all those grumbles and squeaks. Plus his eyes light up and his head tilts, just so."

"She makes me sound like a battery-operated toy," he said. "If she used her inner ear, we could save a lot of trouble."

I gestured for him to simmer down. "Bixby says the first step is to stop ingesting the poison, which makes sense. But we can't afford to wait and see what happens after that. If someone gets worried we're not decaying as planned, they'll get more creative."

"You're right," Sinda said. "We need an antidote to help us hold our ground."

"Not just hold our ground," Ren said, getting up off the floor. "We need to fight back." She slammed her purse on the counter hard enough to make the keys inside jingle. "I am not going to wait around to get poisoned like vermin by my own neighbors. People I've served baked goods to for years. I've even house sat for Candace and Frida and emptied their mousetraps."

"Vermin..." I mused. "Common pests."

"The spell," Sinda said. "The one intended to exterminate you."

"Exactly," I said. "Someone may be using something similar here. They probably don't have all the ingredients they need from us, so it's sort of a slow roll into the grave."

Mr. Bixby chuckled. "I admire that you can keep your sense of humor even while being exterminated."

"What else have I got?" I said.

"Your wits?" he suggested. "The spell book? Perhaps there's an antidote."

"Yes! You're brilliant," I said.

"Not *that* brilliant. You're just extra stupid right now, on account of the poison."

"What's he saying?" Ren asked.

"I refuse to give him the satisfaction of passing it on. He's rude." I headed out of the kitchen. "Hang tight, everyone. I'll be right back."

"Rude, but brilliant," Bixby called after me. "You said it first."

"Braggart," I called back as I went upstairs. It seemed to take forever to get to the attic, and I leaned heavily on the railing.

I had pushed an old wooden filing cabinet over the cubbyhole that hid the book. Moving it back seemed nearly impossible, but I leaned over and put my shoulder into it.

"Whatever are you doing, Miss Brighton?" I jumped at the sound of Sir Nigel's voice. He'd been transfixed by the TV the whole time we were talking in the kitchen but followed me up the stairs.

"I've got a problem, Sir Nigel," I said. "I think someone's trying to kill me and my friends."

"That is a problem," he said. "Though not terribly unusual around Wyldwood Springs. Could I assist you in some way?"

"Possibly," I said. "Can you move the file cabinet?"

"Of course." He nudged it aside as if it were nothing. "Shall I retrieve your book?"

"Please."

He carried *Everyday Spells for Everyday Magic* to the round table. "This reminds me of how I used to help your mother in her work. It was very satisfying, I must say."

Maybe he was recovering from his malaise or just liked being needed. Either way, it was nice to see a glimmer of his old spark.

"You seem more chipper today, Boswell. Have you heard from Mom?"

He shook his head a little too hard. "It grieves me greatly that I cannot tell you where she is."

I turned my back on the spell book. "Do you *know* where she is?"

His shoulders gave a shrug of irritation, either at me or the situation. "Perhaps. But if I know... I don't know."

"Ah. Someone—probably Mom—spelled you into forgetting what happened."

He started straightening the books on the shelves with unnecessary force. "If she did, I'm very disgruntled about it. I cannot do my duty by her and this family without full use of my faculties. Such as they are."

"Boz, your faculties were extraordinary when I was a kid," I said. "I could never ever fool you, and I certainly tried. And as a—"

"Don't say it. I hate that word."

"All right, I'll add it to the lexicon with the words Mr. Bixby and I dislike."

"I dislike Mr. Bixby," he said. "And I know he used to be the word we are not using."

"It's true. He's just a regular dog now. With a little something extra." I joined the butler beside the bookcase. "Bixby looks after me, Boz, just like you used to, and as you would now if circumstances were different."

"If I hadn't lost my faculties, you mean."

The books kept moving but he faded out of sight. "Come back, Boz. I still need you. We'll get this figured out and you'll be firing on all cylinders again."

I thought about telling him I'd seen Mom in the video footage, but at this point, I could only assume she'd deliberately erased his memory. If he knew nothing, he couldn't share information with her enemies. Nor could he send me after her. It was quite possibly for her safety and mine. And even Boswell's. There could be people in town with enough magic to torment the truth out of a ghost.

Going back to the table, I picked up the book. When the time was right—when my skills were right—maybe I could reverse the spell on him and find out what he knew. For now, I'd respect my mother's wishes.

Besides, I had bigger fish to fry. Namely, staying alive long enough to save my friends.

"Boz, I promise we're going to circle back to this problem," I said. "In the meantime, the very best thing for you to do is stay calm and watch *Survivor*."

He reappeared and finished banging the books around. "Is that a request or an order, Miss Brighton?"

It was probably only then, in that moment, that I fully accepted my responsibility for the manor and its inhabitants. Mom might still be alive, but she was most certainly not responsible for us, and probably wasn't in full command of her faculties, either. For the moment, I was. Even Sir Nigel Boswell, our family protector for generations, was deferring to me.

It made me feel all kinds of awkward, as if a crown had been placed on my head that didn't quite fit. In fact, it was so lopsided it slipped over one eye and half blinded me.

But it also felt true, if not exactly right. Mom would hopefully return and reclaim her position, but in the meantime, the ill-fitting crown was mine—along with all the duties that came with it.

"Boswell, it's a request *and* an order. It's what's required to keep you safe for now."

He complained as he followed me down the stairs. "It's my job to keep you safe. Always has been."

"And will be again, I have no doubt about it," I said. "Just as soon as I learn *my* job, which is a lot more complicated than I thought it would be."

"I would imagine you're only just beginning, young lady," he said. "But you're very much up to any job your mother left to you."

Stopping on the landing, I turned and looked up. He was hazy now, or the light was just poor. I hoped he couldn't see that my eyes had filled with tears. Sir Nigel was a remarkable friend and ally but he couldn't possibly understand all the nuances of family relationships. He'd died while still single and relatively young.

"Thank you, Boz," I said. "I don't feel that way."

He came back in full force and even more, lighting up the staircase as if to cheer me on. "You were always so gifted, young lady, even as a toddler. The day you shocked the doctor who was giving you a routine vaccination, I knew you would turn into someone magnificent. That's why I was so vigilant. I wanted to make sure you reached your full potential."

The tears spilled over and ran down my cheeks. "I haven't, though. Reached my potential."

"Yet," he said. "You're barely more than a schoolgirl to me. Be on your way now and use that book well."

"Did Mom have a book like this?" I asked. "The cubbyhole was exactly the right size."

"There's always a spot just the right size for a book like that," he said. "But if she had one, I'm afraid I've forgotten."

I continued to stare up at him. "I order you to tell me what you know about my mom's spell book."

He passed through me as easily as fog, and just as chilly. "I've got a date with destiny," he said. "We're voting people off the island tonight."

CHAPTER TWENTY-FOUR

I wiped the counter down and dried it thoroughly before placing the book on the granite surface.

"*Everyday Spells for Everyday Magic*," Ren said, checking the spine before I opened it. "Wow. This is exciting stuff."

"Wait till you see the one that nearly offed me," I said.

Ren gasped as the pages flipped on their own to the spell I'd first seen at the Briar Estates. I supposed the flipping function kept the user focused. Otherwise, it would be so easy to fall down a rabbit hole and start spelling everything that was amiss in life. There was plenty I'd like to magically set right and plenty I could get wrong.

The pages settled on an ornate calligraphy title that read, "How to Exterminate Everyday Pests," with its special footnote on foolproof extinction. If I hadn't stolen the book and run, another 10 minutes would have sent me where all under-magicked non-witches went. Despite what Sir Nigel had said, "magnificent" was nowhere within reach for me.

"Not without a lot of work," Mr. Bixby said. "You don't get to swan around the world serving cocktails and expect to be suddenly proficient at your calling."

Sinda lightly circled his muzzle with her fingers. As if that would ever stop this dog from talking.

"Ignore him, dear girl," she said. Then she peered at the book I angled toward her. "Oh, my goodness! This is outrageous."

The page on the left featured a large illustrated rat with even larger buck teeth. The page on the right featured a black, hairy spider.

Renata leaned over my shoulder and groaned. "Is that how these people see us? As spiders and rats that need to be wiped out?"

"That's us... everyday pests," I said. "And at least one of these ladies has been gathering samples while serving us samples. By now they have many of the ingredients, especially the critical ones: saliva, hair and possibly fingerprints." I tapped the asterisked note at the end. "Those are guaranteed to exterminate pestilent people... permanently."

"No blood at least," Ren said, reading carefully. "It recommends three drops."

My hand froze over the book. "The handkerchief Sinda gave me when I split my lip... it disappeared before I could launder it."

Mr. Bixby made a wah-wah trombone sound. "Next set of snacks is going to pack quite a punch."

I turned a chilly gaze on him. "Sir Nigel and I just had a beautiful moment, you know."

The dog cocked his head as the volume came up on *Survivor*. "Yeah? What's the stiff done for you lately? It's easy to spout pretty words before collapsing on the couch with the remote." He tapped the spell book lightly with his paw. "I'm on the front lines with you."

"Let's just go over the spell and figure out how to reverse it," Sinda said.

I started to read the ingredients aloud but exclamations from Sinda and Mr. Bixby stopped me.

"Don't read anything like that aloud," the dog said. "Just

speaking the words can cause energy shifts. It's about your intentions."

"How do you know?" I asked.

"How do you *not* know?" he countered. "Did your mother teach you nothing?"

"Nothing of value," I said. "Mom kept these things from me."

Ren touched my arm, hearing only my side of the conversation. "You haven't done this before?"

I shook my head. "Not on purpose. In full disclosure, Bixby and I speculate that the first door blowout may have been a learner's error."

Sinda covered a grin and Mr. Bixby snickered.

Ren didn't see the humor, and I couldn't blame her. Her fingers laced together and tightened till the knuckles turned white. "So you're a total novice?"

"Total. The book fell into my hands less than a week ago, when someone tried to cast this precise spell on me and failed. I took the book and ran."

"So, it's not even yours." Ren's voice had a tremor. "Don't you have to, like... own it?"

"It's more like the other way around," Mr. Bixby said. "At least from what I've seen. This book is yours, Janelle. Otherwise, it would be too hot to handle."

"Literally or figuratively?" I asked him.

"Just trust me, you'd have offloaded it pronto. It's yours to use, and you'll see that soon enough if you stop yammering and do your homework."

I looked back at Renata. "Bixby assures me the book is mine and it's just a matter of experience."

"And purpose," Sinda said. "You've got to come from a good place. That much I know."

Renata ran her hand over the book and nothing happened. "The pages don't flip for me. Does that make you a..."

"We don't use that word," I said, showing her again how the book responded to my energy. The pages fluttered under my fingertips but stayed on the extermination spell. "It packs a huge punch for five letters."

"Maybe we should wait," she said.

"Maybe," I said. "I wish I could promise you're in good hands, but I'd be lying, Ren."

"Someone in town probably has more experience," she said. "I could ask around."

Mr. Bixby started to laugh and I shook my finger at him. "Don't, Bixby. Would *you* trust me to spell you right now?"

"I would," he said, simply. "I trust your intentions, and that's what it's all about. Don't overthink it."

"He's right," Sinda said. "At least in my limited experience. I know your intentions are good and I trust you, too."

Mr. Bixby settled the matter by leaning over and giving Ren a good sniff. Then he made a choking sound, closed his eyes, and went limp in Sinda's arms.

"A little dramatic, but he's making a point, Ren. If we don't act soon, we may not have a chance to act at all. We'll stink worse than the contents of the fridge."

"Okay," she said. "I trust your intentions, too. So let's get on with it before we start falling apart. Like zombies."

"Nice," Mr. Bixby said. "She rallies well."

After that we fell silent, heads together as we read the spell.

"It's so awful," Ren said, crossing her arms and hugging herself. "I can't believe someone thinks they can just wipe us out, like we never existed. Wouldn't the police notice?"

"They would," I said. "Drew especially. But the local police would make it go away, as I'm sure they've done with many other freakish disappearances. The underground police help make that happen." I sighed. "I'm sure there's a spell to wipe memories clean and the bad cops use it on the good cops."

Ren got up and started pacing. "This is all very complicated."

"Luckily I got the 'everyday' version, which I can mostly understand. I bet other spell books are even more complicated."

Sinda directed me back to the page. "Let's hurry, dear girl. Remember who's likely to decompose first."

"You're stronger than you think," Mr. Bixby told her. "There's a book out there for you, too."

I clapped for attention. "Here's another footnote in teeny-tiny print. It says, 'If you have second thoughts, turn to—'"

There was no time to finish before the pages began flipping and came to rest on a spell that read, "A Simple Remedy for Common Errors."

"Now we're talking," Mr. Bixby said. "Especially the simple part."

I read silently alongside Sinda as Ren paced. "It says that many spells can be reversed with this one, when it hasn't been too long."

"Does it specify what 'too long' is?" Ren asked.

"No, but our early state of decay is promising," I said. Running my finger down the page, I added, "We have all this stuff upstairs, although it might take me a minute to find a semiprecious stone."

"I've got that covered," Sinda said. "My jewelry design kit is in my room."

"Teaglove," I said. "We're missing the teaglove."

"What's that?" Ren said.

"It's a healing plant. We need three leaves, one for each of us." My fingers moved quickly over my phone. "It doesn't grow in North America. What's the point of including a plant we can't find in a spell book for newbies?"

"We're out of luck then," Sinda said, slumping so much I was afraid she'd slip off the stool.

I kept googling. "Not necessarily. It's a kissing cousin of teaweed. Looks and smells the same but far more common. I saw it in the garden on Bixby's potty runs."

Ren came back to the island. "Isn't spelling like baking? It's all in the alchemy, and substitute at your peril?"

"Who knows? Probably. For the moment, it looks like teaweed is non-toxic and we have it on hand. What have we got to lose in trying?"

"Or you could just get the real thing," Mr. Bixby said.

"We'd never make it to South America and back," I said.

"Unless I'm much mistaken, there's a supply closer to home. Specifically, in Maisie Gledhill's greenhouse," Mr. Bixby said. "Pretty sure I smelled it when I did my reconnaissance."

I turned to Renata. "He thinks Mrs. Gledhill has some in her greenhouse."

"She'd call the cops on us, just like she did your mom."

Ren started pacing again and I joined her. "Is that why Mom was in her greenhouse in the first place? To find teaglove? Maybe she was trying to do the same thing we are: reverse a spell that was killing her."

"Distinctly possible," Mr. Bixby said. "But Maisie has a wide range of interesting plants in there, including hemlock. I didn't think much of it, given the populace."

Ren wrung her hands and then took mine. "Oh, poor Shelley. No wonder she was behaving so erratically. She was decaying slowly, like we are."

"Not so slowly," Mr. Bixby said. "Quicker than you'd like, with my extensive knowledge of decay in all its stages. From my previous life, of course."

Luckily Ren couldn't hear that, but Sinda had slumped even more. Either she'd gotten a bigger dose of the toxic brew, or age really was working against her.

Not that Ren was doing particularly well, either. The whites of her eyes had turned yellowy-green, and her hands had a pronounced tremor.

I was faring better than either of them, which only made me

feel worse. It was probably just a gift of my genes that helped me withstand it. I bet Mom had been fighting the extermination spell for weeks, if not months, before she succumbed.

"We need to try it with the substitution until we can get the real thing," I said. "Otherwise, we won't have the strength to raid Maisie's greenhouse. Especially when she's on high alert."

Sinda roused herself from a drowsy stupor. "Get my kit, dear, and let's begin."

It only took a few minutes to gather everything listed and place it in a white ceramic bowl that had seen better days. I went outside and came in with the teaweed, adding an extra leaf to be sure we were covered.

Once everything was in the bowl, I shook it up and read the spell out loud. Once again, I felt the thrumming of energy and a whoosh, as if an invisible bird had exploded into flight from my chest and throat.

No sooner had I finished speaking than Sinda leapt off the stool and raced upstairs.

Renata shot out of the kitchen, too, and ran down the hall to the powder room.

"Uh-oh," I said. "I probably shouldn't have used that extra— Oh, my."

There were many good things about coming home but nothing —and I do mean nothing—made me happier than having a third bathroom.

"Good to see that energy coming back," Mr. Bixby called after me. "Better out than in!"

CHAPTER TWENTY-FIVE

The next morning, we gathered early around the old wooden counter at Whimsy. It wasn't officially Whimsy until the sign arrived, but it already felt exactly like the store I'd always wanted—and hadn't known I'd wanted. It made no sense to me that I'd been so successful in hotel management when my secret desire was to run a quirky shop in my hometown. If I'd realized, I could have saved a lot of miles on poor Elsa, not to mention my stilettos.

"You look better, Janelle," Sinda said. "Much better."

I felt much better, although the so-called cure had shown signs of killing me first.

"My spellcasting leaves something to be desired," I said. "Ren seems brighter, but you don't look yourself yet, Sinda."

She sighed. "After that purge, I definitely feel my age. But I do feel like I backed away from death's doorstep."

"Not far enough," Mr. Bixby said, from his cushion on the counter. Once the store opened for business, I might need to withdraw his counter privileges, but for now, I needed him to be part of every conversation—and to stay out of Bijou's way. "The stench of decay has diminished considerably but it's still there. You've slowed the tide."

"Hopefully long enough that we can grab the teaglove," Ren said. "It won't be safe to go hunting in Maisie's greenhouse till after dark."

"The later, the better," I said. "In the meantime, how about we try to figure out who's trying to kill us?"

"But how?" Ren asked.

"By getting them to try to kill us again, obviously." I grinned to lighten the blow.

"Oh, no," Ren said. "Please don't tell me we need to swallow more samples."

"Definitely not. We'll do as you suggested and go store to store—with a little thank you gift for all their kind hospitality."

Ren's eyes lit up. "Did you concoct a nasty brew for them when I was indisposed?"

"We need them awake to spill the truth," I said. "So, we're going to give each woman a cute little necklace from Sinda's collection and I'll try to get a reading off the stone. If one of them is messing with us, something should come up."

"Is your radar back online?" Mr. Bixby asked. "There was an awful lot of flushing."

"I'm not sure, but I'm ready to give it a whirl," I said. "How do I look? Mom always says presentation is half the battle."

"You look sharp," Ren said. "Jilly has great taste."

A prickle of jealousy told me I still had some feelings to work through about my cousin. That probably had less to do with her wardrobe than with the fact I was out here on the front lines being magically assaulted while she got to kick back on the farm and bake cookies. I'd drawn the short straw in the genetic lottery.

"You'll be reunited with your own clothes soon enough," Sinda said. "Your gran told me she'd shipped them when we spoke earlier."

I turned to her quickly. "You didn't tell her we'd been poisoned?"

She shook her head. "No need to worry her. I was just asking her to check in on my store now that Chief Gillock is in Wyldwood."

Ren turned to the dog. "Ask Mr. Bixby if we still smell of... you know."

"Ask him yourself," I said, smiling.

"I adore being consulted," he said. "Even if it means delivering bad news about decomp."

"Did you get any of that?" I asked Ren.

"Not in so many words, but the general tone said we might need this." She dug around in her purse and came up with a smudged and dusty bottle of Angel Tears—the perfume of our youth. "Spritz?"

"Spritz!" I said, laughing as I walked through the cloying cloud she shot into the air.

"Ugh, stop that," Mr. Bixby said. "My nose is a weapon and you're destroying my olfactory glands."

"That's what you get for telling us we smell like the walking dead," Sinda said. "Spritz!"

We were all still giggling as we left the store and linked arms on the sidewalk. It struck me that laughter might indeed be the best medicine, or at least better than a half-baked spell.

Mr. Bixby strutted well ahead of us, sneezing conspicuously. "Don't blame me if I can't pick up anything useful in these stores, giddy girls. You're on your own."

Ginny's Juice Bar was only a few doors down from Whimsy and we hadn't regained our composure when we stepped inside. She looked up from the massive pile of carrots she was peeling and smiled at the sound of our laughter.

"Ladies, how nice to hear you sounding so happy. You've come by to get even fresher juice today. How about a Harvest Stinger?"

"What's the sting?" I asked. "You charging us today?"

She laughed, too. "The sting is my little secret but it's totally on the house."

As the juice machine roared, I raised my eyebrows at Ren and she nodded to confirm she was ready. It was my job to distract Ginny and Ren's to dump the samples into a container in her backpack while Sinda stood guard.

Mr. Bixby was still grumbling under my arm about asphyxiating from the perfume.

"What's troubling Mr. Bixby today?" Ginny asked over her shoulder as she poured three glasses of juice.

"He's just grumpy we haven't given you your gift," I said. "He loves presents, even when they aren't for him."

"A gift? Why on earth would you give me a gift?" Ginny looked taken aback.

"Because you've been so kind and welcoming to me," I said, accepting the drink she slid across the counter. "I was so nervous about coming home but you and the rest of the Welcome Committee have gone out of your way to make me feel like part of the community."

Mr. Bixby sneezed again but I heard the word, "Overkill."

"It was nothing," Ginny said. "Really. You're part of the Main Street family now."

"Well, this is just a small token of my gratitude," I said, reaching into my purse. "It's also a taste of what we'll be serving at Whimsy."

"I see," Ginny said. "You're returning the sample."

"Exactly." I beckoned and walked to the end of the counter, away from the others. "You might want to take off your gloves for this."

As she did, I saw that despite the protection, her fingers and nails were stained orange and green. She cupped her hand, palm up, and I coiled a gold chain into it, starting with a small pendant in the shape of a sunflower. At the center of the pendant was a tiny chip of topaz, which I knew from past experience tended to give me a fast, free pass into people's thoughts. So much so that I normally avoided it like the plague.

Not today. Today I was boldly going where this psychic hadn't gone before: directly into the mind of a possible enemy. There was no time to dance around the point. To protect Sinda and Ren, I needed to act quickly.

"It would be nice to be on that list," Mr. Bixby said. "I won't last long in this town without you."

"Give me a nip if you need to," I said mentally, as I folded Ginny's fingers around the pendant.

She pulled her hand away to swing the pendant. "Oh, how pretty."

I reached out to turn the sunflower to the light. "See the sparkle? It's..."

The word topaz evaded me, because I'd already crossed the barrier and found myself sharing space with Ginny's thoughts.

There were no serpents waiting, but what I saw surprised me. Not only was Ginny as unwelcoming as I feared, she was also downright hostile about my arrival home. Turned out she'd been pestering Laverne Billings for years to let her open a second store—the store of her heart—in Mabel's Fables. Knitting was Ginny's private passion and Oscar Knight didn't see a broad enough appeal in wool. Thus, she was shut out, whereas I, the pariah, waltzed in and got a choice location when no other space was available.

Mr. Bixby poked my arm to make me release the pendant before things got awkward.

"This is so lovely and you're an absolute darling," Ginny said. She stared at the pendant with her mouth hanging open and I saw that her tongue was stained red. No doubt beets had done that job, but she looked like a vampire who wanted to suck the store out of me, if not my life. And worse, the life of my friends.

The dog nudged me again. "No time to dwell. We have more work to do."

Backing away, I found a smile. "Enjoy wearing it, Ginny. And thank you again."

I beat it out of the store with Ren and Sinda trying hard to keep up.

"CAN YOU SLOW DOWN A BIT?" Ren asked, as I charged across the street to Frida's Froyo. "What's the big rush?"

"Well, first, I don't want Ginny warning the others if we can avoid it. And second, we're dying, remember?"

"Not today," Mr. Bixby said. "I'm reasonably sure you'll make it till tomorrow." He added internally, "At least, you and Ren. Sinda might have to fight a little harder."

Picking up even more speed, I said, "You got the samples?"

Ren patted her backpack. "Secure. The yogurt is going to be a little harder to filch."

"Just do your best, and I'll explain everything later. I already know Ginny has motive for not only wanting me gone but killing Laverne. She may not have been working alone."

I figured Ginny would call or text, but Frida looked genuinely surprised when we walked in. "How lovely to see you, girls. I don't allow dogs inside, though. We're serving food, remember?"

"How could we forget those luscious samples you deliver every day?" I said. "We'll only stay long enough to grab our daily pick-me-up and give you a little something in return."

That seemed to silence her complaints about Mr. Bixby and she turned to add ingredients into her stainless steel mixing container. Her gloved fingers worked so fast that if there had been hemlock or anything else we wouldn't have seen it.

After the blender roared for a few moments, she let the frozen yogurt spiral into cups that were twice the normal size.

"All the better to kill you with," Mr. Bixby said, with his wry chuckle, as I led Frida to the far end of the counter to give Ren a chance to collect evidence.

I sang Frida the same song of gratitude that had worked on Ginny, and she took off her latex gloves without my even asking when I swung the little pendant.

"You really didn't need to," she said. "It's been a pleasure getting to know you and Sinda better." She examined the pendant and smiled. "It's adorable. Topaz, I do believe."

"Good eye," I said, reaching out to wrap my fingers around hers, and the pendant.

Ooof. Her thoughts hit me like a kick in my still-queasy gut.

Despite all the sweet frozen treats she'd shared, Frida was full of rage. She hated my gran, hated my mother more, and hated me most of all. I fought hard against the desire to retreat. Wasn't knowing this enough? No. I needed to find out if she hated me enough to kill me, and possibly Laverne as well.

Frida's simmering resentment coalesced into a clear image: my store, only now it had the name Marigold's Marvels on the sign. Marigold was the name of Frida's daughter, I knew. There were gifts and jewelry on display in the store's window. Now I knew there was another thwarted contender for Mabel's Fables. The rumors of haunting hadn't deterred Ginny or Frida at all from taking over the store, and seeing it go to me had created resentment. That ill will had most definitely been directed at Laverne, too, as I could see her through Frida's eyes. The real estate agent pushed her spectacles firmly into place, shook her head and then shrugged. She was the messenger, that's all.

A judicious poke of a damp dog nose told me we were done here. Frida's role in the welcoming committee was as fraudulent as Ginny's, but there was no proof she felt wronged enough to try to kill me. Nor did it appear that she was in cahoots with her friends.

If they were even friends at all. There was no apparent warmth inside these women. They were as hollow and cold as a jack-o'-lantern the day after Halloween.

"Good metaphor," Mr. Bixby said, with another poke. "But let's keep it moving."

"Easy for you to say," I grumbled after we'd bid Frida goodbye and walked out into the sunlit street. "I'm the one getting mentally pummeled and still need to carry on like—"

"Like a professional," the dog said. "That's what you are, now. Don't forget I'm traipsing around inside those ladies with you, and it gives me no pleasure to see the vacant signs where their morals and character should be."

Sinda and Ren fell behind again as I charged forward to The Nutty Chocolatier. "Imagine how it feels to be so reviled over one foolish move as a teen," I said.

"Was it really that foolish? You protected your friends, as you should do. Ren is here with you now because of that."

"She's being poisoned because of that," I said.

The dog shifted under my arm. "Quit getting derailed by emotion. Ren and Sinda said they're happy to be with you on this wild ride. Just focus and find out who's behind everything." When I didn't respond, he gave a harsh yap. "Breathe!"

I pulled in a breath and slowed down. It would do us no good if I walked into that candy store so agitated that I couldn't gather the information we came for. I had to collect my wits and put up a front even more false than the Welcome Committee's.

"Did he talk some sense into you?" Sinda asked, as we gathered on the corner nearest the candy store.

"Tough love," I said. "I guess I needed it."

"Who said anything about love?" Mr. Bixby asked. "It's a little early for that."

"Oh, Bixby," Sinda said. "It was love at first sight or you would never have left me in the dust for this girl."

"Love has nothing to do with it," he said. "She called, and I came. It's a quest. A chance to be a hero. Again."

I gave his silky ears a pat. "I'll grow on you, pal. For what it's worth, you're already my hero, and I look forward to hearing about your earlier escapades."

He relaxed noticeably in my arms. "I do like you. Sometimes I just wonder where exactly you're going to drop me. It's hard to be a hero in a gutter."

"I'd argue that it's much easier," I said. "You can shine like a diamond in the filth."

He snorted. "Just get in and get out this time, okay? Hanging around human garbage will taint your soul."

"Maybe Candace isn't as bad," I said, opening the door and letting the others pass in front of me. "She can't be."

"I wouldn't count on sweet in the sweets store," he said, as the aroma of chocolate enveloped us. "Anyone wafting so much sugar has something to hide."

"Or just wants to make the world a happier place," I said, clipping briskly to the counter.

There was no sign of Candace so I tapped the bell on the counter and she emerged from the back room wearing an apron, hair net and the ubiquitous latex gloves I'd need to talk off her. There was a time I wore leather gloves all the time to form a barrier between me and others. Now I wasn't even knocking before barging inside them.

"I heard you might be coming," she said, gesturing to a silver tray on the counter. "Ready and waiting. A brand new flavor guaranteed to dazzle your tastebuds. Vanilla bean with thyme."

"Sounds like a mouthful of comfort," I said, glancing around the store I'd so loved as a child. Back then, the heavy smell of chocolate was an intoxicant rather than possibly just toxic. I hadn't minded the other stores being sullied but I wished I could hold onto my fondness for the candy store. It was linked in memory with happier times.

"Nostalgia is the enemy of the sleuth," Mr. Bixby said.

Is that what I was now? It didn't sound so bad, actually. A sleuth took action. A sleuth was not a victim of forces bigger than her. A sleuth kicked—

"Janelle?" Candace interrupted my inner monologue. "Are you all right, dear? If you don't mind my saying, you've gone downhill since you came home."

I did mind her saying I was losing my looks, since someone was actually taking them by force.

"Vanity is also the enemy of the sleuth," Mr. Bixby said.

"Just tired, Candace," I said. "I probably won't sleep well till Laverne's killer is caught."

"That may never happen," Candace said. "Unfortunately, there are unsolved crimes in this town. People forget, just as you will."

If I died, most definitely. If I lived someone would need to cast a spell to erase my memory. The entire community's memory, from the sounds of it.

"I brought you a gift to thank you for making me feel so welcome," I said, gesturing to the chocolate. "I really didn't expect anyone to be so neighborly."

"It's not entirely selfless," Candace said, with a smile. "I'm hoping you'll spread the good word about my truffles to your clients. On Main Street, we collaborate. It works for everyone."

"Of course, and I hope you'll do the same for our jewelry after seeing your gift." I pulled out the third necklace and let the pendant swing. "Come, try it on." I gestured to the end of the long counter. "I'll do the clasp for you."

"Try the truffles first," she said. "I like to run my experiments past your tastebuds, ladies."

She crossed her arms, clearly unwilling to accept my gift till I'd consumed hers.

"Candace, I can't speak for the others, but my stomach is touchy today." I leaned over the tray. "They do smell scrumptious."

"Scraped the vanilla beans myself," she said. "Please do try. For me."

"I really wish I— Oh! Oh no!"

While I was still bent over, Mr. Bixby stuck out his long nose and snatched all three truffles.

Candace gave a little scream. "Janelle Brighton! Those are the highest quality chocolate. Take that mutt outside."

"Let me," Renata said, reaching for Bixby. "He's been so patient but all the chitchat is hard on a dog."

I offered Candace the necklace again but she was too disgruntled to take it.

"I'm so sorry, Mrs. Riordan," I said. "He's never been so rude before. Let me make it up to you."

The necklace swayed from my fingertips, and she stared at it. Then she blinked a few times before shaking her head.

"There's no need, Janelle. Pets will be pets, I suppose. I've never been a fan of either dogs or jewelry, to be honest. Save that bauble for someone more trendy. The only thanks I need is for you to try my new flavor and then talk them up."

"Of course," I said. "But then you'll need to part with another."

She walked into the back room, muttering, and Ren came back inside with the dog.

"Got 'em," she said, as I took Mr. Bixby from her. "He really is a hero."

"Candace won't take the necklace," I whispered.

"Let me help," Sinda said. "Just follow my lead, girls."

When Candace placed the new truffles on the counter, Sinda gave a loud gasp and then collapsed with a terrible retching sound.

"Sinda!" I set the dog down and knelt at the older woman's side. "Oh my gosh, she's fainted."

"Bring a cold cloth," Renata called out.

Candace ran some water and then came round the counter and dropped to her knees beside me. "Lock the door and close the blinds, Renata," she said. "I don't want anyone seeing someone dead in my store. They'll get the wrong idea."

"I'm not dead." Sinda's voice was so weak I wondered if this emergency was legit after all. "The cloth, please."

Candace reached out with it and I intercepted her hand. The gloves were gone now, and there was a good-sized diamond engagement ring I could target.

As with most stones worn so long, it was packed full of memories. The ones that flooded me were usually either recent or particularly intense. The key was to do triage, and fast.

A montage of Candace's experiences flashed into my mind and I saw them from her eyes. She was as full of bitterness as Frida, it seemed. It was a Main Street staple. And like Frida and Ginny, she'd faced off with Laverne Billings, who shook her head again and again until her cat eyeglasses fell off and swung from the beaded chain.

The images that came next surprised me more. Candace had also confronted my mother, whose wild-eyed, angry face made my heart race. She barely looked like my mom anymore. But before I could get too caught up, Oscar Knight appeared, his silvery gray eyes narrowed in fury.

"Come out," Mr. Bixby said. "It's disgusting in there."

Sinda heard him call it quits and sat up. She knocked my hand away from Candace's ring, because the storekeeper didn't seem to have noticed.

Ren and I helped our friend to her feet, and then Sinda turned to Candace. "We'd better take our truffles to go," she said.

"Never mind," Candace said, backing away. "We'll try again tomorrow."

CHAPTER TWENTY-SIX

"Thank goodness my grand gesture didn't go amiss," Mr. Bixby said. "I held those toxic bombs in my mouth for nearly a minute before I could spit them out."

"Do you really think they were toxic?" I asked.

"Chocolate can kill a dog, in case you don't know," he said. "But I couldn't tell if they were spiked for human doom. I just got rid of them as soon as I could."

"I hope you're okay," I said, planting a kiss on his head. "Because I love you already."

"Ugh," he said, squirming. "No PDAs, please and thank you. Tell the others what you saw."

I delivered the highlights reel as we walked Renata back to the café to start her shift.

"Basically, it could be any of them, as far as I could tell," I concluded. "They all despise me, and it's not about my old history or even my family. They wanted the store, Mabel's Fables, and they resent me for landing it."

"They all wanted the store?" Ren said. "Why? I thought everyone was scared of the place because it's haunted."

"The Welcome Committee apparently isn't put off by a ghost.

Ginny wants to open a knitting store and Frida wants her daughter to open a gift store. I'm not sure about Candace's plan but she argued with Laverne, my mother and Oscar Knight." I winced. "He was pretty angry, by the looks of things."

"I've overheard people at the café complaining about how hard it is to shoulder in on Main Street," Ren said. "They say you have to wait for someone to die before you can get a storefront."

"Or kill them yourself," Bixby said.

"And yet Mabel's Fables has sat empty for several years," I said. "I thought people just gave up on it."

"They did... until the right ghost-whisperer came home," Sinda said. "I imagine you'll liberate Bijou soon enough."

"I hope so," I said. "That little girl has been there alone far too long."

"The poor thing," Ren said. "I would adopt her, if she were alive."

"Stranger things have happened," Sinda said, with a fond smile at Mr. Bixby.

Ren caught the glance and her eyebrows soared. "Was Mr. Bixby a—? I don't feel right using the word."

"That word doesn't bother him," I said, "although it grates on Sir Nigel. To be considerate, I'll say that Mr. Bixby is formerly deceased."

The dog chuckled. "Good one. I like it."

My old friend's mouth dropped open. "He came back? That can happen?" She swallowed hard and added, "For real?"

"It happened for real with Mr. Bixby. I've never heard of it happening before. I'm sure if Mom or anyone else in the family could have brought Boswell back, they would have, so this might be a one-off."

"Or not," Mr. Bixby said. "But bringing back the Victorian stiff would give you a lot of explaining to do."

"Good point," I said. Grinning at Ren, I added, "Bixby retains some of his former gifts along with some new ones. It's all pretty recent so we're still learning."

"Huh. That is so cool," Ren said.

I had to give my friend credit. Since we were young girls, I'd thrown her a lot of curveballs and mostly she just rolled with them. A family ghost? Check. Psychic abilities? Check. A stun gun at my fingertips? Check.

The disclosure about the spell book was taking her more time to integrate, but I had no doubt she'd accept that, too.

A ghost dog was a breeze in comparison. But Ren had always loved pets, unlike her parents who considered them little better than vermin.

I wondered what her folks would think of someone trying to exterminate *us* like common pests. Both of Ren's parents were buttoned up pretty tight, which is probably why they'd left town as soon as she came of age. Maybe there was more to that story than I knew about, but it wasn't the time to pry.

"We can talk about Mr. Bixby all day," I told Ren. "Nothing would please him more. But that won't save our lives."

"It might," he said. "There are worse strategies."

Ren looked somewhat downhearted. "This morning was a bust, I guess."

"Not at all," Sinda said. "Janelle's impressions may lead to something later. And you have evidence that Chief Gillock can analyze."

Ren's face brightened. "Of course. When magic fails, there's always science."

"Thank goodness we have a decent cop on our side," Sinda said. "He'll be upset to hear someone is poisoning us. Hopefully this won't put him in jeopardy."

We all sighed at once, knowing how hard it was to stay out of jeopardy in Wyldwood Springs.

Ren handed over the samples she'd collected. "So we just wait till we hear the results?"

"Far from it," I said. "Soon there won't be enough Angel Tears left to disguise what's happening to us. So tonight, we'll take a field trip to Maisie's greenhouse to collect the teaglove. Then back to the manor so I can nail that spell. Tomorrow, we breakfast on Ethan's croissants and ponder the future."

"Sounds good," she said, opening the door. "Text me the deets."

When the door closed behind her, I said, "I wish there was more we could do now."

"Maybe there is," Sinda said, nudging me ahead of her down the sidewalk. "I have a little plan of my own."

MINDY TANG COULDN'T CONCEAL her shock when I walked into Eternal Springs Realty. It was a name that better suited a funeral home and made me wonder if Laverne was currently enjoying eternal life... somewhere else. She hadn't seemed better or worse than anyone else on my brief foray into her mind. Her biggest mistake was probably her biggest client. I knew she'd lived on a spectacular acreage outside town. Oscar Knight's business had no doubt financed that.

The desk that had once been Laverne's now appeared to be Mindy's, so the older woman hadn't been irreplaceable after all.

Mindy had been a year behind me in school, and the photos on her desk showed children about the right age for someone who had stuck around town and done what was expected. A couple of kids made more sense here than a dachshund tucked under one's arm.

"I make complete and utter sense, at any time, anywhere," he said, not even bothering to use his inside voice. In fact, he rarely kept quiet anymore. It was on me to control my reactions, which was hard enough when I wasn't being slowly poisoned. "Quit whining," he added. "You're destined for better things than managing property for a man like that."

"An acreage would be nice, though," I thought, rather than said. "For privacy."

"Your mausoleum will suit us well enough with a little sprucing up," he said. "Sinda, what's the plan?"

Mindy stumbled as she pulled another chair around so that we could both sit down opposite her. "Janelle, how are you? Welcome back."

I noticed she didn't say "home." Come to think of it, few did.

"I'm good," I said, although her expression told me I didn't look that way. "I came to talk to you about Laverne Billings. I heard she had an argument with my mother, and I wondered if you knew why."

She picked up a pencil and then a paperclip and dropped both before answering. "It's not my place to speak of private business, Janelle. I'm sure you understand."

"Mindy, it was my mother. My mother who is missing." I pointed at the photos on her desk. "Imagine your kids. Wouldn't they want to know what happened if you vanished?"

Biting her lower lip, she drove color into her cheeks. Her hair was shiny, black and precisely cut in a bob that looked too perfect. Finally she leaned across the desk and whispered, "Shelley wanted to buy Mabel's Fables. Outright. In cash. Made a very good offer, too."

"Close your mouth," Mr. Bixby told me. "Your mommy issues are showing."

I closed my mouth until I could make sense when I opened it. "Really? My mom had no interest in running a store, and clearly she didn't need the money. Why would she make an offer like that?"

Mindy's perfect hair swayed. "I don't know. Laverne didn't say. But we all knew your Mom took it very hard when Mr. Knight refused to sell. I thought he would, when it had sat empty so long."

"So Mom made a great offer and he turned her down?"

"Turned her down flat. Laverne just delivered the verdict but she caught an earful."

"Poor Laverne caught an earful from a lot of people," I said. "It's not an easy job you're taking over."

She picked up the paperclip again and unfurled it. "There will be challenges, I'm sure. But I have kids to put through college."

"Can you tell me why Mr. Knight was so determined not to sell or even rent out my store? It seems like it had become a hot commodity."

"Any property on Main Street is hot these days," she said. "I figured he just got attached to Mabel's Fables after all the misfires." Her face brightened. "But then you talked him into it. People must be a little jealous."

Sinda leaned forward to grip the desk. "They'll be even more jealous when he accepts our offer to buy," she said.

I turned to my friend, expecting a coy smile, but her expression was serious.

Mindy leaned back. "It's not for sale, ma'am, and I didn't catch your name."

"Sinda Joffrey," she said. "I'm new in town and looking to invest."

"I can find you plenty of properties," Mindy said. "But not that one."

"Come now, Mindy," Sinda said. "Everything has a price, including Mabel's Fables. Could you do us a favor and get Oscar Knight on the phone to ask what it is?"

After a moment's hesitation, Mindy got up and excused herself to walk into a meeting room.

"Sinda, are you crazy?" I said. "Who has that kind of money?"

"Your mother, obviously. And your grandmother, who proposed the idea this morning. I'm kicking in, too. We want you out from under Oscar Knight's thumb. He's a dangerous man."

"How I wish he'd sell, and I'm thrilled you and Gran would invest in me like that, but it's too much to ask."

It really was too much to ask, apparently. Mindy's face telegraphed the truth long before she reached her desk. "As I suspected, he has no interest in selling. At any price."

My disappointment took me by surprise. For that one brief moment, I'd imagined actually owning the property with Gran and Sinda, and keeping little Bijou safe in Whimsy forever.

"I'm sorry to hear that," Sinda said. "We'll try him another time."

Mindy sat down opposite me again. "Mr. Knight wants to buy out your lease, Janelle."

"I have no interest in leaving," I said, getting up.

"He'll double what you paid," she added quickly. "It's a very good offer and you could get much more floorspace elsewhere for that money."

"This is my store. I'm responsible for it now." I was responsible for Bijou, in particular, and I certainly wouldn't leave her by choice. "But do thank him for me."

Mindy stood too and leaned across the desk to offer her hand. "Janny, take the offer. It's for the best. Trust me."

I let her grasp my hand and her diamond ring told me just how terrified she was of Oscar Knight. She hadn't volunteered to take over Laverne's role. She'd been coerced.

"Mindy, be careful," I said, releasing her hand. "There's got to be a better way to put your kids through college."

Shaking her head, Mindy's eyes filled as she looked at her family photo. "I guess we'll cross that bridge if we come to it."

"You're not alone in this town full of bridges," I said. "Call me if you need anything."

CHAPTER TWENTY-SEVEN

When Drew Gillock arrived at Withrow Park, I was already sitting on the bench where Ren and I had caught up after Laverne's murder. I'd asked him to meet me here partly because I'd always liked the scenery but mostly because it didn't offer much cover for spies. As a bonus, the falls made so much noise we couldn't be easily overheard.

Drew got out of his rental car, gave me a wave and started walking across the grass. I'd expected a uniform, but he was wearing jeans and a white T-shirt and moved with the easy grace of a Hollywood movie star. The midday sun burnished his thick auburn hair with golden highlights and my fingers twitched as I thought about touching it.

"Down girl," Mr. Bixby said, with a naughty snicker.

"You must have an off switch," I said, while there was still time to get the dog in line. "Where is it? Because if you ruin this, Bixby, so help me, I'll—"

"Ruin what, exactly?" the dog asked. "There's nothing between you, at least from what you told me. Even if there was, now there probably isn't. The chief came all this way from Strathmore County to follow up on what happened at Sinda's store. With a couple of killers spouting nonsense he's not sure what to believe."

"Well, he doesn't believe I killed anyone," I said.

"Maybe not, but he's keeping his eyes wide open." The dog watched Drew and laughed. "Even though he still has trouble looking right at you, unless he's talking business. He's afraid you're a mystical gorgon who'll turn him to stone."

"A gorgon!"

"Like Medusa," Bixby said. "If you saw your hair right now, you'd understand why."

I set him on the seat and smoothed my hair with both hands. The mist from the waterfall was doing a number on my curls. I could feel the frizz rising.

"And his hair is so *very* nice," Bixby said. "Even I want to give it a pat."

"Stop it," I said. "Just. Stop."

"Talking to yourself?" Drew asked, joining us. His smile turned to a grin as he sat down.

"Having a word with the dog, if you must know." I grinned, too. "When you really need to vent, there's nothing like a set of floppy ears."

"That bad?" he said. "Well, mine are available. They aren't floppy, at least as far as I know."

"They could be," Mr. Bixby said. "With the right spell in the right paws, they very well could be. Then we wouldn't need to worry about you mentally lapsing into slow motion when Chief Dumbo walks on screen."

The dog was determined to tease me till I cracked and exposed myself. I couldn't let that happen. The Janelle that Drew Gillock met down south was elegant. Understated. Poised.

"Poised? I never saw that," Bixby said. "You were throwing down with Lexie the first time I saw you and it got worse after that."

I pressed my index finger into the back of his neck and fired one mental word at him. "Off."

Drew gave me a curious look. "You okay?"

"Yes, but not really," I said.

His coppery eyebrows rose. "Which is it?"

"Mostly yes with a whole lot of no." I peered around to make sure we were alone. "I have enemies here and someone's getting serious about it."

"Tell me more." Leaning back, Drew crossed well-muscled arms. He probably did chin-ups before breakfast, whereas the only exercise I got was running from people.

Mr. Bixby stirred, wanting to comment, but I pressed harder and he settled for making kissing noises.

"Do you really want to hear this, Drew? Because it's going to sound crazy."

"It's not like I haven't seen crazy when you're around. Is this any worse?"

I closed my eyes for a second and thought about it. Was it worse? Or just equally bad?

"Think hard," Bixby said. "The next few minutes could be quite pivotal. I'm going to go out on a limb and suggest you be as honest as you think he can handle."

That was the question. What could Drew handle? The other question was why did I care so much? We'd never even been on a date. Heck, I hadn't been on a real date for ages. I was the love 'em and leave 'em type, except for the fact that I was never in love.

"Till now," Mr. Bixby said, with more smooching noises.

That nearly did it. It took all my strength to resist the dog's baiting. I wasn't in love with Drew Gillock. Sure, we'd hung out a lot down south and he'd given me a potted plant, but he didn't really know me. Obviously. And until he intervened during my altercation with Oscar Knight, he'd never touched me. I'd have remembered that feeling. Drew was full of light like the glorious sun overhead now.

"But that's the *only* magic in his holster," Mr. Bixby said. "Sunshine and sweet vibes. Those won't do you much good in a dumpster duel."

I could fight my own battles. What I really needed was the calm between the storms to center me.

"Janelle." Drew rested his hand lightly on my forearm and my eyes popped open. "It seems like you're caught in some sort of inner struggle. Let me help."

There it was again. The sensation of liquid sunshine trailing down to my fingertips and up to my shoulder. If it reached my heart, it could be more undermining than Oscar Knight's negative energy.

"That's exactly my point," Bixby said. "I like Drew well enough but with threats escalating, you can't really afford distractions like romance. You'll hiccup and turn all the local frogs into princes by accident."

Finally, a giggle escaped and I pulled my arm away from Drew. There was no stopping the laughter now, however. Peels of it roared out of me and the dog laughed, too.

Drew slid a little further down the bench.

"There. That's better," Bixby said. "Leave a little room for common sense."

"Just give me a moment, Drew," I sputtered. "I'm sorry. The stress has been getting to me."

I fought hard to regain self control. This wild-eyed, guffawing version of me wasn't going to make Drew—

"Exactly," Bixby said. "You don't want him to fall for you."

I did, though. I really did. More than I ever had anyone before. I craved that inner sunshine. There had been precious little of it in my life.

"But then Drew would be more vulnerable," Mr. Bixby said. "A gun and sunshine are no match for what Oscar's packing."

The warm feeling flushed out of me and left cold clarity behind. For a moment, I'd allowed myself to believe Drew was destined for me. It felt so right for me. But it would be wrong and unfair to him.

Down girl.

It was *my* inner voice this time, not Bixby's.

"At least for now," the dog said. "Things could change with Drew. By then, you may well have met a hunky young warlock with firepower to spare."

I didn't want a warlock... or whatever you called the masculine version of me. Why would I want to go any deeper into this messed up world of magic than I had to? My store, my side hustle of saving ghost dogs, and a small circle of true friends would have to be enough.

Heaving a resigned sigh, I got up and beckoned Drew. "Let's walk around and chat about something else."

"We could talk about the dog," he said.

"Oh, do," Mr. Bixby said. "I just can't get enough."

Drew gave him a quizzical stare. "He's oddly vocal. Do you go anywhere without him?"

"Oddly vocal?" Mr. Bixby reached out and air-snapped at Drew. "Docked again, Big Red."

Jerking his arm out of reach, Drew said, "What's with him? I like dogs. And they usually like me."

"Mr. Bixby is a rescue," I said, speeding up to get ahead of Drew on the sparkling trails that led to the falls. "He has a tortured past."

"True," the dog said. "Something you and I share."

That's why I was destined to be alone. Permanently.

"Fiddlesticks," Mr. Bixby said. "You won't be a spinster."

Spinster! That implied I had no choice in the matter, whereas I was opting to be single for a noble cause. I was on a quest. First I'd restore order in my life, and then broaden my scope to turn this town around.

"You *could* sacrifice yourself to the greater good... or you could just be sensible and choose a guy who can support you in all the important ways," Mr. Bixby said. "I actually remember a time when women made smart decisions instead of melting over chocolatey eyes."

I clenched my teeth. The dog had won and he knew it. Now I couldn't let myself fall for Drew, even though he brought sunshine to my soul. I'd embrace my noble cause and be a lone wolf.

"A lone wolf and a dachshund," Bixby said. "Perfect pair."

Drew caught up with me in time to catch my smile over that image and he smiled, too. I hadn't let myself notice how perfect his teeth were before. In fact, his only potential flaw in the looks department was extremely pale skin. From now on, I'd focus on that to keep me grounded.

"Don't worry," Mr. Bixby said. "I'll help, too."

The dog reached out from my arms, snagged Drew's sleeve and gave it a tug.

"Hey," Drew said. "What did I ever do to you, little guy?"

"Little guy!" Mr. Bixby was so outraged he released the fabric. "The nerve!"

"A little guy with a large ego," I said, setting the dachshund on the grass. "How about you go and be a dog, Bixby?"

"Sure," the dog said. "Just as soon as you commit to being a witch. Which won't happen." He snickered over his own wordplay. "I wish this dude could hear me. My witticisms are wasted."

Maybe the time would come where I had to make that commitment and even tell Drew about it. But it wasn't today. For the moment, I'd share only the essential facts.

When we were as close to the falls as we could get, I turned to Drew. "What do you think?"

"Spectacular," Drew said. "It's a beautiful town, but it always feels like something is churning under the surface."

I nodded. "The twisty politics are nearly as old as these falls, and I'm guessing the police have quite a time keeping order."

"Then they'll be glad to have an extra pair of hands for a while," Drew said, with another flash of perfect teeth. "I've decided to take a leave from Strathmore County and see if I can't help straighten things out here."

"Don't!" I regretted the word instantly because Drew looked confused, and maybe a little hurt. Perhaps he'd felt our connection yesterday, too. Maybe that's why he'd met my eyes more today than ever before. "Drew, I only mean it's not safe for you here. There are criminal factions. Kind of like an underground mafia."

"And it's safe for you?" he asked.

"Far from it. That's why I wanted to meet way out here." I glanced around one more time. "So that I could tell you in private that someone's trying to kill me."

"Kill you! What makes you say that?"

Pulling the evidence out of my purse, I handed it to him. "I think you'll find poison in here. Someone's been plying Sinda, Ren and me with treats laced with toxins. I was hoping you could get these analyzed so I know who's behind it, and what poison they're using. I'll need a complete list of ingredients. On their own, they may be innocuous, but in combination quite deadly."

His eyebrows had taken flight again. "Have you seen a doctor?"

"Not yet." I started walking again, and Drew followed. "The problem is that you never know who to trust around here. I'm afraid of making things worse."

"What's worse than getting poisoned?" he asked.

Mr. Bixby deliberately tried to trip him and failed. Drew was light on his feet.

"Oh, where to start?" the dog said. "Infestation spells? Time travel curses? Watching people you love suffer and die?"

"Poisoning is probably common enough in Wyldwood," I said. "Like a rite of passage. Hazing the new girl. Or worse, the girl who left and came back."

Drew's smile was long gone. "You haven't been looking well.

And you haven't seemed yourself. So I'll put a rush on this. Can you tell me what you know about your enemies?"

"It stems from that long-ago prank after prom."

"That's on record and there was no hard evidence you caused the death of Reginald Corby," Drew said. "Zero. The police of the time believed you used some sort of electrical device to shock the victim and his heart gave out."

"Scapegoating at its finest," Mr. Bixby muttered, nosing around the grass.

"Reggie was vicious that night, but I wouldn't wish that on him."

"Of course not." Drew fell silent and we looped back on the path.

I expected Mr. Bixby to fill the pause with smart aleck chatter, but he seemed to be waiting on tenterhooks, too. Something big was coming and the dog and I could both sense it.

Finally, Drew stopped walking and turned to look at me. And he really looked at me. His gaze was probing and personal. The cop equivalent to mind-reading, I supposed.

"What?" I said.

He held the stare. "Janelle, I like you very much. You know that."

"And...?"

"Oh, what a pregnant pause," Mr. Bixby said. "The kind that says no one's getting pregnant anytime soon."

I nudged the dog with my stiletto, wishing I could punt him into the nearest stream.

Drew took a breath and continued. "And I couldn't help but notice similarities between what happened to Reggie, and the situations in Strathmore County."

Now my eyes shifted to focus on a freckle on his pale forehead. "I'm not really following."

"I am," Bixby said. "Like a dog on a lead."

"According to hospital records, Reggie was extremely confused and stayed that way. The same thing happened to the two killers in my jurisdiction. And you helped sideline all three. Don't you think that's weird?"

"It is weird that I run into so many violent people," I said. "Less than Ivy Galloway, I guess. But still."

"I've been doing a little digging. You've lived in a lot of places. And left in a hurry."

I didn't have the energy to continue the cat and mouse game. "What are you saying, Drew? That you think I'm guilty of killing Reggie Corby? Maybe Laverne Billings, too?"

"Laverne's cause of death was pretty clear." He shrugged broad shoulders. "Mind you, no one knows her state of mind when she passed."

My heart filled with ice so suddenly that Mr. Bixby shivered. "Don't take it so hard," the dog said. "He's just a cop, doing what cops do."

"Accusing me of murder," I said, to the dog, not the cop.

"No one's accusing you of murder," Drew said. "At least, not me. Maybe the contrary."

My heart thawed just a little. "Oh?"

"Some nasty people got taken down when you were around. You probably saved Ivy and Sinda from killers. Or so they told me."

"That sounds so much better," Mr. Bixby said. "Big Red is hard to hate."

"Drew, I was probably just in the right place at the wrong time, or vice versa. But I can assure you I've never killed anyone, and I hope you believe me."

"I do," he said, holding up the package I'd given him. "Otherwise, I wouldn't be sticking my neck out to help."

"Thank you for that," I said. "I promise not to—"

"Don't make promises you can't keep." Two voices overlapped as Bixby and Drew admonished me at the same time.

Drew spoke over the dog's unheard laughter. "I'm just saying there's something you're not telling me. And I'd like to know what it is."

A breeze came up behind us and blew the mist into a cloud that swirled around us. I shivered in the damp chill and nodded. "There's a lot I'm not telling you right now, Drew. It's better if I try to handle this myself."

Disappointment and annoyance did a little dance on his face and disappointment won. "I'm sorry you don't trust me," he said.

I started walking again. "It's not about that. I *need* to handle this myself or I won't be able to stay here. It's like managing schoolyard bullies."

"Why would you even want to live in a place like this?" he asked, following me. "There are scenic towns all over the country."

"I know. I've seen a lot of them," I called back. "They weren't home. This is where I belong, for better or worse."

"Mostly worse, it seems." He caught up with me again, despite the dachshund obstacle course at his feet. "I really don't see the magic in Wyldwood."

"Let's hope it stays that way," Mr. Bixby said.

When the three of us reached my car, the dog turned and cocked his leg... over Drew's leather boot.

"Don't you dare!"

My voice was so loud Drew jumped. Then he looked down and said, "Are you kidding me, dog?"

Mr. Bixby settled for making scratching motions on the pavement as if wiping the dust of Drew off his paws.

There was no way Drew could detect the dog's laughter but there was a suspicious look in those deep brown eyes. I wasn't the only one who baffled this cop.

"I'm ready to go," Mr. Bixby said. "Red bores me now."

I whisked the dog into the car and followed so fast I nearly sat on him.

I didn't apologize, either.

CHAPTER TWENTY-EIGHT

Renata never uttered a word of complaint as we basically bushwhacked our way through a quarter acre of dense woodland behind Maisie Gledhill's home. A flashlight could barely penetrate the darkness, but a half moon helped.

Since my arms were full of dachshund, more of the work fell to Ren than I would have liked—especially when neither of us was operating at peak capacity. As the day had worn on, the effects of the poison intensified again. It felt like a bad flu that did a special number on our GI systems. The hardest part of this midnight mission might be going without a bathroom. No one had warned me magical life could be so unglamorous.

"Wouldn't it have been safer to leave Mr. Bixby at home?" Ren asked.

"Safer for him, yes. For us, no. I'm not at the top of my game and need him more than ever. He'll see and smell what we can't. And he'll stop at nothing to make sure we're okay."

"He's that devoted?" she asked, shoving branches aside. "You two always seem to be quarreling."

"You always nip the ones you love," Mr. Bixby said, burying his muzzle in my armpit. "It's for their own good."

Ren was too busy breaking trail to notice his mumbling, but I knew it was the closest Bixby had come to using the L word. Another week or two and he'd be splashing affection all over me, like a regular dog.

"Don't count on it." His voice was muffled in the fabric of an old black coat. Ren and I had gone through Mom's extensive wardrobe to come up with disguises, including Mardi Gras masks and bandanas. The hardest part was keeping the wigs in place when the trees seemed determined to snatch them.

"Bixby and I went through a lot to be together," I said. "So yes, we're that devoted, even if it doesn't always sound that way."

"They say rescue dogs are the most loyal," Ren said. "If I ever decide to get another dog, I'll check out the local shelters."

"The right dog will come along. Just keep an open mind because Mr. Bixby was a complete surprise in every way."

There was only a grunt from Ren in response because the foliage was becoming impenetrable. Finally, she stopped and said, "I'll need to get a scythe out of my backpack."

"Scythe! You're packing a scythe?"

She laughed as she pulled out a curved blade on a retractable handle. "When you come to dinner, you're going to see quite a collection of tools. I don't have much space so they're hanging on a pegboard on my bedroom wall."

"What kind of tools?" I asked as she snapped the handle in place.

"The kind that might keep someone like me alive in a town like this," she said. "I prepared for assault but not poison. Or random spells that rotted my guts. My mistake."

There was so much I wanted to say but Mr. Bixby pulled his head out and offered his signature verbal prod. "Focus."

Ren's look of grim determination said that while she might not be magical, she was by no means helpless. I was more grateful than ever to have her on my side.

"We should probably keep it down now," I said. "Who knows what kind of security system Maisie might have?"

"Let's get in and get out as fast as we can," Ren said. "We need this spell to work, and fast, for Sinda's sake."

"So, no pressure." I tried to laugh but it was more of a dry cough. "If it fails—if *I* fail—we'll need to take our chances on the hospital later."

"You won't fail," Ren said. "I feel good about this."

I wasn't sure whether to believe her, but she was putting a lot of power behind that scythe. No question, she was going down swinging.

Another 30 yards or so took us to the fence that partitioned Maisie's yard from the wilderness beyond. It was just a regular wooden fence that Ren scaled with ease. She dropped onto the ground with a slight thud and held her hands back over the top. I put Mr. Bixby into them, and even though he was going to Ren, I felt a chill where his warm body used to be. It was amazing how quickly I'd gotten used to his weight.

"Don't be clingy," he said from the other side of the fence. "You've got to stand on your own two feet. Thank goodness you had the common sense to wear sneakers."

I was stylish, not stupid. My brief stint bounty hunting pythons in the Everglades made outings like this seem simple enough.

But we still had to break into the greenhouse.

I took the lead once I was over the fence and Ren held onto the dog. Picking locks was one of my non-magical superpowers but I wasn't sure if Maisie might be fortified with supernatural security. I hadn't noticed magical vibes from the cantankerous woman, but why else would she be growing mysterious plants?

"Black market sales," Mr. Bixby said. "Duh."

"Don't you duh me," I said internally, and signaled for Ren to put him down. "Let's keep the confidence high."

We navigated to the greenhouse door using the moon and a bit of light that reached us from Maisie's back porch. Picking locks was more about feeling and sound than sight anyway.

Mr. Bixby's long muzzle lifted as I eased the door open. My nose came up, too, and we gave a joint sniff.

"This place smells amazing," we said at the same time. My voice was too loud, and I clapped my hand over my mouth.

Ren laughed quietly, as if she'd heard our overlapping voices. "It smells like damp grass to me," she said. "What does it smell like to you?"

"Possibility," I whispered. "Hope. Everything we need is here. We just need to find it."

"Good thing you brought the nose of a sleuth," Mr. Bixby said. "In my last life, I had to forage in the hills for what's at your finger-tips tonight."

"My botanical knowledge is scarce," Ren said. "How will we find anything in the dark? We can't use flashlights without being seen."

"Bixby for the win," I said. "He's got the sniffer."

There was barely enough light to see the mostly black dog set off through the rows of plants in raised containers. We fell behind until Bixby stopped and turned.

Ren and I gasped at the same time. The dog's eyes gave off a spooky greenish glow. I'd been out with him in the dark countless times without noticing that. Maybe it had something to do with the greenhouse... or the risk we were taking.

"Here," he said. "End your bathroom woes with a bit of this."

I pulled out scissors and a plastic baggie, and snipped enough teaglove for the spell with some to spare. Then I gently unearthed a small section of the plant with the roots. There was every reason to think I'd be reversing more spells, so I had better start my own garden of hope and possibility.

"Agreed," Mr. Bixby said. "I admire your foresight. Now, on with your laundry list."

He led me to three more plants I wanted to have on hand, based on a quick perusal of the spell book. There were a couple with intriguing titles that might just help me restore the memory of our family ghost and thereby lead me to Mom.

Excitement made me giddy... and greedy. "I want to grab everything," I whispered. "Just in case."

The dog stared up at me with glowing eyes. "Or we could just go back and save Sinda. How about that?"

"Right, yes," I said. "Just one more thing, Bixby. Please?"

He sighed and led me to the last plant on my list. "You'd better really need it. If this has anything to do with fixing your hair, I'm going on strike."

"It's important, trust me," I said, plucking berries and leaves with gloved fingertips. "We can visit again. This was easy."

As the last word left my mouth a bank of very bright lights came on, blinding me temporarily. After that, a horrible alarm started shrieking.

Ren started running back to the door while I pocketed the berries. I suspected there was something so important about this plant that Maisie had set up a sensor.

"The door's locked," Ren called. "We're trapped."

If there was any doubt, a voice came over a speaker system. "You're trapped! Trespassers will be prosecuted." Maisie gave a wheezy laugh. "More like persecuted."

An overhead sprinkler came on and I was glad of our wigs and plastic masks. There was no way Maisie could identify me.

At least, as long as she couldn't see Mr. Bixby, the great giveaway.

I glanced around for him and saw nothing.

"Bixby," I whispered. "Where are you?"

"Right at your feet," he said. "Is the mask blocking your eyes?"

"You're invisible," I said, crouching to be sure. "Even to me."

"Cool. I thought I felt a breeze." He chuckled delightedly. "I guess that puts me in the lead, ladies. Follow me. Or rather my voice."

Avoiding kicking him was a challenge at the best of times. "Stay well ahead," I said.

Maisie sounded an airhorn that nearly deafened us and then bellowed into her mic, "Stop right there. The police are coming. And not the nice ones."

Bixby urged us on with commands only I could hear. "There's a back door I sussed out on our first visit. I hear sirens. Hurry!"

I picked up speed, hoping I didn't trip over him or squish him. Maybe I'd pass right through him. The thought made me stop suddenly and Ren bumped into me.

What if Bixby had turned back into a ghost? I didn't know what I'd—

A nip on my pant cuff got me moving again. "Do I *feel* dead to you?" he asked.

"No, but—"

"I can still smell the glory of your decay, so trust me, I'm on the same plane," he said. "Now, move it."

Maisie's voice cut in again as I ran a few yards. "Aha! Just as I thought. A Brighton. I'd know that clumsy stride anywhere. Like mother like daughter. Although I don't know which of you my Venus flytrap has caught. I'm guessing the younger because Shelley doesn't have any friends, poor thing. Not a single one."

"Ignore her," Ren whispered, shoving me along. "She's trying to get inside your head and slow you down."

"Ren's right," Bixby said. "Toughen up, Janelle."

Maisie's laughter nearly drowned him out. "If I had doubts before, you've just confirmed it, poor girl. Someone slumped under her mommy issues. But don't take it so hard. You've already surpassed Shelley in many ways. Shame it won't last. Soon you'll be exiled, too. Doomed to die alone like your mom."

My feet slowed despite Ren's efforts to push me forward. I

might have been stuck there, frozen in the glare of my past, had it not been for a set of sharp invisible teeth on my ankle. That bite was going to bleed.

"Get. Moving. Now." He sounded furious. "There's a problem with the door and you need to—"

"Focus. I know." Now I was running to avoid those invisible teeth. "What's wrong with it?"

"No lock to crack," he said, behind me. "She wants people to come in and never leave."

"Like the Venus flytrap." When we got there, I bent over to examine the silver doorhandle gleaming under the bright lights. "I've never seen anything like it. I can't pick it or snap it."

Ren's breath was ragged behind me. "The sirens aren't far off. If we get taken in, we won't get a fair shake. Drew has no pull with the underground police. You'll lose the store and I'll get fired."

Or worse. Much worse.

"Don't count us out," Mr. Bixby said. "You know what to do, Janelle."

"I do?" I said.

"The only thing you *can* do," the dog said. "Use your stunner."

"My stunner? It only works on people."

"Have you tried?" he asked.

"What's he saying?" Ren asked. "What's a stunner?"

I glanced at her over my shoulder. "It's what got us into trouble with Reggie all those years ago."

"Well, it's just a door this time," she said. "Hit it hard."

Peeling off my gloves, I grabbed the handle and tried to summon the pulse of energy. It had been simple the last time, in Sinda's store. Automatic.

"Shooting blanks," I said. "Must be the poison."

"Nah, it's your confidence," Bixby said. "You've let Maisie Gledhill steal your firepower. How do you *feel* about her right now?"

As if on cue, Maisie called out, "We know where your mom is, sweetheart. And we're going to snuff her out like a candle. Just waiting till you were around to see it."

That did it. White-hot energy surged from my wounded, angry heart down through my arm.

The doorhandle simply melted away, leaving silver on my fingertips.

CHAPTER TWENTY-NINE

S inda met us at the store with the spell book.
    On the way back, Ren and I had made our best guess that Maisie would direct the police to the Brighton manor to find us. We'd stripped off our disguises and tossed them over one of the less-traveled bridges. The cops had nothing to identify us except the one bit of evidence we truly needed.

The plants.

I kept only the teaglove and hid the rest outside of town with a promise to come back. They felt alive to me, and I owed them respect.

We parked on a side street, crept up the alley and let ourselves in by the back door. Would there ever be a time that the dumpster didn't make me shudder?

"Nope," Mr. Bixby said. "You've got Post Traumatic Dumpster Disorder. Odd that garbage picking bothered you more than the staking itself. Poor Laverne."

"Focus," I said, letting him into the store ahead of us. It was a relief to have him visible again. He'd materialized in time to be carried through the bushes back to Elsa. I had to give him credit for mastering a new ability so quickly.

Sinda had drawn all the blinds and was waiting in darkness on the window seat, with Bijou perched beside her and the spell book in her lap. She'd taken a cab over and used the spare key I'd left with her.

The fluffy ghost dog leapt down and frolicked around Ren's feet. Despite the circumstances, I couldn't help smiling.

Joining us at the counter, Sinda said, "I called Chief Gillock and suggested he swing by the manor. With any luck, the police will stay busy till we get this done." In the dim light, she looked rather ghastly. "Drew asked me to let you know that the truffles tested positive for toxins, and he's going to bring Candace in for questioning in the morning."

"Candace is behind all this?" It wasn't surprising, but it was disappointing. I'd hoped my sugarplum visions could be salvaged. "Well, I guess we'd better hurry."

I took the book from Sinda and set it on the counter. Then I drew in a deep breath and lifted the heavy cover. Tingling started at my toes and moved up like a tidal wave to my silvery fingertips. Something was different this time.

"*You're* different this time," Bixby said. "The right kind of different. Use it fast before it fades."

Sinda pulled a plastic baggie out of her pocket containing the other "ingredients." Hopefully the magical universe didn't quibble over presentation.

The teaglove leaves were already in my hand and I crushed them lightly before adding them to the bag. It seemed like the sensible thing to do, since they were the most powerful part of the spell. The make-or-break component.

Once everything was combined, I expected an instant whoosh of magic.

It didn't happen.

"Now what?" Ren said, after a pause. "Do you need to read the spell out loud?"

"I don't know," I said. "Bixby, why isn't it working?"

The dog was on the counter beside me. "It's something that goes on under the surface. Like your stunner. I suggest you look inward."

That wasn't what I wanted to hear. I was looking for easy. And fast. Not some sort of deep inner work that required me to face things I wanted to avoid—had spent my entire life avoiding.

"It worked before," I said. "What's wrong with me?"

"You've choked," he said. "It's performance anxiety."

The dog set his paw on my hand that rested on the baggie. Sinda set hers overtop and Ren did the same. I felt the warmth of their friendship filling me, not from the toes, but the heart, and spreading like rays of intense heat. It was similar to the feeling of my "taser" move but more refined and considerably more pleasant.

I was still wondering if I needed to toss in some magic words when Sinda pulled back her hand. Renata did the same. In the slashes of light creeping through the blinds, I saw them straighten. What's more, Bijou was on her hind legs hopping in a circle like a circus dog.

"I feel great," Sinda said. "Younger than I have in years. Or maybe I just didn't know it."

Ren applauded. "You did it, Janny!"

I could feel it myself when I stepped away from the book. Now I was just me again. Me without the queasy innards.

"It's all good now," I said.

"As long as Drew can pin Candace," Mr. Bixby said. "And confirm she killed Laverne, too."

"I don't know," I said. "Something doesn't feel quite right about that."

Closing the book, I followed Bijou into the back room. She poked her nose repeatedly at a space on the wood paneled wall. When I touched it, a little door slid back. As Sir Nigel had said, there was always a space just the right size for a book like this.

The ghost dog turned and raced back to the window seat, where Mr. Bixby had his nose stuck through the blinds.

"I'm afraid our adventure isn't quite over," he said.

"The cops?" I asked.

"Far from it," he said. "I hope we're just in for a tongue lashing."

There was a sharp rap on the door and after peeking through a gap in the blinds, I opened it just a crack. "Why, hello! You're out late."

Frida Dayne shoved the door and hit me hard in the nose. My eyes filled with a billion tiny stars, just like in a cartoon.

"Hey! What kind of Welcome Committee smacks people in the face?" I asked, backing away.

"The kind that doesn't welcome you anymore." Frida stepped inside and closed the door behind her. "You never were, actually."

"Ouch. That's a little harsh, Frida."

"Jimmy Barrow came by tonight to talk to me about Candace and poisoned chocolates. So I've been to the manor and back, looking for you. The police were rolling in as I left."

"Poisoned chocolate?" I said. "What does that have to do with us?"

My mind was racing but all the synapses started connecting. Spellcasting must have greased my mental circuits.

"Don't play dumb," Frida said. "We've called you a lot of things, but not dumb."

"You overestimate me," I said. "My dog calls me dumb all the time."

"Not in so many words," he said. "Oblivious, maybe. Are you seeing the obvious here or do I need to spell it out?"

Frida stared at the dog. "What is he yammering about? He's the noisiest dog I've ever met."

"Me too," I said. "But he's picking up a bad vibe, Frida. He feels you're a threat. I can't imagine why."

"Think about it," Frida said, advancing on me. "Does Candace really seem capable of poisoning people?"

I sent Mr. Bixby a silent message to guide Sinda and Ren to safety. There was an intensity swirling around Frida that unnerved me. She might not be magical, but that didn't make her powerless.

Bixby did as I asked, corralling them in the doorway of the back room. Meanwhile, Bijou circled Frida and me with increasing agitation.

"One thing I've learned is that people are capable of things I never expected," I said. "For good and for ill."

"True enough," Frida said, continuing her advance. I had no doubt now that she was at least partly behind the poisoning. But I'd need to draw her out to see if others had joined her on the mission.

Backing away quickly, I dodged behind the counter and grabbed my phone. Who was I going to call? I didn't want the police —especially Drew—to walk in on this, because I fully intended to use my power if it came to that.

In the end, I just hit the record button. I'd play it by ear and see what happened. Maybe I could talk her down as I had so many hotel guests who tore a strip off me over the years.

"I'm sorry if Jimmy Barrow got the wrong impression about Candace," I said. "Obviously someone poisoned us. We've been so sick, Frida. My friend Sinda, especially. I can understand someone having a grudge against me, and maybe even Ren, though she doesn't deserve it. But not Sinda."

Frida shrugged. "No one wants an old, weak witch around."

I gripped the counter with both hands. "Are you saying you were part of a plot to kill all of us?"

She took another step toward me. There wasn't enough light to see her expression, but I could feel the animosity coming off her in waves.

"Sinda was collateral damage," Frida said. "Renata was asking for it. It's a shame because I've always rather liked her."

"I liked you, too, Frida," Ren called from the doorway behind me. "And I didn't deserve to get poisoned like a common pest. None of us did."

"Ah. So you found the spell," Frida said. Light slid though the slatted blinds at the right point to make her eyes glint. "Then I got here just in time. Before you could find a way to reverse it."

"Plenty of time," I said. "I don't have skills in that regard, unfortunately."

"Neither did your mother," Frida said. "She went down so easily. Like the common pest she was. Just wish I'd found the body so that I could show it to—" She stopped abruptly and took a breath. "Never mind. I'll have three new ones."

"Reminds me of my childhood cat," I said. "She'd leave three mice a night in her food bowl. Tails hanging over the side."

"Breakfast of champions," Frida said.

"Why isn't Candace here to help you?" I asked. "It's three against one. Four counting the dog."

"Candace is useless," she said. "Never even noticed I was injecting her prize truffles. I figured you little piggies were more likely to swallow those than frozen yogurt or vegetable juice."

"You framed your best friend? How sad. What about Laverne? You were old friends, too."

"Laverne was no friend of mine, although she pretended to be. When I asked for something I'd earned, she turned me down flat."

"This store," I said, gesturing around. "You wanted Marigold to be the one selling jewelry and gifts here. Not me."

For the first time, Frida hesitated. "Who told you that? Laverne?"

"Maybe. I know that when she said no, you had to make a big promise to someone else to get this store."

"I earned this store, yet you swanned in and got it handed to you."

"You can have it, Frida," I said. "I've decided to accept Oscar Knight's offer and surrender the place. It's yours."

She shook her head, and the slice of light showed a hint of desperation in her eyes. "No one will be satisfied until—"

"Our tails are hanging over the bowl?"

"Exactly. If I don't do it, someone else will. I'll make it quick and easy now. I know that spell stinks."

"Sure does," I said. "We were up all night after the last round of truffles. Good thing I have three bathrooms."

Frida's teeth glinted in a ghoulish smile as she clapped her hands together briskly. Oscar Knight, among others apparently, had sent her to finish the job she started, and judging by what she'd done to Laverne, she was a very capable old woman. The only thing working in my favor was that she thought I was still weak.

Well, I was still weak, compared to a madwoman with magical backing. But I was pretty sure I'd shed all the toxins.

"I'd call yes to that," Mr. Bixby said. "The reek of decay is gone."

I reached out to him mentally. "What do I do now?"

"Stun her. Stunner." He gave a hollow laugh. "Get it? Always your best option."

But when I used that power earlier, I'd only succeeded in melting a door handle. It would take more than that to disable Frida.

"Have a little faith," Bixby said. "Even at a low ebb you got the job done. You're likely back on full power now, and you've barely scratched the surface of your potential." I hesitated too long and he piled on more motivation. "I expect you're Sinda and Ren's best chance. I'd hate to see what Oscar—"

"Stop," I said.

Frida was moving toward the counter at a brisk clip and she certainly didn't stop. I moved out from behind it and backed to the window, hoping to lure her away from my friends.

"I can't stop," she said. "I've got an assignment, and you've seen what happens when you don't fulfill the duties required. Wouldn't want to end up like Laverne."

Reaching out, I yanked the blinds apart so that I could see a little better. Was she armed, or coming at me with borrowed magic? I doubted she had any of her own.

"Affirmative," Bixby called. "My sniffer says she's a dud."

A dud with a very long blade, though. Ren and Sinda gave a little scream when they saw it, but I was relieved. A blade I could dodge. Hexes, probably not.

I circled more slowly than I wanted. My feet felt like they were submerged in ice water. It was fear... the enemy of firepower. I was neutralizing my own energy.

"Such a pretty young thing," Frida said. "So like your mother and just as weak. I would have liked more of a challenge. The rewards are greater. He always knows. *They* always know."

"Who's 'they'?" I asked. "Oscar obviously has a club."

A club that met in my basement on folding chairs, I guessed. They'd cleaned the crime scene before I found Laverne so there was nothing pinning Frida to the murder. Till now. I had no doubt they'd leave her holding the bag.

Ignoring my question, Frida took a lunge, which I sidestepped. Then another. And another. My goal was to tire her out so that she'd be easier to stun if my powers were low. But she had the energy of the deranged. I could feel that from two yards away.

Still, my evasive maneuvers frustrated her greatly. She'd expected me to go down as easily as... well, a mouse.

My back was to the window seat once again when Frida took a mighty leap. I slipped away, but not before her knife grazed my arm and made me yelp in pain.

Renata left Mr. Bixby and ran at Frida with her scythe raised. The older woman's jumpsuit got sliced from shoulder to knee but the wound wasn't deep enough to stop her. In fact, it seemed to release more crazy, and she turned on Ren.

"Go first, if you insist, Renata," Frida said, before charging at her with blade aloft. "Let Janelle watch you die."

I knew I couldn't reach Ren in time. Scanning the room, I saw Bijou on top of the counter, poised to leap. She was waiting for my cue. All I had to do was pull, and pull hard. For Renata.

"Bijou," I called, centering myself. "*Come!*"

There it was... the whoosh of energy that left me breathless.

Bijou leapt off the counter and by the time she hit Frida's face, she was no longer a ghost.

The thrashing of fur prevented me from seeing exactly what happened, but the screaming told me it was a good time to close in.

Frida was already falling when I caught her arm and sent a burst of energy into her.

She was out cold before she hit the floor.

CHAPTER THIRTY

Renata tossed the scythe aside and sat down hard about two yards from Frida's prone form.

Bijou jumped into Ren's lap. The dog's tail lashed and she licked my best friend's face in a frenzy of joy.

Ren looked as confused as if I'd hit *her* with my stunner but she rolled with it, patting and then hugging the dog. Eventually, she asked, "Is she mine?"

"Looks like she made her choice," I said, as the dog rolled onto her back to invite a tummy tickle.

I went behind the counter again to stop the recording. The police didn't need to hear this particular conversation.

Meanwhile, Mr. Bixby escorted Sinda out of the back room and then turned away in disgust. "Has that dog no dignity at all?"

"Oh, shut up, you self-righteous little—"

"Bijou! Stop." I shook my finger at the dog. "We speak respectfully to each other around here."

"It's my store," Bijou said. "And was for decades before you arrived."

I tipped my head. "Do you want me to go? And take Renata with me?"

The poodle threw herself down again and nudged Ren's hand. "Where she goes, I go," Bijou said. "For years, I watched her get pushed around by this town through no fault of her own. She needed me but I was stuck on that window seat."

Ren's hand moved more slowly over the dog and then stopped. "Thank you," she said. "Where I go, you go from now on."

I looked at Sinda and we laughed in delight. "You did it again, Janelle," Sinda said. "Brought over another ghost dog and united her with the right person. I'm so proud of you."

"I'm proud of Bijou," I said. "She made the choice. And she saved Ren from a killer."

"Speaking of which," Mr. Bixby said. "Perhaps someone should rope up said killer before she revives."

"You mean she isn't dead?" Ren said, proving she could, in fact, hear both dogs now. Perhaps shock had pulled the curtain and revealed her powers.

I shook my head. "Just unconscious. Bixby is right."

"There's some rope in my backpack," Ren said. "And handcuffs."

Sinda collected the backpack and brought it to us. Ren moved Bijou off her lap and helped me secure Frida Dayne to the radiator.

After that, I contacted the police. With the evidence and recorded confession, there was enough to put Frida away.

"As long as Oscar and his posse don't step in," Bixby said. "You did call him out."

"He'll probably let Frida take the fall and spell his way out of anything else," I said. "But this won't go away, I'm afraid. It might even get worse. For all of us."

Bijou pranced over to me, stood on her hind legs, and hopped in a circle. "I can help. I can help. I can help."

"I hate her," Mr. Bixby said. "A crime scene is no place for a circus act."

"Mr. Bixby, remember what I told Bijou. We're respectful to

each other around here. She's perfect for Ren, just like you're perfect for me. That's how this works."

"You know that based on two events?" he said, still sulky.

"Based on what I felt in my heart when it happened," I said. "Now, are you really going to let pride stand in the way of something that might sideline Oscar Knight?"

It was hard for my dachshund to step back to let the poodle pass, but he did it. Sinda and Ren offered to stay and watch over Frida as I went downstairs with the two dogs.

Bixby refused to be lifted. "I have legs for a reason. Do you think hunters run after badgers carrying us in their arms?"

"Grumpy, grumpy, grumpy," Bijou said.

"He's an acquired taste and you'll grow to love him like I do," I said, following the poodle's direction to open the door of the hidden room.

"The bad man," Bijou said. "He's always here. Holding secret meetings."

"Stinking out the place with sulfur and roadkill," Mr. Bixby said. "Welcome to real life, poodle."

"Smelly, smelly, smelly," Bijou said, parading ahead of us to the secret room. "Glad my nose works again."

She went to the corner with the candles and pawed at the wall.

"A cubbyhole?" I asked. "Something hidden?"

"Yes-yes-yes," Bijou said. She bristled with frenetic energy, unlike Bixby, even fresh after his crossing. "Get it. Get it. Get it."

"Honestly," he said. "There's no need for repetition. Janelle may not be the sharpest witch—"

"Or a witch at all," I said. "You just let Bijou be herself. She's been pretty much on her own, whereas you had someone you loved. And TV."

"Fine," he said. "Just hurry. Big Red will be here any minute."

I ran my fingers around the edge of the big cinder block Bijou had indicated and found a little groove. It took a couple more broken nails but the block eventually gave way. Shining my phone light into the cavity, I saw nothing but two dog heads blocking the opening.

"Mind if I take a look?"

They moved back. "Sure, sure, sure," Bijou said. "Give her some room, weiner boy."

"Stop it," I said. "Both of you. Like it or not, we're a team now."

"I like it," Bijou said. "Like it, like it, love it."

"Stab me in the heart now," Bixby said. "Or use that thing on me."

"That thing" in the cavity appeared to be a taser gun, but bigger and clunkier than the modern style. It reminded me of the earliest cell phones I saw in movies, which got smaller and sleeker with every year that passed.

"Touch it," Bijou said. "Touch it. Touch it. Use your woo-woo skills."

Mr. Bixby collapsed dramatically on the floor, although with his short legs, it wasn't that far to go. "She's going to be the death of me," he said.

"Or the life of you," Bijou said. "Thank me later, little sausage."

"Enough," I said. After taking some photos, I reached into the cavity and carefully applied the very tip of my index finger to the electroshock weapon. "There are enough distractions without your squabbling. If you want me to read anything off this thing I need silence. It's so old I can't imagine... Oh. *Oh, my.*"

"Exactly," Bijou said. "You got it. You got it. Now... go get him."

I pulled a bandana from our greenhouse raid out of my pocket and picked up the weapon. Wrapping it carefully, I slipped the taser into my pocket and covered the bulge with my coat. Then I replaced the block and asked Bijou to share every single thing she knew about Oscar Knight and this store.

When she was done, I got up and led the dogs out of the secret room.

"Bijou, don't tell Ren," I said. "Do you hear me?"

"Have to," Bijou said. "No secrets from Renata."

"This is to save Renata," I said. "And if she knew what I was doing—what *you* want me to do—she'd try to stop me."

All animation faded from the poodle as she trailed after me. "Bad girl, bad girl, bad girl."

"She's not that bad," Mr. Bixby said. "Quite good in some ways."

I knew the dog was talking about herself. She felt she was failing Ren already.

Stopping near the stairs, I knelt to face her. "You're a very good girl. A wonderful girl. And I trust you with my best friend's life. Got it?"

"Got it." Her head and tail came up. "I'll protect her. And the other lady. With Mr. Sausage."

"Where Janelle goes, I go, poodle." Mr. Bixby looked up at me. "My ride, please."

I carried him up the stairs, getting a little slower with each step.

"Tackling Frida was a piece of cake compared to facing Oscar Knight," I said. "He's unstunnable, I'm sure."

"Remember, the force is with us," Mr. Bixby said. "Should I repeat it three times and click my heels?"

I sighed and then smiled. At least I would go down laughing.

CHAPTER THIRTY-ONE

The sun was rising as I left the Brighton manor and drove back into town.

"Well, that was an exercise in futility," Mr. Bixby said. "I hope you aren't discouraged by your failure with Sir Windbag."

"Actually, I think it went great."

He stared at me. "You got nothing at all out of him about your mother."

"Maybe not, but I got something *into him*. When you were outside doing your dog business."

"What?" He was outraged. "We're like Renata and Bijou. No secrets."

"Really?" I cast him a bemused glance. "Do I know everything you know?"

"Not yet. But I know everything *you* know and that's a far better arrangement."

I laughed. "Well then, I don't know why you're even asking."

He twisted in the passenger seat, put his front paws on my leg and lifted his nose to my temple, as if trying to draw out my thoughts with a long, loud sniff.

"Where is it?" he said. "You hid that thing and now you're hiding it from me."

"It's a little something I learned from the spell book," I said. "And I hid that, too."

He plopped back in his seat, dejected. "I don't like this one bit."

"I know, and I'm sorry. Especially when you got me the plants to help me do it."

"You're not sorry," he said. "You're jubilant. That I can feel."

"What I feel is relief," I said. "If you can't read these things from me, hopefully Oscar Knight can't either. That's the key, Bixby."

"So you were afraid I would spill secrets?" He sounded incredibly hurt. "I hoped you thought more highly of me than that, after all we've been through."

"I couldn't possibly think more highly of you, Mr. Bixby, and that's why I have to protect you. Oscar is a heartless, snake-pit of a man who would think nothing of using you against me. If he threatened to torture secrets out of you, I would break." I reached out and the dog ignored my hand. "Do you want me to break?"

After a moment, the dog sighed and gave my dangling fingers a reluctant nudge. "No. I want you to put him in his place."

"Good. Then we both need to be at our very best. He's far more powerful than I am."

"*Now*," he said. "You're just getting started."

"Now's the only time that counts. Or there won't be a later."

I drove across town to the Knights' posh neighborhood. Renata had mentioned that Oscar took their dog to a park every morning. My goal was to catch him where there was some privacy, but not too much.

"It's good to have an easy exit," Bixby said.

"That, too." I pulled up to the curb and parked Elsa in the shadows of a weeping willow tree. "I wish you could drive getaway."

"It wouldn't be the first time," he said. "Although it didn't end well. Is there a spell to give me prehensile thumbs?"

I cast an eye over to see if he was joking, but he was already stomping the seat with his chunky paws to get me moving.

"All right, already. Let a girl collect herself." I pulled down my visor and checked the mirror. I'd twisted my hair into a neat knot, put on some makeup and chosen Jilly's sharpest dress and heels.

"Is this really the time to worry about your looks?" Bixby said, as I touched up my lipstick. "Big Red's busy processing another very confused individual who had an altercation with you. He's going to want to hear your story again."

There was no doubt in my mind about that. Especially because my phone had gone missing, taking Frida's confession with it. None of us saw anyone come in, so I suspected Oscar Knight's private security detail had been in the store spying, and pulled off a clever feat. There were plenty of distractions, especially after Frida woke up and started fighting like a wildcat. Maybe someone picked the lock on the back door or used a secret entrance to the store. Either way, I kicked myself for not sticking the phone in my pocket.

"I hope Drew can gather enough evidence from forensics and witnesses," I said, sighing. "Still, I've got to admit I'm a little relieved he won't hear that discussion with Frida about witches and magic. It's a lot to absorb all at once."

"I suppose, but I hope Frida doesn't walk," Mr. Bixby said. "We could have bigger problems than Drew's delicate sensibilities."

Leaning into the visor, I stared at my reflection. It seemed as if the lines around my eyes had smoothed out and my split lip had healed completely. Even the relatively fresh gash in my arm had improved noticeably. Was that due to the teaglove or the Wyldwood waters? Either way, I was all for it.

"If this meeting goes well, Bixby, some of our woes will vanish," I said.

"And if it doesn't go well, *you* might vanish. Like your mom, who got on Oscar's bad side."

"Mom's still around. Somewhere." I tucked up a few stray curls. "Anyway, looks are half the battle with a man like Oscar. This is as much a costume as what Ren and I wore last night."

Using a tissue, I carefully wiped away mascara and then scraped a bit of lipstick off my teeth.

"I'm on my last nerve, Janelle." Bixby nudged my makeup bag till it spilled the contents. "Do you want me visible or otherwise?"

"Visible. To onlookers, we'll just be an attractive pair on a morning walk." I started gathering spilled cosmetics and then gave up. "Just don't provoke Oscar with any of your stunts, okay? No nibbles or snarls or cocking a leg. We need to be chill. Fully in control. Got it?"

"Aye, Captain," he said, as I got out and set him down on the pavement.

Leaving the doors unlocked, we circled Elsa and stepped onto the grass. My stiletto heels instantly sunk into the soil. It happened again and again, and I grunted in frustration.

"Chill. Fully in control," he said. "Got it?"

"This is ridiculous. I can scale tall buildings in stilettos. This is like walking in quicksand."

The dog stopped walking and looked up. "It's okay to be anxious. You just need to hide it, which is one of your superpowers."

I pulled my eyes away from the tall man in the distance and stared down at Mr. Bixby. The dog's eyes were normally full of mockery, but now they shone with empathy in the early light.

"Okay. Getting centered." I took a few deep breaths, forcing myself to appreciate the effervescence of Wyldwood air. The act helped to ground me and then ejected my heels from the turf. "Engaging stiletto superpower and hospitality fakery."

"Atta girl," he said. "It might even be fun. Like the barf-inducing theme park rides we discussed."

I picked up the pace and my shoes coasted over the grass now. "Please tell me no one took you on a roller coaster. It would be so irresponsible."

"I'll tell you all about it later," he said. "If you tell me your secrets, too."

I couldn't help laughing and the sound made Oscar Knight turn. The silver-haired man had been walking away from a rather large pile of steaming poop left by his Rhodesian ridgeback.

"Yoo-hoo," I called. "You missed a bit." I fumbled in my purse for a poop bag from the pack I'd bought after Mr. Bixby's reanimation. "Here. I got you covered."

"If it bothers you, then you get it," Oscar said. "I have my people come by every day and clean up."

I scanned the park and then smirked. "You need to pay your poop patrol better because they've missed a few weeks."

"Janelle, I don't have time for idle chitchat. If you've got a point, make it fast."

Mr. Bixby stared up at the ridgeback with disdain and the larger dog wagged her tail ingratiatingly. "Study and learn," he told me. "It's all in the posture and eye contact."

I straightened my shoulders, looked Oscar Knight in the eye and smiled. "I have two points. The first is that you really should pick up after your dog. It's our civic responsibility. Didn't you say you're all about community?"

"And your second point?"

I flashed a lot of teeth to soften my delivery. "I'm buying my store from you. The property, I mean, including the bistro and the flower shop. The whole shebang."

Oscar Knight actually laughed, if you could call that bark a laugh. "Very funny."

"Oh, I'm not joking. You turned down our first offer, so now I'm making you a lower one."

This time his laugh sounded more genuine. "I see. Well, I've enjoyed the morning chuckle." He gestured to the poop. "Do grab that on your way out."

"Okay, you got me. I am joking about the price. I want to pay fair market value so that people don't talk." I shrugged. "People always talk but they'll talk less."

He started walking and I kept up, even though it meant dodging piles that looked about the right size for a ridgeback.

"The building is not for sale," he said. "Especially not to you. I made that clear through my agent the other day."

"I figured you'd think it over and come to a better decision." I sailed lightly over the grass as he picked up speed. "It's in Jared's best interests."

He stopped abruptly. "Jared? What does he have to do with this?"

"So much, Oscar. Everything, really." I picked up Mr. Bixby just to feel the warmth of his body and draw courage. "You know full well he was behind that high school prank long ago. And you know he killed Reggie Corby."

"Excuse me? There were plenty of witnesses that said you stunned Reggie. Your magic was coursing through the victim when the paramedics arrived. Don't even pretend otherwise."

"I didn't kill Reggie. I just tried to protect my date and my best friend from him. He was going to whip them in the face for a prank Jared dreamed up. Ren and I each threw a single egg and my date none. I'm sure Jared told you."

Oscar started walking again. "I don't have time for this. It's ancient history."

"Not to me. That story has clung to me for nearly fifteen years. Since Jared didn't take responsibility, I had to leave town."

"You're the one who gave Reggie a heart attack," he said. "A few eggs didn't do that."

"I didn't kill him. I've never killed anyone."

He turned and there was a feral gleam in his eye. "No? Well, there's a lot you *could* do with that skill if you mastered it. Since you chose not to, we chose to let you leave town."

"At least you banished Jared, too," I said. "Since he's the one who really killed Reggie. All those years I wondered if I'd overshot, when Jared had done it in cold blood."

Oscar's hand shot out, either to strike me or throw a curse, but Mr. Bixby's snarl made him pause. "You've concocted quite a story, young lady, but you're batting way out of your league."

"Maybe. But I do have proof. The taser you hid in the basement of my store. I understand it was quite a touching moment when you said your goodbyes and sent your son on his way."

Oscar's breath came in short, quick gusts that hung briefly on the cool morning air. Fall was on its way.

"Whatever you think you have, it's not proof."

"Sure, it is. Jared's prints are on it, which means he's not even magical. I imagine that was a disappointment to you and his mother. I know how that kind of thing rips a family apart."

Now steam came out of his nostrils in two jets, like a dragon. "Whatever you found doesn't tie Jared to Reggie in any way."

"Oh, it's just a hop, skip and a jump for the police to connect the dots. And like I said, there was a witness. Apparently, you erased Jared's memory before you sent him off, so I guess his conscience doesn't give him much trouble. He got the fresh start I never did."

"You have no idea what you're talking about, young lady," Oscar said.

"I don't know why you kept it," I said. "Maybe to torture Jared if he got out of line later? Magical families work in strange ways."

Oscar's hands clenched into fists and I worried he'd lash out and hit the dog. But I couldn't and wouldn't back down. I knew without touching his jewelry that his inner snakes were seething.

"Perhaps I'll send a team to search the store and your house," he said. "It wouldn't be the first time. When someone speaks ill of my family, the consequences are dire."

"It wouldn't help," I said. "I've locked the evidence and the story away somewhere safe. The details are completely inaccessible without me alive and well. And *happy*. Let's throw that in because I deserve to be happy now. It's been a long time coming. Jared's happy, isn't he?"

"Do not say my son's name again." He spoke the words through clenched teeth.

I raised an appeasing hand. "Okay. I'm done with that anyway. How about we just leave it there and get on with our lives? You sell me the property so that we don't need to deal with each other, and Renata and I will run that little strip well. She'll probably take over the bistro because Ethan Bogart wants a bigger space. Frida's store might work now that she's out of commission."

He stared at me silently, as if I were a species of insect he'd never seen before.

"Frida didn't turn on you, in case you're wondering," I continued. "I did try to get her to admit you hired her to kill Laverne Billings, as well as my friends and me. But no go."

"Oh, I know," he said, with a flick of his fingers. "I have your phone. It's the only reason you're well enough to annoy me with this discussion right now."

"Ah. I assumed as much. Your secret agents are quite good." I scuffed at the grass with the tip of my shoe. "It was a shame to lose the confession, but maybe the police will make Frida an offer she can't refuse."

"The police have nothing to offer Frida," he said. "And I didn't *hire* her to kill anyone."

I gestured around at the poop in the park. "It's kind of like the poop patrol. You've got to pay well to get the job done right."

Murmuring a command to his ridgeback, Oscar finally started walking again. "I won't say I'm sorry you and your friends didn't die. You're obviously not as cavalier with your gifts as I thought. But you'd better watch your mouth if you want your friends to stay alive and well."

"And happy," I said. "Don't forget happy."

"Maybe you can protect yourself but not the others. I don't know why we bothered keeping the baker around. She's a dud."

"That happens," I said, glad to let him believe my friends were no threat. "Look at Jared."

He reached the exit to the street and stepped onto the sidewalk with his dog. "We're done here. I don't want you as a tenant and you've got a lock on the lease, it seems. I suppose the best thing to do right now is sell you the building to get you out of my hair."

I wanted to scream and laugh and jump around. Instead, I just gave another toothy smile. "Wonderful. I knew we could work this out. My lawyer will call your lawyer and we'll make this fast."

"Nothing with you is fast." Oscar tugged on the leash and spun on his expensive loafers. I was surprised he'd risk high end footwear in this park.

"Wait," I called after him. "You forgot something."

He snorted in exasperation as he turned back. "We've been over this poop situation."

I held out my hand, palm up. "Phone please."

My suspicion that it was in his breast pocket proved correct, and he pulled it out. "We've cloned the data and erased Frida's ramblings."

"As expected. But no point my forking out for a new one."

"Are we done now?" he asked. "Because your voice has become a nail gun in my head."

"Tell me about it," Mr. Bixby muttered. "Imagine being inside it all the time."

I gave the dog a little squeeze that was more about triumph than discipline. "I've been told I have a melodious voice. Like a mythical siren, some say."

Oscar rolled his eyes. "Maybe your smitten cop. And I'll admit you're easy enough on the eyes—unlike your mother the last time I saw her. She wasn't always so haggard."

A prickle of anger started in my belly but the dog poked my hand. "You've won. Stay on that throne and hold onto your tiara."

"I suppose you hired someone to poison her, too?" I asked.

"You've got an overactive imagination," he said. "But you do have a way about you and I'm interested in seeing how you fare in this town. Take enough rope to hang yourself."

"All I want to do is run my little store and hang out with my friends. It's all about community, just like you said."

"I did say that. And I've got community, too."

"I know. They even travel for you. I nearly ran into them down south." My smile finally notched down. "Which reminds me... stay away from my family. That's all part of our deal."

He started backing away. I tried to follow and my heel drove hard into what was likely a fairly recent offering from his ridgeback.

"You were bound to overstep eventually, Janelle. I've turned a blind eye to most of your foolishness, but when it comes to your mother, all bets are off. You'd better hope she doesn't come home. I've been assured she will not."

"What did Mom ever do to you?" I called after him. There was no point following. I could not do my best work with poop on my stiletto.

Waving, he picked up speed. "Sorry to tell you this, sweetheart, but you reek."

"The nerve," Bixby said. "When he shoots sulphurous gusts like a geyser."

I reached into my purse and pulled out the old bottle of Angel Tears perfume Ren had given me. "Sorry, Bixby, but I can't get back into Elsa smelling like this."

He squirmed and I set him down to run ahead of me toward the car. I'd never seen his little legs pump so fast.

The sight did my heart good. In fact, I felt better than I had since my return. But I knew full well I'd won only one battle, not the entire war.

"Wait," I said, running after the dog and letting the turf do some cleanup on my heel. He let me catch up to him and we laughed like kids as we navigated the pocked park.

Only when I was opening Elsa's door did I turn and see Oscar Knight bent over in the field bagging dog poop.

"Maybe you really can teach an old dog new tricks," Mr. Bixby said.

I passed him into the passenger seat. "We'll see, my friend. The game is far from over. But at least we're in the arena fighting."

He tapped the handle for me to roll the window down and then spoke into the breeze. "Good job, Padawan. I'm proud of you."

"I won't let that go to my head," I said, pulling away from the curb.

It would have been nice to leave with a roar rather than a chug, but Elsa always had my back. Just like Mr. Bixby.

"I won't let that go to my head," he said, with a damp sneeze.

CHAPTER THIRTY-TWO

A few days later, Jilly linked her arm through mine as we scaled one of the highest peaks in the area near Wyldwood Springs. She'd hugged me more today than since we were kids. It felt strange but also reassuring.

"Do you really think your mom is out here?" she said. "It isn't like Aunt Shelley to rough it. She likes the finer things in life."

"As do I, but we do what we must," I said. "Look at these boots. Did you ever think you'd see me with tractor soles?"

"No," Ivy said, from my other side. "Whatever happened to Janelle Bond?"

"Common sense," I said. "Possibly maturity. Turns out all those years on the run were just a warmup, and for real life, I'm going to need sensible footwear. At least some of the time."

Normally Mr. Bixby would chime in with some witticisms but he was desperately trying to keep up with Bijou, who had much longer legs. Bijou, meanwhile, was desperately trying to keep up with Keats, who'd taken over the lead role in the search party.

Close behind the dogs came Edna Evans and Gertie Rhodes, Ivy's octogenarian warrior friends. They were both in fatigues that bulged in curious places. A rifle jutted out from under the battered poncho Gertie wore overtop.

Sinda and Renata followed at a bit of a distance. Both had recovered well, but they were taking it slow at my request. Meanwhile, I felt better than I had in ages. It was like my body came back from the attack with more to give.

That was our entire crew.

Ivy had wanted to bring an army. With a large family and an ever-growing circle of friends, hers was a community I could only dream about having at this point. Mine would need to be different from Ivy's—people capable of surviving Oscar Knight and his minions. They would need to have open minds, which is why I had limited the group today. I wasn't sure what we would discover or how it would affect people. Edna and Gertie were prepared for the end of days, including but not limited to zombies. Nothing would faze them.

Ivy, too, had proven herself open-minded and had a mystical connection to her brilliant dog.

The holdout was Jilly, whose mind was still locked tight on the issue of magic. But if she saw something she didn't like today, so be it. Welcome back to family life, where nothing is perfect.

I certainly had mixed feelings about reuniting with Mom, if she was indeed out here. The thing about family was that mixed feelings came with the package. Every day I chose to carry a big fat chip on my shoulder about what happened years ago was a day I wasn't fully enjoying. It was also a day I wasn't fully aware of what was going on around me. If I wanted to exploit the fresh start I'd worked hard to earn, it needed to start from the bottom up. And Mom was ground zero.

"Keats is slowing down," Ivy said, standing on tiptoe. "He thinks we're getting close. Are you ready for this?"

"I'll never be ready for what this crazy life has to throw at me," I said. "I've just got to roll with it. You know that better than anyone."

"Tractor soles are mandatory," Ivy said, with a smile. "Care to tell us how you figured out where your mom is?"

I glanced uneasily at Jilly. "Someone won't want to hear it."

"That's correct," Jilly said. "I don't need to know the details to be supportive."

I tightened my arm through our loop. At one time I'd have felt differently, but now I realized we could support each other in other ways. Jilly particularly didn't want to hear a word about Sir Nigel, the family ghost who severed the fragile ties between our mothers. But he was a big part of our story, whether she liked it or not.

Mom had buried the secret of her location in Boswell. I had tried all the memory spells in my book to unlock it, but it was obviously not "everyday magic." All I had been able to get out of him was a panicky "run for the hills," which sounded like his own reaction to Mom's situation. Nonetheless, I had a feeling she'd done just that, and seeing her alive in that video proved she was capable of harsh survival tactics.

Following Mom's example, I had successfully buried the secret of Jared and Oscar Knight in Boswell. My friends didn't need to know about that, either. What they didn't know, Oscar could never torture out of them. As for the physical evidence, it was in my backpack today and probably wouldn't be when I got home. Mom's hiding place had kept her safe from Oscar and it would do the same for the taser.

"We've got a point, people," Edna bellowed.

We gathered around Keats, whose right front paw had lifted as he stared at a seemingly innocuous bank of hills across a shallow valley.

"I don't see anything," Jilly said.

"That's because you're not a trained survivalist, Jillian," Edna said.

"Maybe we would be if you'd invited us to your classes," Ivy said. "Do you want to lose us to zombies?"

Edna shrugged her camouflage shoulders. "Some days, yes. But to bring you up to speed quickly, this is exactly where I'd build a bunker, and in fact, a backup is never a bad idea. This locale has everything Janelle's mom would need for the long haul: good sightlines, fresh water, a variety of vegetation and plenty of cover."

"All right, let's take a closer look," I said. "If Keats is so sure."

"He's right, he's right, he's right," Bijou said. "The mean lady is here."

Renata and I burst into laughter, and of course the joke was lost on everyone. Even Bixby and Sinda, who could also hear Bijou but didn't know my mother.

"Do we want to know what's so funny?" Jilly asked.

I shook my head. "Suffice to say my mom's reputation is well known."

We bunched up and crossed the valley together. Keats fell back and let Bijou and Bixby lead now. Whether he was yielding to their specialized knowledge or just being polite, I didn't know.

Regardless, the dogs seemed to agree on a particular site that was so buried in thorny overgrowth it would be nearly impossible to penetrate.

"I knew I should have brought the chainsaw," Edna said. "They're so unwieldy. I'm hoping to design and patent something easier to handle and fuel before the end of times."

Gertie flicked her waist-long braid over her shoulder. "It would take us ages to hack through with the small blades we brought, Edna. Better ideas? Do we go back and equip properly?"

Edna stomped her foot. "It irks me to no end to be foiled in bunkery 101."

I wanted to explain that this was, in fact, advanced bunkery. Mom had likely concealed the entrance with both magic and horticultural wizardry. She'd always had a green thumb, unlike me.

Sighing, I reached out mentally for Bixby. "What do we do now?"

"It's not a 'we' but a 'you' this time," he said. "There's no forcing your way in without another few years of magic under your belt. You'd best call her out."

"Call her out? How?"

"She's your mother," he told me. "Do you think she won't hear you?"

"Yeah, I think she won't hear me." This time I said it aloud. "Cover your ears, everyone."

They did and I shouted, "Mom! Mom? It's me, Janelle."

Mr. Bixby laughed. "I meant use your inside voice. Use the gifts she gave you."

Heat rose in my cheeks as I thought about attempting that in front of everyone... and failing. What if I tried my very best to reach my mom and she ignored me, like she had so many times? She had never been easy to reach, even when I was a small child.

"There were reasons for that, I'm sure," Mr. Bixby said.

I glared at him. "Whose side are you on, anyway?"

"You know the answer to that, just as you know the answer to getting her out of that hole. The real question is, do you want to be a slave to this angst all your life?"

"That I don't," I said, out loud.

"Why do I feel like we're missing a really good conversation?" Edna said. "It's like when Ivy is communing with Keats."

I laughed. "It's exactly like that, actually. I'm running some thoughts by Mr. Bixby, but I'll spare you, because he isn't nearly as gallant as Keats."

"Keats can be plenty rude," Ivy said, as her dog returned to sit prettily by her side. "And impatient when I'm not buying what he's selling."

"See?" Bixby said. "We're not alone in our suffering of the imperfect dog-human bond. Now, get to work or you'll disappoint all these people who came out to help you."

It had been easier to face down killers and Oscar Knight than it was to reach out to Mom now, but I did it. Using my backpack as a battering ram, I forced my way through the bushes to the thorn-covered dirt wall. Overhead was a sheer rock face. Had she really managed to carve out a safe house?

"Only one way to find out." Bixby had one paw on my boot, having followed me through the bush. "You'd best pick me up. In case of explosions. I'd be tossed like a pebble."

"There won't be explosions," I said.

From the other side of the bush, Edna called, "Beware of explosions. Or, I could set off something contained if needed."

I twisted the tightly woven vines apart and tapped the dirt. It fell away and when my fingertips came in contact with rock, my doubts fell away, too.

"There you go," Bixby said. "Now just call her again."

This time I reached out silently, through my fingertips and the energy she had indeed given me.

There was a sudden trembling and rocks crumbled. I clutched the dog to my chest as a pale, gaunt woman with wild, gorgon-like hair appeared in the opening and nearly turned me to stone with green eyes.

"Mom?" I whispered.

"Well, it's about time," she said.

CHAPTER THIRTY-THREE

M r. Bixby squirmed under my arm till I adjusted my grip. "I know you were expecting hugs and tears and swelling music," he said. "But that's not how your family rolls. Plus, she's been isolated for ages. She'll come around."

"I expected her to be in far worse condition," I said. "From the stories we heard."

"She's probably been treating herself with medicinal herbs as best she can," Bixby said. "You've said she's very resourceful."

Mom wasn't bouncy, but she was making pretty good time on the trail with Edna and Gertie on either side. She had taken to them immediately and was chattering animatedly about bunker life. Edna wasted no time enlisting Mom to do a series of guest sessions for her survivalist class and my mother had readily agreed.

"She barely acknowledged me or Jilly," I grumbled to the dog. "Let alone asking a single question about the status of things in Wyldwood."

"Even if your mom were the type to spill in front of a crowd, which I doubt she is, she probably didn't need to ask questions," Mr. Bixby said. "I was watching her face and it looked like she picked up everything she needed to know just by brushing by you. The very fact you're bringing her out of hiding tells her you've secured the situation."

"Well, she could have thanked me," I said. "A little appreciation never goes amiss."

The dog laughed. "For some that feels like weakness. You pride yourself on keeping an open mind and I suggest you double down here. No matter what's happened, she's family."

"Sometimes friends make better family," I said. "Because they *choose* to have your back."

"True enough," he said. "But unless I'm much mistaken, your mom has something your friends don't. Namely, a powerful command of magic."

"If she has such a powerful command, why was she holed up in the hills? It wasn't that hard to defeat Oscar Knight if a novice could do it."

"I reserve judgment till I've heard the tale. I suspect she deliberately put herself on the wrong side of powerful people, whereas you got there by accident. Many will excuse the impulsive errors of youth, but not a middle-aged..."

"We don't use that word, remember? Even Mom dislikes it." I sighed. "Or she did, when I used to know her."

"You'll get to know her all over again in a new way. As adults," he said.

"I want her to leave as soon as possible for the Briars," I said. "Gran can find out what happened and report back."

"You don't want your Mom to leave without healing the rift," he said.

"The rift can close just fine from a distance," I said. "It'll just take longer. You know Oscar will come after us now that Mom's out of hiding. The retail property just changed hands and I don't want anything to mess that up. This is my future, Bixby. And Renata's. Ren deserves to have a fresh start after being so loyal to me despite everything that happened. So does Sinda."

"I agree, although I could do without Bijou being right next door. It was gallant of Chef Bogart to vacate for Ren, though."

"He wanted a fresh start, too. Wyldwood is ready for something upscale, so he's going to renovate Frida's space into a proper restaurant. Oscar didn't put the kibosh on that."

"I have a good feeling about all of this," he said. "Don't you? I mean, deep down."

I didn't want to poke around deep down right now. My disappointment over Mom's reaction was seething and swirling like bad magic.

"There's not a hint of sulphur in the air," Bixby said, tipping his muzzle. "Your mother is full of good magic, if not maternal skills. Just give it time."

"Oscar won't give it time," I said. "I'll be lucky to get my store launched before he plows me under."

"You never used to be so negative," he said. "What happened to Janelle Bond, drunk on the champagne of Wyldwood air?" He took another sniff. "I love it here, for what it's worth."

"Uh-oh. Mom's falling back, Bixby. The crowd is parting around her. There's still time to plunge off the cliff. Are you coming with me?"

"Not unless you've been hiding wings from me. Or a state-of-the-art broomstick." He rose up in my arms to watch Mom. "Did you see that? She squeezed Jilly's wrist! How affectionate."

I laughed. "She was picking Jilly's pocket, Bixby. More specifically, pulling thoughts from Gran's bracelet under the guise of being a fond aunt."

"It's possible to do both," he said. "It might be best for you to think of your mom as a warrior like Edna and Gertie. She's using the tools she's been given and trying to survive whatever apocalypse happened here while you were gone."

"Great, just great," I said. "I've inherited an apocalypse as well as substandard gifts."

"Your gifts are fine. It's the skills that need work. Nothing time can't fix there, either."

The words were barely out of his mouth when Mom fell into step beside me. "I see you've found your familiar," she said.

"My... what?"

"Your familiar," Bixby said, as if that clarified anything. "That would be me. Your handsome and talented sidekick."

Mom actually cracked a smile. She looked like a backwoods hillbilly, but her smile was quite nice. "He's witty. I like that in a dog."

"Perhaps we misjudged her," Bixby said to me, silently.

"You didn't," Mom said. "Or not by much."

"Do not eavesdrop on my private conversations, Mom," I said.

"Then use another frequency," she said. "That was one of the lessons you didn't want to learn, back in the day."

I ran my free hand through my hair, which had blown loose in the wind and probably looked nearly as wild as hers. "Can we not fight? Please? I haven't seen you in fifteen years."

She reached out and I sidestepped her. If she wanted to read my mind, she'd have to work harder for it.

"I don't though," she said. "You're an open book to me. I'm your mother." Scanning me from head to foot, she shook her head. "I don't know where you got your style sense. Must have been your gran."

My hackles started to rise but then I felt the undercurrent of humor. It was a joke on my hippie grandmother, and something we could share.

"Gran wants to see you, Mom," I said. "She's been pining for years."

"I know, and I miss her too," Mom said. "But I can't go right now. There's a—a situation."

"With Oscar Knight. I know."

"Oscar and others," she said. "We can talk about it later. I need to make sure Boswell is okay."

"If you don't mind my asking, Ms. Brighton," Mr. Bixby said. "Is the, er, butler, your familiar?"

Mom shook her head. "Not exactly, no. Boswell is my best friend. My keeper of secrets."

"He's kept them admirably," I said. "And now he has one of mine. I hope you don't mind. It's about settling feathers in the community. So I can run my store in peace."

"Janny, there won't be peace as long as Oscar Knight and his ilk are around."

"Oscar and I came to an agreement," I said. "He said there will be peace as long as *you're* not around. So it's time to take a little break and visit Gran. She needs protection at the Briars."

"I'm not leaving you to handle this alone," she said. "What kind of mother would I be?"

That was such a loaded question. It would take me at least a year in therapy to answer it. But the fact that she wanted to support me meant a lot.

"See?" Mr. Bixby said. "Maternal sentiment. She just needs more training in how to use her gifts. Like you."

"He's a snarky one," Mom said, smiling again.

"You can carry me," Mr. Bixby told her. "Janelle's been carrying a lot lately."

Mom didn't wait to be asked twice, and soon the two of them were chattering away as they walked ahead of me down the trail. She didn't bother to use her inside voice and no one seemed to think twice about her having an animated one-sided conversation. They just assumed she was crazed from isolation.

Meanwhile, I felt bereft... like my dog had indeed sided with the enemy.

A little voice popped up inside, like a thought bubble. "Does Janelle Bond wallow in self-pity?"

He was using another frequency and proving I still came first.

"I guess not," I said. "She buys a whole new wardrobe."

"That's more like it. Now whose side am I on? The lady who brought me back to life, or the one who just crawled out from under a rock?"

"Mine, I guess. My footwear game rocks, and you do spend a lot of time down there."

"Exactly," he said. "That's my place."

Though I was alone for the moment, my heart soared.

CHAPTER THIRTY-FOUR

H ome.

The meaning of the word had changed for me since I arrived in Wyldwood Springs.

It wasn't about the old manor, or Boswell or even Mom.

It was about Whimsy. The sign with its old-fashioned swirly typography had gone up that morning, so it was official. The merchandise and shelving hadn't arrived so I had to settle for buffing the old oak counter to a high gleam. Mr. Bixby kept pacing back and forth across it, keeping an eye on the street and giving me fresh paw prints to polish off.

I loved the place, and more importantly, I loved my small but growing community here. Running this store would introduce me to the people who waved now as they passed. On top of that, I would hang out at Ren's yet-to-be named café and join any club in town that would take me. My goal was to become so well known and well liked that I wouldn't end up in a hole in either a cliff or the ground. That's where Mom had tripped up, I figured. She'd chosen to be a lone wolf and that decision left her fully exposed when the tides turned against her.

I'd made the same decision when I left town all those years ago and I might still be on the run, alone, had I not been given the opportunity to reunite with Jilly and see the community springing up around her at Runaway Farm like sunflowers. I studied and learned that it was better to trust people. To be part of a pack who truly cared about you.

"Agreed," Mr. Bixby said. "Although dachshunds are an independent breed. Since my return I've liked the idea of being part of the crowd. Except for the clumsy feet."

"Well, your paws rarely touch the ground anymore," I said. "My real calling seems to be carrying you around."

"About that," he said. "A velvet cushion would be nice. Royal blue suits me."

I was still laughing when the little bell I'd hung over the door jingled and Ren walked in with Bijou on a pink, rhinestone-studded leash.

"You look great," I said, eying her dress and heels. "Hot date with a hotter chef?"

Her faced flushed but she shook her head. "Walking with Bijou has made me realize how long I've been slinking around town to evade notice. My dog deserves better than a shrinking violet."

The poodle pranced around Ren and said, "Good enough as you are. Plenty good enough for me, thank you."

"She's really very sweet, isn't she?" I asked, looking pointedly at Bixby.

He hacked, as if coughing up a hairball.

"So smart, too," Ren said. "She's perfectly trained and our only challenge is not getting caught chatting. I don't have your other channels to fall back on."

"Yet," I said. "We're just getting started, my friend."

"Does that mean you're embracing this whole magical lifestyle?" Ren asked. "Spelling up a storm?"

"No." The word shot out like a bullet and Ren literally ducked. "Well, only enough to stay out of trouble. All I really want is to run my store alongside my best friends, and immerse myself in the community."

"Staying out of trouble sounds good to me," Ren said. "I can't believe my dream of opening a bakery is finally coming true. Thanks to you, Janelle."

"Thanks to Sinda, and Gran and Mom, really. We're just paying the mortgage on their investment."

"Best investment I ever made," Sinda said, coming out of the back room. She'd arrived even before me to start refurbishing the secret room downstairs as a jewelry design workshop. We'd done half a dozen spells on it to cleanse the place and it felt livable now. "I've already started a new piece in my dog collection, Janelle. I have the feeling there's another dog in need of rescue. A big one."

"Terrific," Bixby said. "That's just what we need."

"It's exactly what we need," I said. "An army of former ghost dogs behind us."

Sinda pulled a small velvet box out of the pocket of her white smock and handed it to Ren with a smile. "I created this design of Bijou as a brooch a long time ago. I notice young people seem to prefer pendants nowadays so I updated it."

Opening the box, Ren's big eyes filled with tears. After hugging Sinda, she handed the pendant to me so that I could fasten it around her neck. Meanwhile, the model bounced around the store, springing from the window seat and sliding across the counter, nearly taking Bixby with her. He snapped at Bijou as she skidded by.

"So much pent-up energy," I said. "I hope you can keep up with her, Ren."

"She's exactly what I need. I've been afraid to get out in the world and now I have no choice."

Sinda cleared her throat. "Which reminds me... there's something Ren and I need to tell you, Janelle. Before you hear it from others."

"Hit me," I said. "Nothing you can say will shock me."

"Zombies," Bijou shouted, leaping off the counter. "Zombies. Zombies."

It was joyous, not a warning.

"What my furry friend is trying to say is that Sinda and I joined Edna's survivalist course," Ren said.

I laughed. "Really? You want to learn all about bunkers?"

She laughed, too, but there was an anxious note in it. "These are dangerous times and we want to be prepared—both to help you, and to protect ourselves so you don't have to." Leaning down, Ren scooped her wriggling dog into her arms. "I have a dependent now."

"Forever dog," Bijou said. "Forever and ever."

Bixby made more hairball hacking noises.

"You're beautiful together," I said. "The best part about coming home was matching you two up."

"Not seeing your mother?" Ren said, with a mischievous grin.

"You notice I'm at the store and not at home? Mom and Boswell are spending quality time reconnecting, and cleaning out the fridge, thank goodness. Four's a crowd."

"She's restored his memory?" Sinda asked.

"Yes, apart from the secret I hid in there. And she's fully recovered from the poison as well. Turns out Frida had also been plying Mom with toxic truffles via Candace, only on a much slower schedule. It was so subtle and gradual Mom didn't know till she was barely able to drag herself up that hill. Once she figured it out, she treated herself with the herbs she could find and now she's cleared out the last of it with teaglove."

"Shelley really should take a vacation," Sinda said. "She deserves to feel safe for a while and the Briars is that." After a beat, she added, "Mostly. I suppose it will be when Chief Gillock goes back."

"She's safer there than here," I said. "And so are we. Oscar Knight has her in his sights and she still won't tell me why."

Ren rocked Bijou like a fluffy baby and said, "What exactly happened when you visited Oscar? I haven't heard the full story."

"Ask him yourself," I said. "There he is now."

I felt him before I saw him. The snakes roiling in my gut announced his presence. Bijou's hackles came up instantly and she thrashed to be let down to charge the door. Ren chased the leash and pulled the dog back.

"Bad man, bad man, bad man," Bijou said.

"For once the repetition is warranted," Bixby said. A ridge of fur came up along his back and settled just as quickly. He didn't like having his worries on display.

The tall man opened the door and stepped inside. Instead of jingling, the bell overhead gave a strident squawk that made him look up in surprise. I was surprised too but tried not to show it.

"Welcome to Whimsy, Mr. Knight," I said. "You've met my friends, I believe?"

He waved the pleasantries away. "I'm here about the matter we discussed. Would you prefer to speak in private?"

"There's nothing you can't say in front of all of us."

"Your call," he said. "It's about your mother. We had an agreement."

I came around the counter, collecting Bixby under my arm as I passed. "I couldn't make an agreement on behalf of my mother, sir. She's her own person. But I can assure you I'm working hard to convince her to leave town."

"Work harder," he said, looking around. "Or I wouldn't count on launching this store."

"Mr. Knight, don't be like that. The launch party is going to be amazing. Please come and buy something nice for Mrs. Oscar. I bet she deserves a bauble or two. I've heard she's a nice lady."

His eyes landed on me again. "She is. I suggest you study and learn from her. From a distance."

"Challenge accepted," I said. "Is there anything special you had in mind as a gift? My friend Sinda does custom orders and we're eager to please. You have such influence in this town."

Mr. Bixby gave another hairball hack. "Overkill. Are you high on fumes?"

I couldn't help laughing and Oscar smiled himself. "You're difficult to dislike, Janelle. But it's a project I can get behind."

Opening the door for him, I gestured for him to leave. "You say the sweetest things, sir. Now, take care and we'll see you at the launch."

He literally brushed past Drew Gillock outside and both men lunged backward as if they'd touched a hot stove.

Drew came inside, saying, "I don't like that guy. He sets off all kinds of alarm bells."

"He sure does," I said. The bell overhead, on the other hand, sounded a rather flirtatious tinkle as Drew closed the door. "Oscar sold us the property, but he's still threatening the store's launch."

"I'm sure he had something to do with Laverne Billings' death," Drew said. "But without your recording, there was no hard evidence against him and Frida isn't making a bit of sense." His coppery eyebrows rose and waggled. "Isn't that strange? It's like her mental wiring got scrambled. Like others before her."

"That is strange," Sinda said, on my behalf. "But since she poisoned us, I can't say I'm sorry she's babbling."

Drew looked from one of us to the other and shook his head. "Secrets, ladies. They'll make you sicker than toxic truffles."

"I don't know about that," I said. "We felt pretty rough for a while."

"Let's tell Big Red about the bathroom situation," Mr. Bixby said. "Total romance killer."

I shook my head at the dog and resisted his teasing.

"Well, I'm glad you're all well and I look forward to the launch party," Drew said. "I've decided to stay in town for a while."

My heart gave a happy twirl, just like Bijou. Then the dog leapt onto the window seat and growled. Outside, leaning against a lamp-post, was the cop with the slick, gelled hair. Oscar Knight's henchman.

"What does *he* want?" Drew said. "I haven't been able to get a straight answer out of Chief Dredger about this secret security team. It's like another police force that revolves around Oscar Knight."

"See?" Bixby said. "No flies on Big Red."

I walked over and flipped the blinds closed. "Probably trying to scare me off, but it won't work."

No doubt Officer Slick was there to remind me about a future tempest in a dumpster. Hopefully I'd have some time to prepare for it.

"What's life without a little drama?" Bixby said. "Peace isn't all it's cracked up to be. And you've got your army now. Starring me, your pedigreed arm candy."

I planted a kiss between Bixby's silky ears. It was the first time I'd dared take the liberty, and I expected umbrage. Instead, the dog chuckled. "Take that, Big Red," he said. "The bells may tinkle for you, but I'm the true gatekeeper here."

"Why is he always looking at me and mumbling?" Drew asked, matching the dog stare for stare.

"Another mystery waiting to be solved," I said.

"I've had enough thrills for one week," Sinda said. "Haven't all of you?"

"It's enough to make a girl hungry," I said. My stomach had settled quite quickly after Oscar's departure. "How about ordering some food?"

Everyone gathered at the counter and the cold fingers of dread on my throat released. Despite all that had gone wrong in Wyld-wood Springs and the threats to come, when I looked around at my friends—both human and canine— knew I was exactly where I belonged.

Join Janelle and Mr. Bixby on their next great adventure in *Any Way You Haunt It*.

Whimsy is set to launch when a canine specter with a little extra arrives and stirs up a whirlwind of trouble. The feisty furball's visit coincides with an unexpected death on Main Street that leaves Renata on the hook for murder. Solving the crime means cracking a complicated canine code and conquering magical mishaps. No one said rescuing ghost dogs would be easy... but there's never a dull moment.

Have you read the free series prequel, *I Want You to Haunt Me*? Join my newsletter group at **ellenriggs.com/mystic-mutts-opt-in** to discover how Janelle and Mr. Bixby started their journey together. You can also try my Bought-the-Farm Mysteries series for free and hear all about my adorable dogs. Hope to see you there!

More Books by Ellen Riggs

"Mystic Mutt Mysteries" Paranormal Cozy

- *I Want You to Haunt Me*
- *You Can't Always Get What You Haunt*
- *Any Way You Haunt It*
- *I Only Haunt to be with You*

"Bought-the-Farm" Cozy Mystery Series

- *A Dog with Two Tales (prequel)*
- *Dogcatcher in the Rye*
- *Dark Side of the Moo*
- *A Streak of Bad Cluck*
- *Till the Cat Lady Sings*
- *Alpaca Lies*
- *Twas the Bite Before Christmas*
- *Swine and Punishment*
- *The Cat and the Riddle*
- *Don't Rock the Goat*
- *Swan with the Wind*
- *How to Get a Neigh with Murder*
- *Tweet Revenge*
- *For Love Or Bunny*
- *Between a Squawk and a Hard Place*
- *Double Dog Dare*
- *Deerly Departed*
- *Think Outside the Fox*

"Bought-the-Farm" Mysteries Boxed Sets

- *Bought the Farm Mysteries - Books 1-3*
- *Bought the Farm Mysteries - Books 4-6*
- *Bought the Farm Mysteries - Books 7-9*
- *Bought the Farm Mysteries - Books 1-10*

Dog Town Series

- *Ready or Not in Dog Town* (The Beginning)
- *Bitter and Sweet in Dog Town* (Labor Day)
- *A Match Made in Dog Town* (Thanksgiving)
- *Lost and Found in Dog Town* (Christmas)
- *Calm and Bright in Dog Town* (Christmas)
- *Tried and True in Dog Town* (New Year's)
- *Yours and Mine in Dog Town* (Valentine's Day)
- *Nine Lives in Dog Town* (Easter)
- *Great and Small in Dog Town* (Memorial Day)
- *Bold and Blue in Dog Town* (Independence Day)
- *Better or Worse in Dog Town* (Labor Day)

Dog Town Boxed Sets

- *Mischief in Dog Town – Books 1-3*
- *Mischief in Dog Town – Books 4-6*
- *Mischief in Dog Town – Books 7-9*

Made in United States
North Haven, CT
27 January 2023

31708072R00163